Also by Georgette Heyer

Romance

The Black Moth
These Old Shades
The Masqueraders
Beauvallet
Powder and Patch
Devil's Cub
The Convenient Marriage
Regency Buck
The Talisman Ring
The Corinthian
Faro's Daughter
Friday's Child
The Reluctant Widow
The Foundling
Arabella
The Grand Sophy
The Quiet Gentleman

Cotillion
The Toll-Gate
Bath Tangle
Sprig Muslin
April Lady
Sylvester
Venetia
The Unknown Ajax
Pistols for Two
A Civil Contract
The Nonesuch
False Colours
Frederica
Black Sheep
Cousin Kate
Charity Girl
Lady of Quality

Historical Fiction

Simon the Coldheart
The Conqueror
An Infamous Army

Royal Escape
The Spanish Bride
My Lord John

Mystery

Footsteps in the Dark
Why Shoot a Butler?
The Unfinished Clue
Death in the Stocks
Behold, Here's Poison
They Found Him Dead

A Blunt Instrument
No Wind of Blame
Envious Casca
Penhallow
Duplicate Death
Detection Unlimited

Contents

Pistols for Two

I

*I*N THE END, THE QUARREL, SMOULDERING FOR SO MANY
weeks, flared up over such a trifle that anyone, Tom
reflected, would have laughed to have known the cause. Only
they had not really reached pistol-point because Jack had stepped
backward in a doorway, and cannoned into him, making him
spill his glass of champagne, and treading on his foot. Nor had
Jack turned pale and tight-lipped with anger because he had
cursed him for being a clumsy oaf. If you had known a fellow
from the cradle, had played with him, gone to school with him,
shot, fished, and hunted with him, you could curse him with
impunity, and either it ended in a bout of fisticuffs or in laughter:
not in a meeting in the chill morning, attended by seconds. Even
had they not been such close friends that sort of thing was out of
date: rubbishing stuff, fit only for the stage! Tom's grandfather,
of course, had been out five times, if the family legends were
to be believed, on the most trifling provocation. He had once
fought Jack's great-uncle George – and very comical they must
have looked, Jack and he had often thought, giggling over it,
with their shaven polls (for they had worn wigs, both of them),

and the absurd ruffles they affected in place of wristbands, and had to tuck up, and their bare feet probably much bruised by the unkind ground. Nowadays, if one fought a duel, one chose pistols, and one didn't make a cake of oneself over the business. But very few people did fight duels, and certainly not because they had been jostled in doorways.

Only it wasn't that. This unthinkable situation had arisen out of something far more serious. Not that one could call Marianne Treen serious: she was the gayest and most light-hearted of all possible causes of dissension.

Strange what changes a few years could wreak in a female! There had been nothing remarkable in little Marianne Treen before she went south to boarding-school: in fact Tom could distinctly recall that he and Jack and Harry Denver had thought her a silly creature, with freckles on her nose, and a tiresome way of intruding where girls were not wanted. Her departure from Yorkshire left their withers unwrung; and since she spent her holidays in London, with her grandmama, they were very soon able to forget her.

But she had come back to Yorkshire. She had enjoyed a brilliant London season, and when most of the *haut ton* had gone to Brighton, Mrs Treen had brought her home to Treen Hall, and the neighbourhood had renewed their acquaintance with her at one of the assemblies at High Harrowgate. A stunning shock that had been to all the young gentlemen for miles around, for who would have supposed that this dazzling beauty was none other than freckled little Marianne, who was used to whine: 'Let me come with you! Oh, pray, let me come too!'

They rarely had let her, and now she had her revenge on them. Only she was too sweet and too gay to care for that, and if she did favour some more than others it was easy to see that she used her best endeavours to be impartial.

Jack and Tom were her favourites, as they were certainly

the most assiduous, of her courtiers. Everyone laughed at this, and they were roasted a little for doing everything together, even when it came to falling in love for the first time. That did nothing to soothe exacerbated tempers. It was a strange and a deplorable circumstance that one's relatives were unable to see when one was in earnest, but, on the contrary, laboured under the delusion that if one had not yet come down from Oxford one was too young to think of marriage.

Each knew himself to be an eligible suitor. Perhaps Jack had a little the advantage over Tom, for his father was a baronet. But Tom's father was the Squire, which counted for something, and Tom was his only son, whereas Jack had two younger brothers to be provided for.

At first their courtship had been unattended by any rancour. They were agreed that Marianne was incomparable, and their rivalry had been conducted in the friendliest spirit. Perhaps neither knew when the change had crept into their relationship with one another. Perhaps Jack was jealous of Tom's superior height, and breadth of shoulder (sure to appeal to a female!); perhaps Tom envied Jack his air of elegance, and his handsome profile. Whatever the cause, the rift appeared between them. They had become hostile, each eyeing the other with suspicion, each on the watch for any cause for offence. A dozen times they had come within an ace of indulging in a maul; but never until this disastrous night had they considered the possibility of settling their quarrel at dawn, in Stanhope's Clearing – by tradition an honourable meeting-place.

That Marianne would choose one or other of them before the summer ended neither doubted. The only question was which it would be, and this made it of paramount importance that neither should steal an unfair advantage over the other. After one or two squabbles they had agreed to this – or so Tom had believed, until on this night of the Treens' Dress Party he had beheld with his own eyes the proof of Jack's perfidy. Both had meant to send Marianne a posy of flowers to carry at the ball, with a suitable message attached to the holder: which posy she chose would clearly indicate her heart's preference. Tom had bullied the Squire's head gardener into making up an exquisite bouquet of pink roses and sweet-peas. He had ridden over to Treen Hall himself that morning, to leave the tribute with the Treens' quelling butler, and the most shocking mischance had occurred. The mare had been stung by a horsefly, and Tom, that bruising rider, lost in some beatific dream, and riding with a loose rein and his head in the clouds, had abruptly parted company with Bess. Alas for the delicate bouquet grasped in his right hand! A shower of petals in the road, a dismal array of broken stalks in the filigree holder: that was all that remained of it.

He had only just caught Bess when, as ill-fortune would have it, Jack came driving along the road from Melbury Court in his smart new tilbury. A bouquet of yellow roses lay on the seat beside him, so that there was no need to enquire his errand.

Three months earlier Jack would have roared with laughter at Tom's mishap; today Jack was politeness itself, and not even the sight of that abject posy did more than make his lip quiver. Jack had had the infernal impudence to behave with magnanimity. He had said that since misfortune had overtaken Tom he should not present his own bouquet. This was precisely what Tom had been about to demand as his due, under the terms of their agreement. He said so, hating Jack for his punctiliousness. So Jack smiled in a slighting way, and had more than hinted that only a cork-brained fellow like Tom would have thought of offering pink roses to a goddess whose hair was a glorious Titian red.

Tom had brooded over it all the afternoon, but it was not then that the thought of calling Jack out had even remotely occurred to him. It hadn't really occurred to him when, on arriving at Treen Hall that evening, he had seen Marianne, adorable in a cloud of jonquil gauze over a white satin robe, holding in one gloved hand a posy of yellow roses. If any reasoned thought found room in his brain, it was merely a vague resolve to give Jack a leveller at the first convenient opportunity – if (for Jack was a clever boxer) Jack did not first plant him a heavy facer.

It was a very grand party, with several London swells, who were staying at Treen Hall, much in evidence. At any other time, Tom, aspiring to fashion, would have taken careful note of the folds of the neckcloth worn by the Tulip talking to Mrs Treen, or regarded with envy the cut of the coat moulded across the shoulders of the gentleman from London who was dancing with Marianne. He would not have been jealous of this personage, for all his handsome face, and exquisite bearing, for he was quite old – thirty at least, Tom judged – and probably already the father of a hopeful family.

All his jealousy, all his seething rancour, was reserved for Jack, his closest friend. Mr Treen's excellent champagne did nothing to assuage it. Before an hour had elapsed it must have been a very obtuse person who failed to realize that the two handsome boys from the Manor and Melbury Court were itching to be at one another's throats.

And then Jack, stepping back politely for an elderly gentleman to pass him, trod on Tom's toes, and made him spill his champagne.

2

Somehow they were confronting one another in the small saloon that led out of the ballroom, and Tom was cursing Jack, and Jack, instead of punching him in the ribs, or meekly apologizing for his clumsiness, was standing straight and stiff, white-faced and close-lipped, his pleasant grey eyes as cold and as hard as the granite of the country. Then Tom had uttered the words from which there could be no retreat. 'I shall send my friends to wait on yours!' he said, in a grand way that was only marred by his shaking voice of fury.

Dear, good Harry Denver, who had seen the encounter, and had followed the injured parties into the saloon, tried to make peace, urging them not to be gudgeons, to remember where they were.

'Harry, will you act for me?' demanded Tom.

Poor Harry stuttered and floundered. 'Now, Tom, you know this is the outside of enough! Jack meant no harm! Jack, for God's sake – !'

'I am perfectly ready to meet Mr Crawley, when and where he pleases!' replied Jack, in a chill, brittle voice.

'Be good enough to name your friends, Mr Frith!' said Tom, not to be outdone in formality.

'Jack, *you're* not three parts foxed!' Harry said urgently. 'Don't be such a damned fool, man!'

Then he saw that they were no longer alone. The gentleman from London, who had been waltzing with Marianne, had come into the saloon, and closed the door behind him. All three young men glared at him, the hostility of the native towards the stranger patent in their eyes.

'You must forgive me!' he said affably. 'An affair of honour, I collect? So much better to shut the door, don't you agree? Can I be of service to either of you?'

They stared at him. Harry, in desperate need of an ally, blurted out the ostensible cause of the quarrel, and besought the gentleman from London to assure the sworn enemies that they were behaving like idiots.

Jack, who had been mentally passing in review his acquaintances in the district, and rejecting them all as being unsuitable candidates for the post of second, said haughtily: 'I am persuaded no man of honour would advise another to refuse a challenge. Of course, if Mr Crawley cares to withdraw his rash words –'

This was a studied insult, as Tom well knew, for Jack was by far the better shot. He snapped out one word: 'No!'

'But they mustn't fight!' Harry protested, distress writ plain on his honest countenance. 'Sir, tell them so!'

The gentleman from London said apologetically: 'But I am in agreement with Mr Frith. A man of honour, sir, cannot refuse such a challenge.'

Jack looked at him with a certain approval, but said stiffly: 'You have the advantage of me, sir.'

'My name is Kilham,' said the gentleman from London. 'May I again offer my services? I shall be happy to act for you, Mr Frith.'

Three pairs of young eyes stared at him. One might live remote from London, but one was not such a Johnny Raw that one had not heard of Sir Gavin Kilham, friend of princes, member of the Bow Window set at White's, amateur of sport, Nonesuch amongst whips, arbiter of fashion. No wonder the folds of his neckcloth baffled the closest scrutiny! no wonder his coat fitted him like a glove!

Jack, bemused at the thought of having such an exalted person for his second, swallowed, and only just managed to achieve a creditable bow; Tom ground his teeth in rage that Jack should yet again have all the luck; and Harry, in relief, supposed that Beau Kilham must know as well as any man what ought now to be done. He ventured to say: 'I – I shall call upon you, sir, at your convenience!'

'That might be a trifle awkward,' said Sir Gavin, to whom the tragic situation seemed to be the merest commonplace. 'I am only a guest in this house, you see. Let us settle it here and now!'

Harry, who had a dim notion that the correct behaviour of a second was to seek a reconciliation between the principals, looked doubtful, but the prospective duellists emphatically applauded the suggestion.

Sir Gavin, drawing out his snuff-box, flicked it open, and took a delicate pinch. 'Since we, sir, have the choice, we shall elect to fight with pistols, at twenty-five yards, tomorrow, at an hour and a place which I shall ask you to suggest.'

Deep trouble was in Harry's face, for the longer range gave all the advantage to the better shot. Before he could speak, Jack said, quite insufferably, Tom considered: 'I prefer to fight Mr Crawley at a range of twelve yards, sir.'

'Well, I won't fight you at twelve yards!' retorted Tom furiously. 'Twenty-five, and be damned to you!'

'Tom, do, for God's sake – ! Now, listen, you crazy fools, this is nonsense! The quarrel can be composed in a trice!' exclaimed Harry.

They rounded on him, all their pent-up feelings finding expression in the loathing with which they commanded him to hold his tongue.

So there was nothing for poor Harry to do but to appoint the time and the place, both of which Sir Gavin accepted with the utmost amiability.

Then a paralysing thought occurred to all three young gentlemen.

'The – the weapons?' uttered Harry, exchanging an anguished glance with Tom.

For a moment no one said anything. Sir Gavin's lazy eyes were lowered to the contemplation of his charming snuff-box, and if his lips twitched it was so tiny a betrayal that it passed unnoticed. Bitter reflections on the ways of fathers, who kept under lock and key their duelling-pistols (if indeed they owned such things) possessed the minds of Jack and Tom. Anyone would have thought that a prudent parent would have given his son a good pair of Manton pistols instead of a pair of shot-guns, and would have taught him how to conduct himself in such a situation as this. Neither Sir John nor the Squire had made the least push to be of real service to their heirs; and intimate knowledge of both gentlemen could only lead those heirs to face the disagreeable fact that an appeal to them now would end in nothing but the summary end to their quarrel.

Harry, anxious though he might be to stop the affair, was not going to allow the gentleman from London to suppose that his principal owned no duelling-pistols. He said that unfortunately Tom's pistols had been sent back to the maker for a trifling repair. Jack was not going to be outdone by this sort of thing, and since he could not think of any reason that was not grossly plagiaristic for failing to produce a pair of pistols of his own, he said, with an odiously curling lip: 'Strange that I should not have been permitted to see Mr Crawley's weapons!'

'You have none either, so be damned to that humbug!' instantly replied Tom.

'In that case,' said Sir Gavin, restoring the snuff-box to his pocket, 'I will be responsible for the weapons. And since the hour of the meeting is not far distant, may I suggest that you should both now retire from this party, and go home to get what sleep you can? Mr Frith, I shall call for you in my curricle at half-past five; Mr Denver, I should like a word with you before we part!'

3

It was easy to talk of sleeping if you were only the second in an encounter, Tom reflected bitterly. He had slipped away from Treen Hall, and had driven himself home by the light of a full moon. The chill air sweeping over the moors cooled his head, and, to a great extent, his rage. By the time he reached the Manor, and had stabled the cob, he was finding it increasingly difficult to look forward with any pleasure to the morrow – no, not the morrow: it was past midnight, he observed, as he entered the Manor, and saw the tall-case clock at the foot of the stairs.

His mother had gone to bed, but as ill-luck would have it, the Squire was still up, and called to him from the library. 'Is that you, Tom?'

He was obliged to go into the room, and there was his father, and not alone either. He was playing chess with Sir John Frith. Tom regarded Sir John in the light of an uncle, and was much attached to him, but there was no one he wanted to see less tonight.

'You are back very early,' remarked the Squire, shooting a look up at him under his bushy brows.

'Yes, sir,' he said, in a careless voice. 'It was such a squeeze – and Harry and I mean to go out early, to fish the Brown Pool.'

'Oh!' said the Squire, his gaze bent again on the board. 'You have me, John, I fancy.'

'I think so,' agreed his guest. 'Jack going with you, Tom?'

Tom knew the tell-tale colour was rising to his cheeks. 'Yes – oh yes!' he stammered, feeling like a Judas – only that it was more likely that it would be he, and not Jack, who would be brought home on a hurdle so few short hours ahead.

'Glad to hear it!' said Sir John. 'Better than dangling after a petticoat at your age, pair of young fools that you are!'

That was the way dotards of forty-five (and very likely even older) talked to one, so senile they had forgotten what it meant to be young, and in love! Tom said stiffly that he would go to bed.

'Yes, you go,' agreed his father. 'Good night, my boy: don't wake the whole household when you get up! The mistake I made, John, was in moving my queen's bishop when I did.'

Tom went away, quite unnoticed by the insensate old men, who were already playing their game all over again. The last thing he wanted was for either of them to suspect the truth, but somehow it made him feel ill-used and resentful that they didn't even notice that something was amiss.

When he got into bed he hoped that Harry would not oversleep. Harry was coming to fetch him in his gig, and it would be a dreadful thing if he were to be late on the ground, perhaps oversleeping himself. The gentleman from London would certainly bring his man punctually to the rendezvous.

He soon found that there was no fear of his oversleeping. He could not sleep at all. He tossed and turned; threw off blankets; pulled them over him again; punched his pillows – all to no avail. He was wide awake, his mind so lively that his thoughts crowded in on it, jostling one another in a restless, worrying way he was not at all accustomed to.

He was not, he thought, afraid – or, at any rate, not more afraid than one was before going out to bat at Eton; but he felt sorry for his father, who would in all probability come down to breakfast to be greeted with the pleasing intelligence that the hope of his house was either a lifeless corpse, or hideously wounded. His mother would never recover from the blow; and what a terrible thing it would be for Sir John and Lady Frith, with their heir obliged to fly the country, and all communication with the Manor severed from that hour! Poor, deluded Uncle John, asking so casually if Jack were going fishing too!

Suddenly, as that thought flitted into his head, it was elbowed out by another: if only it had been true, and he and Jack were going to tramp off through the dewy early morning, sandwiches in their pockets, rods in their hands, creels on their backs, and nothing between them but the comfortable, idle chat of close friendship! No need for Harry on that expedition; in fact, better without Harry, though he might come if he chose, for he was a good sort of a fellow – a very faithful friend, really, though not to compare, of course, with Jack. He was apt to be a little in the way sometimes, as when he had gone with them when – Tom checked that thought quickly. Fatal to remember all the things he and Jack had done together, and the sport they had had, and the scrapes they had plunged into! That was all over; and even if their encounter did not end in the death of one of them, nothing would ever be the same again between them. But he couldn't help remembering, and it didn't seem to be of any use to dwell on Jack's miserable double-dealing today, because whether Jack gave Marianne flowers behind his best friend's back, or whether he behaved as impeccably as one had been so sure he would, he was still the friend who had shared one's every thought, helped one out of tight corners, called on one for instant aid himself, so that one would as readily have doubted Father's loyalty as his.

And it was all because of freckled little Marianne Treen, who was a shocking flirt, when one came to consider the matter dispassionately, and probably didn't care a rap for either of them! One dance each – and only country dances at that! – had she granted them tonight, but she had waltzed twice with Sir Gavin Kilham, and had engaged herself to another town-buck for the quadrille. When one thought of the time one had wasted, trying to fix her interest – yes, wasted *was* the word! All these summer months, when he and Jack might have been so much better employed, squandered on toadying a chit who had never been anything but a dead bore to either of them!

The more one thought of it the less vivid grew Marianne's present image, the clearer the memory of a tiresome little girl with freckles, spoiling one's sport by insisting on accompanying one, and then falling into the brook, or complaining that she was tired, or dared not cross a field with cows grazing in it. The idea that he and Jack – *Jack!* – should stand up to shoot at one another for the sake of Marianne Treen would have been a grand jest if it had not been so tragic. And just suppose that by some quirk of fortune it was not Jack's bullet that found its mark, but his? Why, if that happened he would blow out his own brains, because there would be nothing left in all the world for Jack's friend to do!

4

When his thoughts had slid into unquiet dreams he did not know, but he must have dozed a little, for he opened his eyes to find that the moonlight was no longer sliding between the chinks of the blinds, but a disagreeable morning-light instead. His watch informed him that it was after five o'clock, so he sprang out of his tumbled bed in a hurry. By the time he heard stealthy footsteps on the gravel-walk below his window, he was dressed, and he leaned out to tell Harry so. Harry had been about to throw a handful of pebbles up, but he dropped them, and made signs indicating that it was time to be off.

Tom stole downstairs, and slipped out of the house by a side door. No one was stirring. He and Harry went in silence down the drive to where Harry had left his gig.

Harry said, unhitching the reins from the gate-post: 'You know, I don't like this above half, old fellow.'

One could not draw back from an encounter, particularly when it was one's first, and one had never had the chance to prove one's mettle. 'Do you imagine I am going to cry off?' demanded Tom.

'Well, I don't know,' said Harry, climbing up beside him into the gig. 'After all, you and Jack – !'

'Don't waste your breath on me!' recommended Tom. 'Try what Jack will say to you! If I know him you'll have a short answer!'

'You couldn't expect Jack to draw back,' said Harry.

'I don't!'

'No, but I mean it wasn't his challenge! You were foxed, Tom – you know you were!'

'No, I was not,' said Tom.

'Dash it, to call a man out only because he jostles you in a doorway, without in the least meaning to –'

'It wasn't that,' answered Tom. 'And it's no use to prose at me: I shan't listen!'

So Harry said no more, and the rest of the drive was accomplished in silence. They came punctually on to the ground, just as a white-winged curricle with a pair of magnificent bays harnessed in the bar bowled up the broad woodland ride. Only two men sat in it, nor was there any sign of a doctor. Tom wondered if his stolid second would point this omission out to Sir Gavin. It was not, he decided, for himself to mention the matter. He stole one look at Jack, alighting from the curricle, and casting off the drab overcoat he wore, and then averted his gaze. Jack was still wearing his flint-face, and his eyes did not warm an atom as fleetingly as they met his. Tom looked instead at those match-bays, thinking how much he would like to ask Jack if they were the sweet-goers they looked to be, and whether Sir Gavin had allowed him to handle the ribbons.

Sir Gavin was walking unhurriedly across the clearing to meet Harry. He wore top-boots polished till you might almost see your face in them; and a many-caped benjamin; and he carried an ominous case under one arm. He and Harry conferred together, and inspected the wicked-looking weapons in that case, and paced out the ground. Tom felt queasy, and rather cold, and a leaden weight seemed to have settled in his chest. He wished the seconds would make haste: they were being maddeningly deliberate. Another glance at Jack showed him that Jack was perfectly cool and collected, only rather pale.

Harry was coming towards him, to conduct him to his position. Sir Gavin was holding the pistols by their barrels; Jack took one in his right hand, and stood with it pointing downwards, his body turned sideways from his adversary.

Sir Gavin gave Harry the second pistol. He saw that it was cocked, and took it carefully, thankful to see that his hand was quite steady. He listened to what Sir Gavin was saying, about dropping his handkerchief, and nodded. Then Sir Gavin and Harry both stepped back, and he was looking straight at Jack, across, as it seemed to him, a vast stretch of greensward.

The handkerchief was fluttering aloft in the light breeze; it dropped, and Tom deliberately fired high in the air. His eyes were fixed on Jack, and even before he realized that his weapon had misfired he saw Jack's hand jerk up, so that his gun too pointed skywards. Only Jack didn't even take the trouble to pull the trigger, apparently, for nothing happened – not even a flash in the pan. Suddenly Tom was indignant with Jack for behaving in this heroic style, and he flung down his pistol, and strode forward, exclaiming: 'What the devil do you mean by that? *Shoot*, damn you! Deloping – not even pulling the trigger – !'

'I did pull the trigger!' Jack retorted. 'The curst piece misfired! It was *you* who didn't shoot! You crazy fool, I might have killed you!'

'You aimed in the air!' said Tom. 'Serve you right if *I* had killed *you*! I won't have it! Damn it, it's insulting!'

'So did you fire in the air!' Jack flung at him. 'And you might as well have aimed at me, because you couldn't hit a barn at twenty-five yards!'

'Oh, couldn't I?' said Tom.

'No – or at twelve!'

'Oh?' said Tom. 'Well, there's one thing I can do, and that's draw your cork!'

'You may try!' said Jack, casting his own pistol from him, and putting up his fists.

They closed with enthusiasm, far too anxious to get to grips to waste time in taking off their coats. It was rather a scrambling fight, because the coats hampered them, and mingled relief and exasperation made them spar wildly, and soon fall into a clinch, each striving to throw the other a cross-buttock. Since Tom was the larger and the stronger of the two the outcome of that was never in doubt.

'Damn you!' panted Jack, picking himself up, and rubbing one elbow.

They looked at one another. Tom's fists sank. 'Jack,' he said uncertainly, 'we – we came to fight a duel!'

Jack's mouth quivered. He bit his underlip, but it was to no avail. If Tom had not begun to grin, like the gudgeon he was, he might have kept his countenance, but Tom was grinning, and the huge bubble of laughter which had been growing within him burst.

5

The same thought occurred to both of them, as the gusts of mirth died, and they wiped their streaming eyes. '*Neither* pistol went off!' Jack said.

'By God, you're right!' Tom said, and swung round to confront the seconds.

Both he and Jack had forgotten the presence of the gentleman from London when they came to fisticuffs. Torn between wrath at his suspected falsity, and dread of his contempt for their schoolboyish behaviour, they glared at him, flushed, and still panting.

Sir Gavin, who was seated negligently on a tree-stump, rose, and strolled forward, saying approvingly: 'Excellent! Rather glaringly abroad sometimes, perhaps, but I should like to see you both stripped. When you come to London you must tell me of your visit, and I'll take you to Jackson's Boxing Saloon.'

This gratifying invitation, from a noted Patron of the Ring, could not but mollify the injured feelings of the late combatants. Decency, however, had to be preserved. 'Sir,' said Jack accusingly, 'neither my friend's gun nor mine was loaded!'

'Do you know, that notion has just crossed my mind?' said Sir Gavin. 'I have such a wretched memory! Really, I must apologize, but I am quite famous for my lapses, and you must forgive me.'

They had a suspicion they were being laughed at, but it was very difficult to pick a quarrel with the gentleman from London. Tom solved the problem by rounding on Harry, and saying sternly: 'You should have inspected the weapons! You're my second!'

'I did!' said Harry, going off into a guffaw.

It might be difficult to know how to deal with the gentleman from London, but there was no difficulty at all in deciding how to deal with Harry – who had had the effrontery to make fools of two persons who, out of sheer compassion, had suffered him to join them occasionally in their chosen pursuits. They eyed him measuringly, and they advanced upon him in a purposeful way.

The gentleman from London seemed to be in the path. He said: 'The blame rests entirely on my shoulders. Er – did you wish to kill one another?'

'No!' said Jack. 'And it was – it was dashed officious of you, sir, to leave out the ball, for we meant all the time to delope!'

'My lack of tact often keeps me awake at night,' apologized Sir Gavin. 'You see, I was requested – by a lady – to intervene in your quarrel, so what else could I do?'

Jack looked at Tom, a little trouble in his face, as he recalled the events of the previous evening. 'Tom, *why*?' he asked.

Tom flushed. 'It don't signify! I dare say all's fair in – in love and war, but it was the roses! I never thought you would use me so!'

'What roses?' Jack demanded.

'Yours. The ones she carried!'

'They were *not* mine!' Jack said, his eyes kindling. 'By Jupiter, Tom, I have a mind to call you out for thinking I would serve you such a backhanded turn! It passes everything, so it does!'

'*Not* yours?' ejaculated Tom.

Sir Gavin coughed deprecatingly. 'If you refer to the roses Miss Treen carried last night, they were mine!' They stared at him. 'I hope you will not both call me out,' he said, 'but the fact is that Miss Treen has done me the honour to become my affianced wife. Our betrothal was announced at supper last night.'

This was shocking news. Each unsuccessful suitor tried to realize that his life was blighted, and failed. Tom said, with dignity: 'You might have told us so last night, sir!'

'I might, of course, but I had the oddest notion that it wouldn't have been of the least avail,' confessed Sir Gavin.

They thought this over. A reluctant grin overset Tom's dignity. 'Well, perhaps not,' he conceded.

Jack executed his best bow. 'We must beg leave to wish you happy, sir,' he said nobly.

'I am very much obliged to you,' responded Sir Gavin, with great civility.

'I suppose,' said Tom, blushing, 'you think we have made great cakes of ourselves, sir?'

'Not at all,' said Sir Gavin. 'You have conducted yourselves with perfect propriety, and I am happy to have assisted in an affair of honour so creditable to both parties. Let us repair to the inn beyond this charming coppice, and partake of breakfast!

I bespoke it half an hour ago, and I am sure it will by now be awaiting us. Besides, I do not care to keep my horses standing any longer.'

'I should think not indeed!' Tom exclaimed. 'I say, sir, what a bang-up set-out it is! Real blood-and-bone!'

'I am so glad you like them,' said Sir Gavin. 'Do, pray, try their paces as far as to the Rising Sun! If you will allow me, I will drive the gig.'

It was rather too much to expect two budding whips to nurse their broken hearts when offered the chance of driving a match-pair of thoroughbreds. Briefly but fervently thanking Sir Gavin, Tom and Jack hurried off to the curricle, arguing with some heat on which of them was first to handle the ribbons.

Sir Gavin, devoutly trusting that his confidence in their ability to cope with a high-couraged pair had not been misplaced, took his fellow-second by the arm, and pushed him gently towards the humbler gig.

A Clandestine Affair

MISS TRESILIAN SURVEYED THE YOUNG COUPLE BEFORE her with perturbation in her usually humorous grey eyes. Not that there was anything in the picture presented by Mr Rosely and Miss Lucy Tresilian to dismay the most captious of critics, for a better-looking pair would have been hard to find: the lady was a glowing brunette, the gentleman a fair youth with golden locks, classic features, and a graceful figure. He was dressed very correctly for a morning visit in a blue coat, with fawn pantaloons and Hessian boots; and if the folds of his neckcloth did not aspire to dandified heights it was easy to see that he had arranged these to the best of his ability. Mr Rosely, in fact, was doing justice to a momentous occasion: he had come to make an offer for the hand of Miss Tresilian's niece.

He said, with a shy smile: 'It can't, I fancy, come as a surprise to you, ma'am! You have been so kind that I'm persuaded – that is, I have ventured to indulge the hope that you wouldn't be displeased.'

No, it had not come as a surprise to Miss Tresilian. It was nearly a year since Mr Rosely had been introduced to Lucy in the Lower Rooms, at Bath; but although Lucy did not want for admirers, and it was scarcely to be supposed that anyone so handsomely endowed in face and fortune as Mr Rosely had not had a great many caps set at him, neither had swerved in allegiance since that date. Nor could Miss Tresilian deny that she had favoured the match: it had seemed so eminently suitable!

'Of course she's not displeased!' said Lucy. 'You knew from the start how it was, didn't you, Aunt Elinor?'

'Yes,' acknowledged Miss Tresilian. 'But I didn't know until I brought you to London, love, that the connection was disliked by Arthur's family.'

'Oh, no!' he said quickly. 'Only by Iver! My sister likes it excessively!'

'And Lord Iver is only Arthur's cousin,' said Lucy. 'Removed, too! Scarcely a relation at all!'

He demurred at this, saying diffidently: 'Well, it's more than that, for he has been my guardian, you know. I wouldn't for the world displease him, only that in *this* case he fancies we are both of us too young – or some such nonsense! He will come about! Particularly if I am able to tell him *you* don't frown on the marriage, ma'am!'

'No, I don't *frown* upon it,' said Miss Tresilian, 'but I agree with Lord Iver that you are very young. This is Lucy's first season, you know, and –'

'How *can* you, aunt?' protested her niece. 'I may not have been regularly presented until last month, but you know you would have brought me to town a year ago if Aunt Clara hadn't insisted she was too unwell to be left alone! Why, I am nineteen, and have been out in Bath above a twelve-month!'

'Yes, my dear, but I never knew until just the other day how awkwardly Arthur is situated. Or even that he had a guardian, much less –'

'No, no, ma'am!' interrupted Mr Rosely anxiously. 'Iver isn't my guardian now that I am of age, but only my trustee! He has no power to prevent my marriage – no authority over me at all!'

'It appears to me that if he holds your purse-strings until you are five-and-twenty he has a great deal of power over you,' responded Miss Tresilian dryly.

He looked troubled, but said: 'He wouldn't – I *know* he wouldn't! People think him tyrannical, but he has never been so to me! The kindest of guardians – and he must have wished me at the devil, for I was only eight when my father died, and *he* not much above five-and-twenty. I wonder he didn't leave me to be reared in my own house, for I was used to follow him about like a tanthony-pig!'

Miss Tresilian refrained from comment. It seemed to her unlikely that Mr Rosely had ever offered Lord Iver the least pretext for a display of tyranny, for while she could not but acknowledge the sweetness of his disposition she did not feel that resolution was amongst his many virtues. No hint of a strong will was to be detected in his delicate countenance, none of the determination that characterized Lucy.

'And even if he doesn't consent, we shall come off all right,' said Lucy cheerfully. 'After all, I have quite a genteel fortune of my own, and we can subsist on that, until your stupid Trust comes to an end.'

But at this Miss Tresilian intervened, saying firmly that neither she nor Lucy's papa could countenance an engagement entered into without Lord Iver's sanction. Lucy, always outspoken, said: 'Dearest, you know that's fudge! All Papa would say is that you must settle it as you think best!'

Miss Tresilian laughed, but said: 'Well, I can't settle it, precisely, but I can and must forbid an engagement at this present. I am very sorry for you both, but unless Lord Iver should change his mind I am afraid there is nothing for it but to wait until Arthur's fortune passes into his own hands.'

It was not to be expected that two young persons deep in love could view with anything but dismay the prospect of waiting more than three years before becoming engaged. Mr

Rosely took a dejected leave of the ladies, and went away, saying that he was sure he *must* be able to prevail upon Iver to relent; and Lucy at once set about the task of convincing her aunt that her attachment to her Arthur was no girlish fancy to be speedily forgotten.

It was unnecessary. Although she had been virtually in her aunt's charge since her childhood only fifteen years separated them, and the bonds of affection between them were strong. Miss Tresilian knew that her niece was neither volatile nor impressionable. She had been much courted in Bath, but none of her suitors, before the arrival on the scene of Mr Rosely, had done so much as turn her head. But she had fallen in love with Mr Rosely at first sight, and not for the sake of his handsome face. 'Handsome?' said Lucy. 'I suppose he is – oh, yes, of course he is! Everyone says so! But, to own the truth, I don't in general care about fair men, and try as I will I *cannot* admire Grecian profiles!' She added, such a glow in her eyes as Miss Tresilian had never before seen: 'His nature is by far more beautiful than his countenance. He has so much sensibility – such quickness of apprehension! It is as though we had known each other all our lives. Oh, my dearest aunt, I never dreamed I could be so happy!'

No, Lucy was not likely to fall out of love, nor was it possible to suppose her to be infatuated. She seemed to be aware of the flaw in his character, for when her aunt ventured to suggest that his amiability perhaps made him a trifle too persuadable she replied without hesitation: 'Exactly so! I don't mean to say that he could be persuaded to do wrong, for his principles are fixed; but his nature is gentle, and his diffidence leads him to rely more on another's judgment than his own. That is one reason why I can't and won't wait for nearly four years before marrying him!'

'Lucy dear, could you be *happy* with a husband who would allow you to rule the roast?'

'To own the truth,' replied Lucy mischievously, 'I have a

strong notion that I couldn't be happy with any other! You know what a detestably managing disposition *I* have!' She added, in a more serious tone: 'Please help me, dear Aunt Elinor! If there were any *reason* for Lord Iver's refusal to give his consent I promise you I would respect it! There is none! But Arthur has been so much in the habit of deferring to him that if all must remain at a stand for nearly four years – Oh, aunt, he is the *horridest* creature, and my enemy besides! I couldn't mistake! I have met him only once, when Mrs Crewe took me to the Waltons' ball, and Arthur brought him up to me, but he looked at me in *such* a way! If I had been a shabby-genteel wretch on the catch for a rich husband he couldn't have been more repelling! But he must know I'm nothing of the kind, for Lady Windlesham does – and if Arthur's *sister* likes the match I wish you will tell me what right Lord Iver has –' She checked herself. 'Well! Talking won't pay toll. Think for me, Aunt Elinor! Useless to suppose that Arthur will be able to bring that creature about!'

❦

Even less than her niece did Miss Tresilian believe that Mr Rosely's efforts would meet with success, and much more astonished than Lucy was she when, two days later, Lord Iver came to call at the slim house in Green Street which she had hired for the season. Indeed, the news that he was awaiting her in the drawing-room startled her into exclaiming: 'Oh, no! No, no, I cannot – !' However, she recollected herself almost immediately, sent the servant down again to tell his lordship she would be with him directly, and turned to cast an anxious glance at her reflection in the mirror.

With the buoyancy of youth, Lucy was much inclined to think that Lord Iver had miraculously capitulated, and had come to discuss the marriage settlements. Miss Tresilian, with no such expectation, begged her not to indulge optimism, and trod resolutely downstairs, pledged to support the lovers' cause.

❧

The visitor was standing with his back to the room, looking out of the window, but when he heard the door open he turned, and stared with hard, challenging eyes at his hostess.

She shut the door, but remained by it, meeting that fierce scrutiny resolutely. For a minute neither spoke, but each scanned the other, the lady perceiving a powerfully-built man, harsh-featured and swarthy, whose close-cropped hair, sporting neckcloth, and gleaming top-boots proclaimed the Corinthian; the gentleman gazing at an uncommonly pretty woman. Miss Tresilian was on the shady side of thirty, but although she had lately taken to wearing a cap over her soft brown curls, and bore herself with the assurance of her years, she retained the face and figure of a much younger woman.

It was she who broke the silence, saying, as she moved forward: 'You wished, I think, to see me, sir. May I know why?'

He bowed stiffly. 'I am obliged to you for receiving me, ma'am. As to my *wishes* – ! I thought it best to come here in person, that there should be no misunderstanding between us.'

'Pray be seated, sir!' said Miss Tresilian, disposing herself gracefully in a winged armchair.

He did not avail himself of this invitation, but said abruptly: 'I imagine you must know what my errand is. If you are indeed your niece's guardian – but you will permit me to say that I find it incredible that you should be! She has a father, and you are by far too young to be her guardian!'

'Certainly she has a father,' replied Miss Tresilian coldly. 'When he married again, however, it was agreed that his daughter should remain in my charge. Let me remind you that I am no longer a young woman, sir!'

At this point, the conversation, which had been conducted with the appearance at least of formality, underwent a change. 'I know to a day how old you are, so don't talk nonsense to me!' said his lordship impatiently. 'A more ramshackle arrangement – ! Is your sister with you?'

'No,' said Miss Tresilian, eyeing him with hostility, 'she is not! The indifferent state of her health –'

He gave a crack of sardonic laughter. 'You needn't tell me! Still suffering spasms and vapours to throw a rub in your way, is she?'

'Pray, did you come here merely to discuss my sister's constitution?' demanded Miss Tresilian.

'You know very well why I am here! This lamentable affair between your niece and my cousin – which you appear to have encouraged!'

'I can assure you, however, that had I known of Mr Rosely's relationship to you, sir, I should have done my utmost to *dis*courage an affair which I dislike quite as much as you do!'

'A pretty sort of guardian, not to have made it your business to enquire who were Arthur's relations!' he said scathingly.

'And did you make it your business to acquaint yourself with all Lucy's remote cousins?' she retorted.

'It was unnecessary. I knew her to be your niece, and that was enough! In plain words, I don't wish for the connection, and shall do what I may to put an end to it. Don't under-rate me! you'll find I can do a great deal!'

'Do rid your mind of the notion that the connection is any more welcome to me than it is to you!' begged Miss Tresilian. 'Nothing could be more repugnant to me than an alliance with any member of your family!'

'So I should suppose – since you made it plain enough when you jilted me!'

'If you mean by that that I terminated an unfortunate engagement which you were regretting quite as much as I –'

'I didn't come here to discuss ancient history!' he interrupted roughly.

'Well, if you came merely to inform me that you don't wish your precious cousin to marry Lucy you've wasted your time!' she countered.

'Ah!' instantly responded his lordship. 'So you do support them, do you? I might have known it!'

She was about to repudiate this suggestion when it occurred to her that to do so would scarcely be in accordance with her promise to help her niece. It cost her a severe struggle, but she managed to summon up a smile, and to say with creditable composure: 'Come! It won't serve for us to rip up at each other, Iver. We may regret this business, but a twelve-year-old quarrel between *us* doesn't constitute a bar to these children's marriage.'

'Have you told your niece?'

'No – any more than you, I collect, have told your cousin! Much good would that do! They would say, and rightly, that it was no concern of theirs!'

'Well, I won't have it!' he announced.

'Now, don't fly into a pelter!' she begged. 'Our differences apart, what is there to be said against the match? Nothing, I dare say, could be more suitable!' She hesitated, and then added, with a little difficulty: 'How odiously selfish we should be if we were to let them break their hearts only because we once quarrelled!'

His lips curled disdainfully. 'Hearts are not so easily broken!'

'No one knows that better than I!' she retorted.

'We need not, then, discuss such an absurdity.'

Realizing, too late, the infelicity of her retort, she tried to recover lost ground. 'Neither of us is in a position to judge what may be the sufferings of two people who *truly* love one another! Lucy's character is unlike mine: her affection is not easily won, and is by far more tenacious than mine.'

'It could hardly be less!' he interpolated. 'Spare me any more moving speeches! She is young enough to recover from her disappointment, and will no doubt transfer her affections soon enough to some other, and, I trust, equally eligible suitor!'

Stung, she retaliated: 'She might well do *that!*'

'Oh, play off no airs for my edification!' he said angrily. 'You won't hoax me into believing that you are not well aware that my cousin is one of the biggest prizes in the Matrimonial Mart! A feather in any girl's cap!'

Rising hastily to her feet, she said: 'If I have anything to say to it, he won't be a feather in Lucy's cap, and that, my lord, you may depend on!'

'Thank you!' he replied. 'You have given me the assurance I sought, and I have nothing further to do here than to take my leave of you! Your obedient servant, ma'am!'

'Lucy,' said Miss Tresilian, with determined calm, 'if your pride doesn't revolt at the imputation of having snared a rich matrimonial prize, mine does! I am not asking you to put all thought of Arthur out of your head: I am merely saying that until he is in every respect his own master, and you have come of age, I will neither countenance his visits to this house, nor allow you to go where there is the least likelihood of your meeting him.'

The youngest Miss Tresilian said, with a brave attempt to speak lightly: 'Dearest, do you mean to lock me up? I must meet him at all the ton parties, and at Almack's too!'

'I know it,' said her aunt. 'And *you* know I don't mean to lock you up! I have a much better scheme in mind, and one which I think you must like. Indeed, I know you will, for you have always wished to visit foreign countries, only, of course, while that dreadful Bonaparte was at large it was impossible. *Now*, however –'

'Oh, no, no!' Lucy cried. 'I don't care a straw for anything Lord Iver may think! He has no power to forbid my marriage to Arthur, and if he is so spiteful as to cut off Arthur's allowance we shall contrive to live tolerably comfortably on *my* inheritance. And no one will think ill of Arthur for doing so, because the instant he is five-and-twenty he may pay me back every groat, if he feels he ought! All we need is Papa's consent – which is to say yours, my dear aunt!'

'And you won't get it!' said Miss Tresilian, with unusual asperity. 'Dear child, consider! How can you expect me to behave so improperly as to support a marriage which the person most nearly concerned with Arthur's affairs has expressly forbidden?' She saw that her words had struck home, and lost no time in representing to Lucy all the advantages of her scheme. She was listened to in silence, but had the satisfaction, when she had talked herself out of arguments, of being caught into a warm embrace, and tightly hugged.

'You are the best and kindest of aunts!' Lucy declared. 'I do understand what you must feel – indeed, I do! *Never* would I ask you to do what you think wrong! I had not reflected how impossible it must be for you! Forgive me!'

Much heartened, Miss Tresilian recommended her not to be a goose, and wondered how speedily she could put her plans into execution, and what her exacting elder sister would say when she learned that she meant, instead of returning to her home in Camden Place, to embark on an extended foreign tour.

It could not have been said that Lucy entered into any of the arrangements which occupied Miss Tresilian's every moment during the following week, or evinced the smallest enthu- siasm for any of the promised treats in store, but she uttered no protests, and that, in Miss Tresilian's opinion, was as much as could be hoped for in the natural oppression of her spirits.

Calculating ways and means, Miss Tresilian paused to consider the likelihood of Mr Rosely's following his inamorata. Probably Lord Iver would scotch any such scheme, but she determined nevertheless to add her prohibition to his.

❧

In the event, she was denied the opportunity of private speech with Mr Rosely. Returning to Green Street just after eleven one morning, after a protracted appointment in the City, she was met by her personal maid, who did not scruple to read her a scold for having sallied forth alone on what this severe critic apparently believed to have been an expedition fraught with peril. 'And breakfast waiting for you this hour past!' said Miss Baggeridge, relieving her of her shawl and gloves. 'Now, you sit down this instant, Miss Elinor! Traipsing all about the town, and knocking yourself up like you are! What your poor mama would have said I'm sure I don't know!'

Accustomed from her childhood to her henchwoman's strictures, Miss Tresilian only said, as she removed her becoming hat of chip-straw: 'Where's Miss Lucy? I suppose she breakfasted an hour ago.'

'It's what anyone *might* suppose of a young lady of quality,' said Miss Baggeridge grimly. 'Though why they should, with you setting her the example you do, miss –'

'– you are sure you don't know!' supplied Miss Tresilian.

Miss Baggeridge fixed her with a kindling eye. 'Well do I know it's not my place to utter a word, miss, and far be it from me to unclose my lips on the subject, but when it comes to a young lady gallivanting about the town without so much as the page-boy to escort her, and carrying a bandbox on her arm like a common person, I couldn't reconcile it with my conscience not to speak!'

'If she was carrying a bandbox, she has only gone to take back that French cambric half-robe which must be altered,' said Miss Tresilian prosaically.

Miss Baggeridge sniffed, but refrained from further comment. Having seen her mistress supplied with fresh coffee and bread and butter, she produced from her pocket a sealed missive, saying, in a grudging tone: 'There's a letter from Miss Clara. There was a shilling to pay on it, too. I suppose you'd better have it, but if I was you, miss, I wouldn't worrit myself with it till you've eaten your breakfast.'

With these sage words of advice she withdrew; and Miss Tresilian, never one to shirk a disagreeable duty, broke the wafer of her sister's letter, and spread open three crossed pages of complaint.

While she sipped her coffee she perused these. Nothing could have been more discouraging than the eldest Miss Tresilian's account of her health, but as her detailed descriptions of the torment she endured from rheumatism, nervous tic, spasm, and insomnia were interspersed with the latest Bath on-dits, and some animadversions on the wretched cards she had held at the whist-table, Miss Elinor Tresilian's withers remained unwrung. She gathered that Clara was contriving to amuse herself tolerably well; was relieved to read no very serious criticism of the indigent lady engaged to act as companion to the invalid; and got up to place the letter in her writing-bureau. She never did so. No sooner had she raised the lid of the bureau than she found herself staring down at a letter addressed to herself in Lucy's handwriting. Clara's missive dropped to the floor, and Miss Tresilian, with a premonition of disaster, snatched up her niece's letter, and tore off the wafer that sealed it.

Dear, dearest aunt, she read. *This will come as a Shock to you, and I can only implore you to forgive me, and to understand (as*

I am persuaded you will) the Exigency of my Situation, nothing less than which could have prevailed upon me to act in a manner as Repugnant to me as, alas, it will be to you. By the time your eyes alight on these lines I shall be many miles distant, and when I Cast myself at your feet to beg your Pardon it will be as the Bride of my Adored Arthur. Oh, my dear aunt, believe that I have not reached this Momentous Decision without an Agonizing Struggle, for to Approach the Altar without your Blessing, or your presence to support me at that Solemn Moment, so sinks my spirits that only my Conviction that your Refusal to sanction my Engagement sprang not from your Heart but from your sense of Propriety gives me courage to pursue a Line of Conduct which must Shock you and all the world. My only Comfort (besides the Bliss of being united to the Best and Noblest of men) is that You cannot be held accountable, even by Lord Iver, for what I must call (though my hand shrinks from penning the Dreadful Syllables) my Elopement....

Stunned by this communication, Miss Tresilian could not for many minutes collect her scattered wits. With every will in the world to spring to instant action she felt as though she had been smitten with paralysis. From this distressing condition she was reclaimed by the sudden opening of the door, and the sound of a harsh, too-well remembered voice saying: 'Thank you, I'll announce myself!'

She raised her head, and stared blankly across the room at Lord Iver.

He was dressed for travel, and had not stayed to put off his long, many-caped driving-coat of white drab. It was plain, from his blazing eyes and close-gripped lips, that he was in a towering rage, but he did not immediately speak. After a searing moment, his gaze dropped to the letter in her hand, and he said: 'Mine is an empty errand, I apprehend! Is that from your niece?'

Hardly knowing what she did, she held it out to him. He rapidly scanned it, and said contemptuously: 'Very affecting! – if you have a taste for the romantic! I have not!' His eyes searched her face; he gave a short laugh. 'Don't look so tragic! You don't imagine, do you, that I shan't stop this crazy project?'

She pressed her fingers to her throbbing temples. '*Can* you do so? Do you know where – Has Arthur written to you?'

'Yes – like the silly widgeon he is!' he replied. 'As for knowing *where*, there was no need to tell me *that*! Or you either, I imagine!'

'But I haven't the least notion!' she said distractedly. 'Where *could* they have gone? She's under age! Even if Arthur has a special licence, no one would marry them! *She* knows that, and surely *he* must?'

'Of course they know it, and also the one place where they may be married, with no questions asked!' He read bewilderment in her face, and strode up to her, and gave her a rough little shake. 'They've set off for the Border, my innocent! This is to be a Gretna Green affair: a charming scheme, isn't it?'

'*Gretna Green?*' she repeated. The colour rushed up into her face; she thrust him away, exclaiming: 'How dare you say such a thing? *Never* would Lucy behave with such impropriety!'

'Then have the goodness to tell me where else she has gone – with a wedding as her acknowledged goal!'

'I don't *know!*' she cried, unconsciously wringing her hands. 'Unless – Oh, could they have hoaxed some cleric into believing Lucy to be of age?'

'They can hardly have needed a post-chaise-and-four for that fetch! Oh yes, I've ascertained that much already – and also that the chaise has been hired for an unspecified time, and the postboys for the first two stages. To Welwyn, in fact, and Welwyn, I would remind you, is on the Great North Road!'

'Oh *no!*' she protested. 'I don't believe it!'

'Well, that's of no consequence!' he said unkindly. 'I have discharged *my* duty, at all events, and must now be off. I shall overtake them long before they reach the Border, and will engage myself, to restore your niece to you with as little scandal as may be possible, so don't fall into despair!'

'Wait!' she uttered. 'If this is true – What was it she wrote? – repugnant to her as it must be to me – agonizing struggle – shock the world – Good God, she must be out of her senses! Iver, she left the house before ten o'clock! *Can* you overtake them?'

'Do you care to hazard a bet on the chance that I shan't have done so before nightfall? I shouldn't, if I were you!'

'Then grant me ten minutes, and I'll be ready to go with you!' she said, hurrying to the door.

'Don't be so absurd! I'm not taking you with me on this chase, or anyone! Not even my groom!'

'I should hope you were not taking your groom! But me you are taking, make up your mind to that, Iver! Who is to protect Lucy's reputation if I don't! *You* cannot! – in fact, you would be very much more likely to blast it!'

'Thank you! Let me tell you that I am not travelling in a post-chaise, but in my own curricle!'

'So I should suppose! And let *me* tell you, my lord, that this won't be the first time I've travelled in a curricle – or driven one, if it comes to that!'

'It will *not* come to that!' declared his lordship, flinging these words after her retreating form.

❦

The first few miles of the journey were accomplished in silence, since Miss Tresilian was absorbed in her agitating reflections, and Lord Iver's attention was fully engaged by the task of guiding a spirited team through the noise and bustle of the crowded streets. His curricle was lightly built and well sprung; and since, like every other sporting blood of his day, he had not two but four horses harnessed to it, and was himself a Nonesuch of the first stare, it bowled over the ground, when the streets were left behind, at a speed that allayed one at least of Miss Tresilian's fears. The June day was bright and warm, the road in excellent condition, and these circumstances helped materially to restore her spirits. When my lord swept through Barnet without a check she asked him where he meant to change horses. He replied curtly that his team was good for two stages. Miss Tresilian relapsed into silence, but, after some twenty minutes, said suddenly: 'Try as I will, I can't believe we haven't come on a wild goose chase!'

'Then perhaps you will tell me why you forced yourself upon me?'

'On the chance that you might be right – but the more I consider it the less do I think you can be!'

But at Welwyn, where my lord arranged for the stabling of his own horses, and had a fresh team put-to, her optimism was quenched. One of the waiters at the White Hart had had ample opportunity to observe the handsome young gentleman who had jumped down from a chaise to procure a glass of lemonade for his lady; and he described him in terms which left no room for doubt. Miss Tresilian's rising spirits went into eclipse, and were not improved by his lordship's saying, as he drove out of the yard: 'Satisfied?'

Spurred by this unhandsome taunt, she responded: 'A very odd notion you must have of me if you suppose I could be *satisfied* by such intelligence! I was never more shocked in my life!'

'I should hope you had not been! If anything had been needed to prove me right in thinking you wholly unfit for the post of guardian your niece has supplied it!'

'Well, if it comes to that, you've made a sad botch of *your* ward, haven't you?' she retorted.

'I have not the smallest doubt that Arthur was cajoled into this escapade by your niece's wiles!'

'To own the truth,' said Miss Tresilian frankly, 'nor have I! Lucy has ten times his spirit! There is a want of resolution in him which I can't but deplore, even though I perfectly understand the cause of it. Poor boy! It must have been hard indeed to have developed strength of character, bullied and browbeaten as he has been almost from infancy!'

'*Bullied and browbeaten?*' echoed his lordship.

'I dare say you never knew you were crushing his spirit,' she offered, in a palliative tone.

'No! Nor he either, let me tell you! You have only to add that fear of me has driven him into this elopement, and you will have gone your length!'

'Well, of course it has!' she said, turning her head, in genuine astonishment, to scan his grim profile.

'God grant me patience!' he ejaculated. 'So you mean to shuffle off the blame on to my shoulders, do you? Well, you won't do it! *You* are to blame, not I!'

'*I?*' she gasped.

'Yes, you! With your henwitted scheme to carry the girl out of the country! Of all the cork-brained, ill-judged —'

'This,' interrupted Miss Tresilian, 'goes beyond belief! Next you will say that it was I who forbade the marriage!'

'You were the only person with the authority to do so, at all events!'

'Indeed? I collect I merely dreamed that you said you would put an end to the project, and warned me not to under-rate your power?'

'When I said that I gave you credit for having enough sense not to precipitate a crisis which any but a confirmed pea-goose must have foreseen!'

'No, that is too much!' she exclaimed. 'And don't dare to tell me that you are without power, Iver, because I know very well that you hold Arthur's purse-strings, and can withhold every penny of his fortune from him!'

'Don't be so ridiculous!' he said irritably. 'How could I possibly do so? A pretty figure I should cut!'

'You threatened to do it!'

'Very likely I may have, but if he believed I meant it he's a bigger gapeseed than I knew! If he was in earnest, there was nothing I could do to prevent the marriage – eligible enough in the eyes of the world, if not in mine! Had *you* refrained from interfering, I could have handled him: it wasn't any threat of mine which goaded him into this clandestine start, but *your* determination to carry the girl out of his reach!'

'Well, of all the wickedly unjust things you have ever said to me, this is without parallel!' she exclaimed. 'So I *interfered*! And for what other purpose, Iver, did you call in Green Street than to prevail upon me to do so?' She saw a slight flush creep into his lean cheek: a sign of discomfiture which afforded her far more gratification than she was prepared to admit. After a tiny pause, she added severely: 'If there is any virtue in you you'll own yourself at fault, and beg my pardon!'

That drew a disconcerting reply from him. He glanced at her, fire in his eyes. 'Oh no! Not again! *Once* I did so – took on myself the blame for a quarrel which was *not* of my making – begged you to forgive –' He checked himself, and said bitterly: 'Even Arthur isn't as big a gudgeon as I was!'

He reined in, for they had reached a toll-gate. She was never more glad to be spared the necessity of answering. While he bought a ticket to open the pikes on the next stage she had time to recover her countenance, and was able to say, quite calmly, as the curricle moved forward: 'If that man is to be believed, we have certainly gained on them, but they must be a great way ahead still. Where do you expect to overtake them?'

'Not short of Stamford, unless they meet with some accident.'

They were entering Baldock, and neither spoke again until they had proceeded for some way along the road beyond the town. Lord Iver then demanded abruptly: 'Why did you never answer me? Did you think it cost me nothing to write that letter?'

She shook her head, a constriction in her throat making it for a moment impossible for her to speak. She overcame it, and said, keeping her eyes lowered: 'I thought it better not to reply – not to reopen – when it reached me, you see, Mama had suffered the stroke which left her paralysed. You know what our house-hold was at the Manor! My father so dependent on her – Lucy motherless – Clara – well, there can be no need for me to explain why it was useless to suppose that Clara could fill Mama's place!'

He had listened to her in thunderstruck silence, but at this he said, with suppressed violence: 'And equally useless for me to tell you that nothing ever ailed Clara but jealousy, and a selfish-ness I have never seen surpassed! We have quarrelled enough on *that* head!'

She smiled. 'We have indeed! Must I own that you were right? Perhaps you were – though it would be unjust to deny that her constitution was always sickly.'

'I told you years ago that she would spoil your life, if she could do it! I learn now that she spoiled mine as well, thanks to your blind, obstinate refusal to credit me with more wit than you had!'

'Nonsense!' said Miss Tresilian. 'You know very well that no two persons could have been less suited than we were! As for spoiled lives, I hope you don't mean to tell me you've been wearing the willow for the past twelve years, because I know very well you haven't! In fact, if only half the tales I've heard are true you've never lacked consolation!'

'Is that what the Bath quizzes say of me? No, I haven't worn the willow, but one tale you've never heard: that I was hanging out for a wife!'

'Very true, and I think you are wise to remain single. I am persuaded you must have a much more amusing time as a bachelor.'

A muscle quivered at the corner of his mouth. 'You haven't altered! How often have I wanted to wring your neck for just such a remark as that!'

'No doubt! But there is nothing to be gained by discussing what you very rightly called ancient history. We have a more important matter to decide. What's to be done with those abominable children when we do catch them?'

'Wring *their* necks!'

'Quite impractical! *I* have no fancy for Newgate, if you have!'

He laughed, but said: 'You may at least depend upon my giving Arthur the finest trimming of his life!'

'I do, and shall be strongly tempted to do the same to Lucy! But it won't answer, Iver: we shall be obliged to give our consent, and with as good a grace as we may.'

'Oh, why stop at that? Let us escort them to the anvil!'

She regarded him with misgiving. 'Iver, don't, I implore you, get upon your high ropes! You said yourself that you could not stop the marriage if Arthur was in earnest! You can hardly want more proof of that!'

'I can want no more proof that he hasn't outgrown his puppyhood! Good God, only a scoundrel or a paper-skulled schoolboy would do such a thing as this!'

'It's very bad, of course, but –'

'And if he, or your hoydenish niece, think they can force my hand, they will very soon learn to know me better!'

'Yes!' said Miss Tresilian bitterly. 'I might have guessed you'd turn mulish, might I not? You always did make bad worse, and you always will!'

❦

By the time Stamford was reached, Miss Tresilian was herself so weary that she could only suppose her companion to be made of iron. More than eighty miles had been covered, often at a pace which demanded the strictest concentration, and in six hours of fast driving he had allowed himself only two brief respites. During one of these Miss Tresilian had found the time to swallow a mouthful of ham, and a few sips of scalding coffee, and on this meagre fare she had been obliged to subsist, encouraged by a disagreeable reminder from his lordship that he had warned her how it would be if she insisted on accompanying him. She forgave him for that: he sat as erect as at the start of the journey, his hands as steady and his eyes as watchful, but she knew, without the evidence of the crease between his brows, how tired he must be. No conversation had been held during the past hour; Miss Tresilian, in fact, had fallen into an uneasy doze, and woke up in the yard of the George, demanding to know where she was.

'Stamford,' replied Lord Iver, looking down at her. 'Quite done up?'

'A little tired – nothing to signify!'

'I'll say this for you: you were always full of pluck! Our runaways are not here, but there are two other posting-houses in the town, and several smaller inns. They may well be racking up at one of them for the night.'

'But it is still daylight!'

'It will be daylight for some hours yet, but it is nevertheless past six o'clock. If they knew they were being followed no doubt they would go on, but I've no reason to believe that they do. They have been travelling at a fair rate, but with no suggestion of flight. Come, let me help you down! You will have time to dine while I am making enquiries at the other houses.'

She agreed to this, but when he left her installed in a private parlour she discovered herself to be too anxious to be hungry. She ordered some tea, however, which revived her, though it drew a sharp rebuke from his lordship, when he presently returned to the George. 'Don't scold!' she begged. 'It was all I wanted, I promise you. And *you* have eaten nothing!'

'On the contrary, I had a sandwich and some beer at the Swan.' His frown deepened. 'I've been unable to get any news of them: they are certainly not in the town. If they changed horses here, no one recalls having seen them – though that's not wonderful: the ostlers are kept too busy to take particular note of all the travellers who pass through the place.'

Her heart sank, but she said: 'There's nothing for it but to go on, then.'

He said roughly: 'You've come far enough! I'll have that portmanteau of yours carried up to a bed-chamber, and you may remain here. You needn't be afraid I shan't catch that pair: I shall, and will bring Lucy to you at once, so don't argue with me, if you please!'

'I don't mean to,' said Miss Tresilian, tying the strings of her bonnet. 'Nor do I mean to be abandoned in this very noisy inn!'

'Now, listen to me, my girl!' said his lordship, in menacing accents.

'Go and order the horses to be put-to!' said Miss Tresilian, unimpressed.

∾

No reliable news was to be gained at either of the two first pikes north of Stamford, but at Greetham, where they stopped for a change, an ostler clearly remembered the young lady and gentleman, for he had helped to fig out four lively 'uns for them, and not so many minutes ago neither. He'd suspicioned all along that there was something havey-cavey about them. Argufying, they were, the young gentleman being wishful to put up for the night, and Miss being that set on going on she was ready to nap her bib. Nothing would do for her but to get to Grantham, so off they'd gone.

'Having made it plain that they were an eloping couple!' said Miss Tresilian, as they drove away. 'How Lucy could be so dead to shame – !'

Lord Iver returned no answer, and she sat staring with unseeing eyes at the fading landscape, lost in the gloomiest reflections. From these she was presently recalled by his lordship's voice, ejaculating: 'At last!'

The curricle had swept round a bend, and brought into view a post-chaise and four, bowling ahead at a spanking pace. 'Hand me the yard of tin!' commanded his lordship grimly.

'You look after your horses!' returned Miss Tresilian, already in possession of the long horn. 'I can sound this quite as well as you can!'

In proof of this statement, she raised the horn to her lips and produced an ear-splitting blast.

'That should startle them!' observed his lordship. 'Oh, my God, of all the infernal *cawkers* – !'

This outburst of exasperation was provoked by the sudden widening of the gap between the two vehicles: the post-boys, instead of making way for the curricle to pass, were springing their horses. 'Hold on tightly!' snapped his lordship, following suit.

'Iver, for heaven's sake – !' she uttered, as the curricle swayed and bounded alarmingly.

He paid no heed; and one glance at his face showed her that to suggest that he might just as well, and far more safely, drive behind the chaise until the fugitives realized the folly of trying to escape from him would be a waste of breath. This foolish gesture of defiance had thoroughly enraged him: he was going to pass the chaise at the first opportunity that offered.

Feeling sick with apprehension, Miss Tresilian fixed her eyes on the road, and tried not to speculate on what would happen if some vehicle were to come round one of the bends towards them. My lord had swung out to the right, not yet attempting to pass, but obviously ready to open out his leaders. The road was narrow, and the chaise held obstinately to the centre. They rocked round another bend, and Miss Tresilian saw a straight stretch ahead. It was a little broader, but not broad enough yet, she decided. Then she saw his lordship drop his hands, and shut her eyes, realizing that her last hour had come. Rigid with fright, she awaited the inevitable crash.

'Good girl!' said his lordship approvingly.

Her eyes flew open. 'You don't mean to say you've *done* it?' she gasped.

'Of course I've done it! What, were you afraid I should lock the wheels? Absurd creature!' He glanced over his shoulder, saw that the post-boys had reined in their horses to a trot, and checked his own team. In another minute he had brought them to a halt, swinging them across the road to form a barrier. He gave the reins into Miss Tresilian's hands, and, as the chaise drew up, sprang down, and strode towards it.

The post-boys eyed him in some trepidation, but he paid no attention to them. He lifted a hand to wrench open the door of the chaise, but before he could grasp the handle the door was thrust open from within, and a fresh-faced youth, not waiting to let down the steps, jumped out, saying, in an impetuous, rueful voice: 'I beg your pardon, sir! I didn't mean – at least, I – oh, by Jupiter, sir, *how* you did give us the go-by! It was the most bang-up thing I ever saw in my life! But I'm afraid you're very vexed!' he added, gazing up in dismay at Lord Iver's countenance.

His lordship was, in fact, thunderstruck, but his expression was certainly alarming. The unknown youth said contritely: 'We shouldn't have done so – *indeed*, I am very sorry! We were only funning – that's to say – well, I dare say you know how it is, sir, when one is in spirits, and – and –' His voice petered out unhappily, for he perceived no understanding at all in the eyes that stared so fiercely at him.

At this point, there was an intervention. A damsel, clad in the demure raiment suitable for a school-room miss, peeped out of the chaise, and said, with an engaging mixture of mischief and penitence: 'It was all my fault! Because I wouldn't put up at Stamford, and so we came on, because it is a whole year since I was at home, and I couldn't have slept a wink, and it's not so *very* much farther! Only when we changed horses at Greetham Jack said the light had begun to go, and Papa would say we shouldn't have come on, but *I* said we might easily reach Grantham if we drove fast, and give them all *such* a surprise, for they don't expect to see us until tomorrow. So Jack said: "*Oh, very well!*" but we should have everyone thinking we were eloping to Gretna Green, which sent us both into whoops, of course! And *that* was what put the notion into our heads!'

'I should explain, sir, that she's my sister,' interpolated the youth, anxious to throw light upon dark places. 'She has been at school, you see.'

'Yes, but Mama let me come away before any of the others, so that Jack could bring me home. Isn't it *famous*?' rapturously exclaimed his sister. 'Because Jack, you know, is *my* particular brother, just as Ned is Cecy's!'

His lordship, stunned as much by all these whirling words as by the shock of finding that he had waylaid two complete strangers, could think of nothing to say but: 'Oh!' and that in a blank voice which made it necessary for Miss Tresilian, deeply appreciative of the scene, to take her underlip firmly between her teeth. .

Frowning down his sister's irrelevance, the young gentleman embarked manfully on an explanation of his conduct. 'The thing was, sir, that I always *meant* to spring the horses, if the road was clear, because we have still more than twenty miles to go before we reach home, and my father – Oh, I should have told you that Father is Sir John Holloway, and we live near

Grantham! Well – well, we were joking each other about being a runaway couple when you blew up to pass us, and I shouted to the post-boys to put 'em along – just cutting a lark, you know! But, of course, I shouldn't have done so!' he added hastily. 'And I didn't mean to keep it up. Only – well, when you gave chase it was so exciting – and when I saw you were going to make the attempt – well, I *do* beg your pardon, sir, but I wouldn't have missed it for anything! You drove to an inch!'

'I see,' said his lordship. 'Well, when next you try your hand at racing on the road, don't do it in a post-chaise, and don't take your sister with you! Tell me, have you come from London?'

'Oh no! From Oxford, sir. One of the old tabbies at Bella's school brought her up from Bath – Oh, I should have told you that I'm at Magdalen!'

'Are you? Well, if you are to reach home before dark you'd best lose no more time. Up with you!'

'*Thank you!*' said Mr Holloway, greatly relieved. 'I'm excessively obliged to you for not – Oh, you go first, sir!'

'No, I should only hold you up: I'm not going to drive at your hell-for-leather pace!'

Laughing heartily at this, Mr Holloway, after fervently shaking hands with his lordship, hoisted himself into the chaise, and it moved forward, Miss Tresilian having by this time drawn the curricle to the side of the road. His lordship, heavily frowning, walked back to it. He observed that Miss Tresilian had succumbed to her emotions, and regarded her balefully.

'Oh, don't look at me like that, Iver!' she begged, wiping her streaming eyes. 'If you could but have seen your own face – !'

'Much help *you* were!' he said, with a reluctant grin. 'Yes, it's all very well for you to laugh yourself into stitches, my girl, but where the devil *are* those pernicious brats?'

'I *said* we had come on a wild goose chase! Have we all the time been pursuing that enchanting couple?'

'Certainly not! Didn't you hear the boy say they had come from Oxford? They can never have been on our road until they entered Stamford. I have not the smallest doubt that when *we* entered Stamford we were hard on the heels of our own pair.'

That sobered her. She said, in dismay: 'Do you mean that they are ahead of us still?'

'No, I don't,' he said decidedly. 'They haven't passed any of the pikes. From Stamford we have been following the Holloways.'

She was disturbed, but could not resist quizzing him. 'Flying from a scent, Iver? *You?*'

He smiled, but absently, and remained for some moments in frowning silence. He said suddenly: 'If the line was crossed in Stamford – Good God, why didn't I think of that before? He has taken the girl to Grantley, of course!' He saw that Miss Tresilian was bewildered, and added impatiently: 'Windlesham's place, beyond Market Deeping! You've met Arthur's sister, haven't you?'

'Lady Windlesham! Yes, but what could he hope to achieve by that?'

'Depend upon it, he has a special licence in his pocket, and means to be married under Caroline's ægis.'

'But *she* has no authority to sanction Lucy's marriage!'

'Much she would care for that! Arthur can bring her round his thumb any time he chooses to do it: she dotes on him! She's of a romantic disposition, what's more, and to judge by the impassioned entreaties she addressed to me on this subject has confused that precious pair with Romeo and Juliet.'

'Iver, she *could* not be so unprincipled as to –'

'Nothing of the sort!' he interrupted. 'She knows that Arthur is his own master, and if she doesn't know already that you liked the connection well enough until you discovered that I was Arthur's guardian, it wouldn't, I assure you, take Arthur more than five minutes to convince her that if only the knot could be tied without your knowledge you would be more likely to fall on her neck than to try to overset the marriage!'

He climbed into his seat again as he spoke, and took the reins from her. She relinquished them unheedingly. 'If that is indeed so, I can't deny that it is a great deal better than a flight to the Border, but a marriage performed in such circumstances *must* give rise to the most odious gossip! I *cannot* allow it!'

'There's no need to fly into high fidgets,' said his lordship, possibly to soothe alarm, but with a sad lack of sensibility. 'Caroline is a pretty ninnyhammer, but Windlesham is a man of excellent good sense, and can be depended on to put his foot down on such a scheme.'

'Yes, but –'

'Oh, for God's sake – !' he exclaimed. 'Can't you think of anything but that addle-brained pair? For my part, they may go to the devil! I'm sick and tired of both, and have been thinking them a dead bore for the last three hours!'

Jerked by this sudden violence from her preoccupation, she realized that the horses had been set in motion. 'Pray, where are we off to?' she demanded. 'If Arthur has taken Lucy to his sister's house we have no need to proceed farther north! How can you be so idiotish, Iver?'

'I'm not idiotish,' he replied, with an odd laugh. 'We set out for Gretna Green, and to Gretna Green we'll go! Our immediate destination, however, is Coltersworth. We shall spend the night at the Angel, and tomorrow, unless you should very much dislike it, we will resume our journey to the Border.'

'I should dislike it excessively,' said Miss Tresilian, after a little pause.

He halted his team and turned, laying his hand on one of hers, and strongly grasping it. 'Nell!' he said, in quite another voice. 'So many years wasted – so much bitterness – ! Nell, my dear love, don't say it's too late! You *must* marry me – you *shall*!'

Her fingers clung to his, and there was the sparkle of tears in her smiling eyes, but she replied with great dignity: 'I have every intention of marrying you, but *not*, I promise you, in such a clandestine fashion as that! Iver, for heaven's sake – ! There's an Accommodation coach coming towards us – *George!*'

But as his lordship, with his usual top-lofty disregard of appearances, paid no heed whatsoever to this warning, and Miss Tresilian was powerless (even had she made the attempt) to free herself from his embrace, the roof passengers on the coach were afforded a shocking example of the decay of modern manners, one moralist going so far as to express his desire to see such shameless persons set in the stocks. 'Kissing and hugging on the public highway!' he said, craning his neck to obtain the last possible glimpse of the disgusting spectacle. 'Calling themselves Quality, too!'

But in this he was wrong. With her cheek against his lordship's, Miss Tresilian said, on a choke of laughter: 'What a *vulgar* couple we are, love!'

'Well, who cares a rush for that?' he demanded. 'Oh, my darling, what *fools* we have been!'

Bath Miss

I

*P*APA,' SAID MISS MASSINGHAM, 'IS PERSUADED YOU WOULD
have not the least objection, or you may be sure I should
not have ventured to ask you, dear Charles, for perhaps you
might not quite wish to oblige him in this way.'

She paused, and glanced doubtfully up at dear Charles. It
could not have been said that his handsome countenance bore
the expression of one delighted to oblige his Mama's old friend,
but he bowed politely. Miss Massingham reminded herself that
this elegant gentleman, with his great shoulders setting off a
coat of blue superfine, and his shapely leg encased in a skin-
tight pantaloon and a Hessian boot of dazzling gloss, was the
bouncing baby on whom, thirty years before, she had bestowed
a coral rattle. She said archly: 'You are grown so grand that I
declare I stand quite in awe of you!'

The expression of boredom on Sir Charles Wainfleet's countenance became more pronounced.

'I am sure, a most notable dandy!' said Miss Massingham,
hopeful of giving pleasure.

'Believe me, ma'am, you flatter me!' said Sir Charles.

The third person present here came, as her duty was, to his rescue. 'No, Louisa!' she said. '*Not* a dandy! *They* only care for their clothes, and Charles cares for a great deal besides, such as prize-fighting, and cocking, and all the *horridest* things! He is a Corinthian!'

'Thank you, Mama, but shall we leave this subject, and discover instead just what it is that the General feels I shall have not the least objection to doing?'

Encouraged by this speech, Miss Massingham plunged into a tangle of words. 'It is so very obliging of you! The notion came into Papa's head when I mentioned the circumstance of your Mama's going to Bath next week, and that you mean to escort her! "Well, then," he said, "if that is so, Charles may bring Anne home!" I instantly demurred, but, "Balderdash!" exclaimed Papa – you know his soldierly way! – "If he fancies himself to have become too great a man to escort my granddaughter home from school, let him come and tell me so!" Which, however, I do beg you will not do, Charles, for Papa's gout has been very troublesome lately!'

'Have no fear, ma'am! I should not dare!' said Sir Charles, his weary boredom suddenly dissipated by a smile of singular charm.

'Oh, Charles, you are so very – ! The thing is, you see, that ever since the Mail was held up in that shocking way at Hounslow last month we have not known how to bring Nan home in safety! You must know that she has been a parlour boarder this year past at the Misses Titterstone's seminary in Queen's Square, and we have promised that she shall come home at Christmas. But for the circumstance of Papa's illness last winter, we had intended – but it was not to be! And now we find ourselves at a stand, and how we may entrust my poor brother's only child, left to our care when he was killed in that dreadful Peninsula – how we may entrust her, as I say, to the perils of the road, without some gentleman to escort her, we know not! And I am confident,' added Miss Massingham earnestly, 'that she would not tease you, Charles, for we shall send her old nurse down to Bath, and you need do no more than drive your curricle within sight of the chaise, and so we may be easy!'

If Sir Charles wondered why General Sir James Massingham should consider that his presence, within sight of his grand-daughter's chaise, would afford a better protection against highwaymen than an armed escort, he did not betray this. Nor did he betray the reluctance of a Nonpareil to assume charge of a Bath miss. It was Lady Wainfleet who raised an objection. 'Oh, but I depend on having Charles with me for Christmas!' she said. 'Dearest Almeria has been to visit me today, expressly to tell me that she will be in Bath herself for several weeks. She is to stay with her aunt, in Camden Place, and her brother, Stourbridge, is to bring her to town only a few days after we ourselves shall have left.'

Miss Massingham's face fell. The notice that Sir Charles Wainfleet, wealthiest of baronets, had at last fulfilled the expectations of the impoverished Earl of Alford, by offering for the hand of the Lady Almeria Spalding, eldest daughter of this improvident peer, had appeared some weeks previously in the *Gazette*, and she recognized that Lady Almeria's claims must take precedence of her niece's.

It was at this point that Sir Charles shook off his air of detach-ment. 'Almeria is going to Bath?' he said.

'Yes, is it not a happy chance? I was about to tell you of it when Louisa was announced.'

'On the contrary!' he returned. 'It is unfortunate that I should not have been apprized of this circumstance earlier. It so happens that I have engagements in town which I must not break. It will not be in my power, ma'am, to remain in Bath above a couple of nights.'

'You cannot mean to do such an uncivil thing as to leave Bath before Almeria arrives!' cried his mother. 'Good God, you would very likely meet her on the road!'

'Were I to delay my departure until after her arrival,' said Sir Charles glibly, 'I dare say I should find it impossible to tear myself away. I could not reconcile it with my conscience to disoblige so old a friend as the General. I shall be happy, Miss Massingham, to afford your niece all the protection of which I am capable.'

It was impossible for Lady Wainfleet to say more. Miss Massingham was already overwhelming Sir Charles with her gratitude. She said that she could not thank him enough, and she was still thanking him when he escorted her out to her carriage. But when he strolled back to the drawing-room, Lady Wainfleet begged him to consider before deciding to leave Bath so soon. 'Now that Almeria is to go there —'

'That circumstance, Mama, *did* decide me,' interrupted Sir Charles. 'Within a few months I shall be obliged to spend the rest of my life in Almeria's company. Allow me to enjoy what is left to me of my liberty!'

'Charles!' she faltered. 'Oh, dear! if I had thought that you would dislike it so much I would never — Not that I have the least power to force you into a marriage you don't like, only it has been an understood thing for so many years, and it is not as though you had ever a *tendre* for another eligible lady, and you are past thirty now, so that —'

'Oh yes, yes, ma'am!' he said impatiently. 'It is high time that I settled down! I have no doubt that Almeria will do me great credit. We were clearly made for one another — but I shall not spend Christmas in Bath!'

2

Eight days later, having sustained an interview with two genteel spinsters in mittens and mob-caps, who were much flustered to find their parlour invaded by a large and disturbingly hand-some gentleman, wearing a drab driving-coat with no fewer than sixteen shoulder-capes, Sir Charles made the acquaintance of his youthful charge. He beheld a demure schoolgirl, attired in a plain pelisse, and with a close bonnet almost entirely concealing her braided locks. She stood in meek silence while Miss Titterstone assured Sir Charles that dear Anne would be no trouble to him. Miss Maria, endorsing this statement, added, with rather odd anxiety, that she knew Anne would behave just as she ought. Both ladies seemed to derive consolation from the presence of Mrs Fitton, who all the while stood beaming fondly upon her nurseling.

Sir Charles, amused, wondered whether the good ladies suspected him of cherishing improper designs towards a chit of a schoolgirl in the most unbecoming hat and pelisse he had ever seen. Their evident uneasiness seemed to him absurd.

Farewells having been spoken, the travellers went out into the Square, where two vehicles stood waiting. One was a post-chaise and pair; the other a sporting curricle. Miss Massingham's large grey eyes took due note of this equipage, but she made no remark. Only, as Sir Charles handed her up into the chaise, she said: 'If you please, sir, would you be so *very* obliging as to permit me to stop for a few minutes at Madame Lucille's, in Milsom Street?'

'Certainly. I will direct your post-boy to drive there,' he replied.

Upon arrival in Milsom Street, one glance at Madame Lucille's establishment was enough to inform Sir Charles that Miss Massingham proposed to visit a mantua-maker. Assuring him that she would not keep him waiting for very long, she disappeared into the shop, followed by Mrs Fitton, whose smile, Sir Charles noticed, had given place to a look of decided anxiety.

Time passed. Sir Charles drew out his watch, and frowned. Speenhamland, where rooms for the night had been bespoken, was fully fifty-five miles distant, and the start of the journey had already been delayed by the chattiness of the Misses Titterstone. The horses were on the fret. Sir Charles walked them to the top of the street, and back again. When he had repeated this exercise some half a dozen times, there was a sparkle in his eye which made his groom thankful that it was the young lady and not himself who was keeping Sir Charles waiting.

At the end of another twenty minutes there erupted from the shop a vision in whom Sir Charles with difficulty recognized Miss Anne Massingham. Not only was she now arrayed in a crimson velvet pelisse, but she had set upon her head an all-too dashing hat, whose huge, upstanding poke-front was lined with gathered silk, and whose high crown was embellished with a plume of curled ostrich feathers. This confection was secured by broad satin ribbons, tied in a jaunty bow under one ear; and it displayed to advantage Miss Massingham's dark curls, now released from bondage, and rioting frivolously. A tippet and muff completed this modish toilet; and she carried, with its forepaws drooping over the muff, a curly-tailed puppy of mixed parentage. This circumstance did not immediately strike Sir Charles, for his gaze was riveted to that preposterous hat.

'Good God!' he ejaculated. 'My good child, you are not, I trust, proposing to travel to London in that bonnet?'

'Yes, I am,' asserted Miss Massingham. 'It is the high kick of fashion!'

'It is quite unsuited to a journey, and still more so to your years,' said Sir Charles crushingly.

'Fiddle!' said Miss Massingham. 'I am not a schoolgirl now, and if it had not been for Grandpapa's illness I should have ceased to be one a year ago! I am nineteen, you know, and I have been saving all my money for months to buy just such a hat as this! You could not be so unkind as to forbid me to wear it!'

Sir Charles looked down into the pleading, upturned face; Sir Charles's groom stared woodenly ahead. 'What,' demanded Sir Charles, turning upon the unhappy Mrs Fitton, 'possessed you to let your mistress buy such a hat?'

'Oh, don't scold poor Fitton!' begged Miss Massingham. 'Indeed, she implored me not to!'

Sir Charles found himself quite unable to withstand the look of entreaty in those big eyes. A whimper from the creature in Miss Massingham's arms provided him with a diversion. 'How did you come by that animal?' he asked sternly.

'Is he not the dearest little dog? He came running into the shop, and Madame Lucille told me that her pug has had six puppies just like him! She let me buy this one very cheaply, because she is very desirous of disposing of them all.'

'I imagine she might be,' said Sir Charles, viewing the pup with disfavour. 'However, it is no concern of mine, and we have wasted too much time already. If we are to reach Speenhamland in time for dinner we must make haste.'

'Oh, yes!' said Miss Massingham blithely. 'And may I ride with you in your curricle, Sir Charles?' She read prohibition in his eye, and added coaxingly: 'Just for a *little* way, may I? For your groom, you know, may easily go with Fitton in the chaise.'

Again Sir Charles found it impossible to withstand the entreaty in those eyes. 'Very well,' he said. 'If you think you won't be cold, you may jump up beside me.'

3

By the time the curricle had reached Bath Easton, Miss Massingham had begged Sir Charles to call her Nan, because, · she said, everyone did so; and Sir Charles had reprimanded her for saying that her friends in Queen's Square had greatly envied her her good fortune in being escorted to London by one who was well-known to be a buck of the first head.

'A *what*?' said Sir Charles.

'Well, it is what Priscilla Gretton's brother said, when she rallied him on the way he tied his neckcloth,' explained Nan. 'He said it was just how you tie yours, and that you were a buck of the first head.'

'I am obliged to Mr Gretton for his approval,' said Sir Charles, 'and I dare say that when he has learnt to refrain alike from trying to copy my way with a neckcloth and from teaching cant phrases to schoolgirls he may do tolerably well.'

'I can see that it is an expression I should not have used,' said Nan knowledgeably. 'Must I not call you a Nonpareil either, sir?'

He laughed. 'If you wish! But why should you talk about me at all? Tell me about yourself!'

She was doubtful whether so limited a subject could interest him, but since she was of a confiding nature it was not long before she was chatting happily to him. When the horses were changed, there was very little about Miss Massingham that he did not know; and since he found her curious mixture of inno-cence and worldly wisdom something quite out of the common way he was not sorry that she spurned a suggestion that she should continue the journey in the chaise. She was not, she said, at all chilly; she had been wondering, on the contrary, whether she might perhaps be allowed to take the ribbons.

'Certainly not!' said Sir Charles.

'You are such a famous whip yourself, sir, that you could very easily teach me to drive,' argued Miss Massingham, in persuasive accents.

'No doubt I could, but I shall not. I dislike being driven.'

'Oh!' said Miss Massingham, damped. 'I don't mean to tease you, only it would be *such* a thing to boast of!'

He could not help laughing. 'Absurd brat! Well – for half an hour, then, but no longer!'

'*Thank* you!' said Miss Massingham, her air of gentle melancholy vanishing.

When she was at last induced to give the reins back to her instructor, the Beckhampton Inn had been passed, and the chaise had long been out of sight. Sir Charles put his pair along at a spanking pace, and would no doubt have overtaken the chaise had his companion not announced suddenly that she was hungry. A glance at his watch showed him that it was past one o'clock. He said ruefully: 'I should have stopped to give you a nuncheon rather than have let you take the ribbons.'

'We could stop now, could we not, sir?' said Miss Massingham hopefully.

'If we do it must only be for a few minutes,' he warned her.

She agreed readily to this; and as they were approaching Marlborough he drove to the Castle Inn, and commanded the waiter to bring some cold meat and fruit as speedily as possible. Miss Massingham and her puppy, whom she had christened Duke, in doubtful compliment to his Grace of Wellington, both made hearty meals, after which Miss Massingham, while Sir Charles settled the reckoning, took her pet for a run on the end of a blind-cord, which she abstracted from the coffee-room, and for which Sir Charles was called upon to pay. She said that she would walk along the broad village street, and that he might pick her up in the curricle. Ten minutes later he ran her to earth outside a bird-fancier's shop, the centre of a small crowd of partisans and critics. Upon demand, he learned that Miss Massingham, discovering a number of songbirds cooped inside small wicker-cages, which were piled up outside the shop, had not only released the wretched prisoners, but had hotly harangued the fancier on the cruelty of his trade. It cost Sir Charles a sum grossly in excess of the birds' worth, and the exercise of his prestige as an obvious member of the Quality, to extricate his charge from this imbroglio, and she was not in the least grateful to him for having done it. She censured his conduct in having given the man money instead of knocking him down. 'Which I am persuaded you might have done, because Priscilla's brother told us that you are a Pink of the Fancy,' she said severely.

'I shall be obliged to you,' said Sir Charles, with asperity, 'if you will refrain from repeating the extremely improper remarks made to you by Priscilla's cub of a brother!'

'Now you are vexed with me!' said Nan.

'Yes, for your conduct is disgraceful!' said Sir Charles sternly.

'I did not mean to do what you would not like,' said Miss Massingham, in a small voice.

Sir Charles preserved an unbending silence for several minutes. It was then borne in upon him that Nan, having apparently lost her handkerchief, was wiping away large teardrops with a gloved finger. The result was not happy. Sir Charles, pulling up, produced his own handkerchief, took Nan's chin in one hand, and with the other removed the disfiguring smudges. 'There! Don't cry, my child! Come, smile at me!'

She managed to obey this behest. He knew an impulse to kiss the face he had upturned, but he repressed it, released her chin, and drove on. By the time Froxfield was reached, he had succeeded in diverting her mind, and the rest of the way to Speenhamland might have been accomplished without incident had not Duke, who had been sleeping off his meal, awakened, and signified, in no uncertain manner, his wish to leave the curricle.

4

Pulling up beside a spinney, Sir Charles set down his passengers, adjuring Miss Massingham not to allow her disreputable pet to stray. Unfortunately, she had neglected to tie the cord round his neck again, and no sooner did he find himself on the ground than he dashed into the spinney, yapping joyfully. She ran after him, and was soon lost to sight. Sir Charles was left to study the sky, which was developing a leaden look which he did not like. When a quarter of an hour had passed, he alighted, patience at an end, led his horses into the spinney, tied the reins round a sapling, and strode off in search of the truants.

For several moments there was no response to his irate shouts, but suddenly he was checked by a hail. It came from quite near at hand, but it was disturbingly faint. Alarmed, he followed the direction of the cry, rounded a thicket, and came upon Miss Massingham, trying to raise herself from the ground. Beside her sat Duke, with his tongue lolling out.

'*Now* what have you done?' said Sir Charles, exasperated. Then he saw that Miss Massingham's face was paper-white, and he went quickly up to her, and dropped on to one knee, saying in quite another voice: 'My child! Are you hurt?'

Miss Massingham, leaning thankfully against his supporting arm, said: 'I am so very sorry, sir! I didn't perceive the rabbit-hole, and I tripped, and I think I must have d-done something to my ankle, because when I tried to stand up it hurt me so much that I f-fainted. Indeed, I did not mean to be troublesome again!'

'No, of course you did not!' he said soothingly. 'Put your

arm round my neck! I am going to carry you to the curricle, and then we'll see what can be done.'

But although, when he had set her gently in her place, one glance at her ankle was enough to inform him that the first thing to be done was to remove her boot, a second glance, at her face, equally certainly informed him that to subject her to this added pain would cause her to faint again. He untethered the horses, and led them back on to the road, telling Nan curtly that he was going to drive her to Hungerford.

'Duke!' she uttered imploringly.

Sir Charles looked round impatiently, found Duke at his feet, and, grasping him by the scruff of his neck, handed him up to his mistress.

The short distance that separated them from Hungerford was covered in record time. Miss Massingham endured the anguish of the journey with a fortitude that touched her protector, even contriving to utter a small, gallant jest. Sir Charles, lifting her down, and carrying her into the Bear Inn, said: 'There, my poor child! You will soon be easier, I promise! You are a good, brave girl!'

He then bore her in to the empty coffee-room, laid her on a settle, and, while the waiter hurried to summon the landlady, removed the boot from a fast-swelling foot. As he had feared, Nan fainted. By the time she had recovered from this swoon, she had been established in a private parlour. She came round to find herself lying on a sofa, with a stout woman holding burnt feathers under her nose, and two chambermaids applying wet cloths to her ankle.

'Ah!' said Sir Charles bracingly. 'That's better! Come now, my child!'

Miss Massingham then felt herself raised, was commanded to open her mouth, and underwent the unpleasant experience of having a measure of neat brandy tilted down her throat. She choked, and burst into tears.

'There, there!' said Sir Charles, patting her in a comforting way. 'Don't cry! You will soon feel very much more the thing!'

Miss Massingham, a resilient girl, began to revive. The visit of the local surgeon, fetched by one of the ostlers after prolonged search, tried her endurance high, but as he pronounced that, although she had badly sprained her ankle, she had broken no bones, she soon took a more hopeful view of her situation, and was even able to think that she might very well be driven on to Speenhamland.

But this was now impossible. Not only was she in no state to be conveyed thirteen miles in an open curricle, but the short winter's day had ended, and the snow had begun to fall. Sir Charles was obliged to disclose to his charge that she must remain at the Bear until the following morning.

'To own the truth,' confided Nan, 'I am excessively glad of it. I am a great deal better, I assure you, but I would as lief not drive any farther for a little while.'

'Just so,' agreed Sir Charles, with a wry smile. 'But as I can place not the slightest dependence upon Mrs Fitton's feeling alarm until it will be too late for her to return in quest of you, I have thought it advisable to inform them here that you are my young sister.'

'Now, that,' said Miss Massingham, betraying at once her innocence and her sophistication, 'is a truly splendid thing, sir, for it shows that *at last* I am a grown-up lady!'

'Let me tell you,' said Sir Charles severely, 'that if you had refrained from buying that outrageous hat I should have had no need to employ this subterfuge! Never in my life have I encountered such an abominably behaved brat as you are, Nan!'

'I have been very troublesome to you, sir,' said Nan penitently. 'Are you *very* much vexed with me?'

He laughed. 'No. But you will ruin all if you call me "sir" in this inn! Remember that I am your brother, and say "Charles"!'

5

A night's rest did much to restore Miss Massingham to the enjoyment of her usual spirits. She partook of an excellent breakfast; hoped that Duke, in whose company Sir Charles had endured a disturbed night, had not discommoded her protector; and demonstrated the ease with which she could, with the aid of a stick, hop about on one foot. Sir Charles, who had been relieved to find, on pulling back his blinds, that only a light powdering of snow lay upon the road, recommended her to sit quietly on the sofa, and went out to see a pair of horses put-to. It was upon his return to the inn that, entering from a door at the back of the house, he was halted in his tracks by the sight of a handsome young woman, who had just come in through the front door.

This lady, catching sight of him, exclaimed: 'Charles! You here?'

'Almeria!' returned her betrothed, in hollow accents.

'But how comes this about?' demanded her ladyship, advancing towards him with her hand held out. 'Is it possible you can have come to meet me? We spent the night at the Pelican, you know. A broken trace has made this halt necessary, or we must have missed you. There was not the least occasion for you to have come all this way, my dear Charles!'

'I am ashamed to say,' replied Sir Charles, dutifully kissing the hand extended to him, 'that such was not my intention. I am bound for London – to keep an engagement I must not break!'

She did not look to be very well pleased with this response, but just as she was about to demand the nature of his engagement, the landlady came down the stairs, with a large bolster in her arm. 'This will be just the thing, sir!' she announced. 'It has been laying in the loft these years past, and I'm sure Miss is welcome to take it, the sweet, pretty young lady that she is! I'll carry it out directly, and see if it can't be arranged so as to make her comfortable!'

With this kindly speech, she disappeared through the door opening on to the stable-yard. Sir Charles, closing his eyes for an anguished moment, opened them again to find that his betrothed was regarding him through unpleasantly narrowed eyes.

'Miss?' said the Lady Almeria icily.

'Why, yes!' he returned. 'I am escorting the granddaughter of an old friend home from her school in Bath.'

'Indeed?' said Lady Almeria, her brows rising.

'Oh, good God, Almeria!' he said impatiently. 'There is no occasion for you to assume the air of a Siddons! It's only a child!'

'A new come-out for you, Charles, to be taking care of children! May I know why a bolster is necessary to her comfort? An infant in arms, I collect?'

'Nothing but a romp of a schoolgirl, who had the misfortune to sprain her ankle yesterday!'

It was at this inopportune moment that Nan, dressed for the road, hopped out of the parlour, Duke frisking beside her, and announced brightly that she was ready to set forward on the journey. Duke, perceiving that the door to a larger freedom stood open, made a dash for it.

'Charles! Stop him!' shrieked Nan.

The voice in which Sir Charles commanded Duke to come to heel startled that animal into cowering instinctively. Before he could recover his assurance, he had been picked up, and tucked under Sir Charles's arm.

'You frightened him!' said Nan reproachfully. She found that she was being surveyed from head to foot by a lady with an arctic eye and contemptuously smiling lips, and glanced enquiringly at Sir Charles.

'So this,' said Lady Almeria, 'is your schoolgirl!'

Sir Charles, only too well aware of the impression likely to be created by Miss Massingham's hat, sighed, and prepared to embark on what was (as he ruefully admitted to himself) an improbable explanation of his circumstances.

'Sir Charles is my brother, ma'am!' said Miss Massingham, coming helpfully to the rescue.

Lady Almeria's lip curled. 'My good girl, I am well acquainted with Sir Charles's sister, and I imagine I need be in no doubt of the relationship which exists between you and him!'

'Be silent!' Sir Charles snapped. He put Duke into Nan's free arm. 'Go back into the parlour, Nan! I will be with you directly,' he said, smiling reassuringly down at her.

He closed the parlour door upon her, and turned to confront his betrothed. That he was very angry could be seen by the glint in his eyes, but he spoke with studied amiability. 'Do you know, Almeria, I never knew until today how very vulgar you can be?' he said.

The Lady Almeria then lost her temper. In the middle of the scene which followed, her brother walked into the inn and stood goggling. His intellect was not quick, and it was several minutes before he could understand anything beyond the appalling fact that his sister, whose uncertain temper had chased away many a promising suitor, was engaged in whistling down the wind a bridegroom rich beyond the dreams of avarice. He looked utterly aghast, and seemed not to know what to say. Sir Charles, who had been refreshing himself with a pinch of snuff, shut his box, and said: 'The lady in question, Stourbridge, as I have already informed Almeria, is a schoolgirl, whom I am escorting to London.'

'Well, then, Almeria – !' said his lordship, relieved.

'Don't be a fool!' said Almeria. '*I* have seen the creature!'

'I should be loth to offer you violence, Almeria,' said Sir Charles, 'but if you again refer to that child in such terms I shall soundly box your ears!'

'You forget, I think, that I am not unprotected!'

'Stourbridge?' said Sir Charles. 'Oh, no, I don't forget him! If he cares to call me to book I shall be happy to answer him!'

At this point, Lord Stourbridge, who wished to come to fisticuffs with Sir Charles as little as he wished to expose his portly person to that gentleman's deadly accuracy with a pistol, attempted to remonstrate with his sister. A glance silenced him; she said furiously: 'Understand, Sir Charles, that our engagement is at an end! I shall be obliged to you if you will send the necessary notice to the *Gazette*!'

He bowed. 'It is always a happiness to me to obey you, Almeria!' he said outrageously.

6

Rejoining Miss Massingham in the parlour, he found her conscience-stricken. 'Who was that lady, sir?' she asked anxiously. 'Why was she so very angry?'

'That, my child, was the Lady Almeria Spalding. If you are ready to go –'

'Lady Almeria! Are – are you not engaged to her?'

'I *was* engaged to her!'

'Oh!' she cried. 'What have I done? Did she cry off because of me?'

'She did, but as we are not at all suited to one another I shall not reproach you for that. Foisting a repellant mongrel on me, however, which whined the better part of the night, is another matter; while as for your conduct in Marlborough –'

'But – but don't you care that your engagement is broken?' she interrupted.

'Not a bit!'

'Perhaps she will think better of it, and forgive you,' suggested Nan, in a somewhat wistful tone.

'I am obliged to you for the warning, and shall insert into the *Gazette* the notice that my marriage will not take place the instant I reach London,' he said cheerfully.

'It is very dreadful, but, do you know, sir, I find I *cannot* be sorry for it!'

'I am glad of that,' he said, smiling.

'She did not seem to me the kind of female you would *like* to be married to.'

'I can imagine none more unlike *that* female!'

She looked enquiringly up at him, but he only laughed, and said: 'Come, we must finish this journey of yours, if your grand-father is not to think that we have perished by the wayside!'

'Do you think he will be angry when he hears all that has happened?' she asked uneasily.

'I fear that his anger will fall upon *my* head. He will say – and with truth! – that I have made a poor hand at looking after you. However, I trust that when he has heard the full tale of your atrocious conduct he will realize that it was experience, and not goodwill, that was lacking in me, and give me leave to study how to do better in future.'

'I know you are quizzing me,' said Nan, 'but I don't precisely understand what you mean, sir!'

'I will tell you one day,' promised Sir Charles. 'But now we are going to drive to London! Come along!'

She went obediently with him to where the curricle waited, but when he lifted her into it, and disposed her injured foot upon the folded bolster, she sighed, and said shyly: 'Shall I ever see you again, once I am fixed in Brook Street?'

'Frequently!' said Sir Charles, mounting into the curricle, and feeling his horses' mouths.

Miss Massingham heaved a relieved sigh. 'I am so glad!' she said simply. 'For I don't feel that I could ever like anyone half as well!'

'That,' said Sir Charles, flicking a coin to the expectant ostler, 'is what I mean to make very sure of, my dear and abominable brat!'

Pink Domino

I

*I*T WAS A SILKEN DOMINO, OF A SHADE OF ROSE–PINK ADMI-
rably becoming to a brunette. One of the footmen had
carried up the bandbox to the Blue Saloon in the great house
in Grosvenor Square, where Miss Wrexham was engaged in
solving a complimentary charade, sent to her by one of her
admirers. This was abandoned; Miss Wrexham pounced on
the bandbox, and lifted the lid. The domino was packed in
sheet upon sheet of tissue-paper, and as Miss Wrexham lifted
it from the box these fluttered to the ground, and lay there in
drifts. Miss Wrexham gave a coo of delight, and held the cloak
up against herself, looking in one of the long mirrors to see
how it became her. It became her very well indeed: trust the
most expensive modiste in London for that! Somewhere, on
the floor, there was a rather staggering bill, but Miss Wrexham
cared nothing for that. Bills were of no consequence to a
Wrexham of Lyonshall. Being under age, one existed upon
an allowance, and frequently outran the constable. But that
was of no consequence either, since there was always Mama
to come to one's rescue, or even, at a pinch, Giles. But only

at a pinch. A brother who was eight years one's senior, and one's legal guardian into the bargain, could not be thought an ideal banker. He had never yet refused to pay one's debts, but there had been several distressing scenes, and one in particular, when she had lost a considerable sum of money playing loo for high stakes, which she preferred not to remember. For several quaking hours she had expected to be banished to Lyonshall, in charge of her old governess; and Mama, who seemed to have incurred more blame even than herself, had had one of her worst spasms. She had been forgiven, but she still thought it astonishingly mean of Giles to grudge her a few paltry hundreds out of his thirty thousand pounds a year.

All this, however, was forgotten, for she had a new and absorbing interest to distract her. Still holding up the pink domino, she wondered how the new interest would like it; and came to the conclusion that he must be hard indeed to please if he did not.

She was so lost in these agreeable speculations that she did not hear the door open behind her, and had no notion that she was not alone until a dry voice, which made her jump nearly out of her skin, said: 'Charming!'

She spun about, instinctively bundling the domino into a heap. 'Oh! I thought you was gone out!' she gasped.

Mr Wrexham shut the door, and walked forward. He was a tall man, with raven-black hair, and uncomfortably penetrating grey eyes. His air of distinction owed nothing to his dress, for this was careless. Stultz certainly made his coats, but he was never permitted to give his genius full rein. Mr Wrexham preferred to enter his coats without the assistance of his valet; and was so indifferent to the exigencies of the mode that when every Pink of the Ton was to be seen abroad in pantaloons and Hessians it was the Bank of England to a Charley's shelter that he would emerge from Jackson's Boxing Saloon attired in riding-breeches and top-boots, and with a Belcher handkerchief negligently knotted about his neck. In a lesser man such conduct would have occasioned severe censure; but, as his mama pointed out to his sister, if you were Wrexham of Lyonshall there was nothing you might not do with the approval of Society.

'It – it is a gown I chose yesterday!' said Letty.

'Do you take me for a flat?' replied her brother. 'It is a domino.' He picked up from the floor Madame Celestine's bill, and his brows rose. 'Quite an expensive domino, in fact!'

'I am sure there is no reason why I should not buy expensive things!' said Letty, trying to turn the issue.

'None at all, but this seems an extortionate price to pay for something you will not wear.'

Colour rushed up into her exquisite little face. 'I shall! I *shall* wear it!' she declared.

'I have already told you, my dear sister, that I will not permit you to go to a Pantheon masquerade, least of all in the company of a military fortune-hunter!'

Her eyes blazed with wrath. 'How dare you say such a thing? You have never so much as set eyes on Edwin!'

'He would appear to have taken good care of that,' said Mr Wrexham, with a curl of his lip.

'It is untrue! He would have been very glad to have met you! It was *I* who forbade it, because I knew how horrid you would be!'

At this moment, the door opened, and a faded lady came in, saying in a voice that matched her ethereal mien: 'Oh, here you are, my love! If we are to visit the Exhibition – Oh, is that you, Giles?'

'As you see, Mama. Pray postpone your visit to the Exhibition, and look at this!' He twitched the domino out of Letty's hands as he spoke, and shook it out before his mother's eyes.

Lady Albinia Wrexham, realizing that a scene highly

prejudicial to her enfeebled constitution was about to take place, sank into a chair, and groped in her reticule for her vinaigrette. 'Oh, dear!' she sighed. 'Dearest child, if your brother dislikes it so very much, don't you think – ?'

'No!' said Letty. 'Giles dislikes everything I wish to do, and – and *every* gentleman who admires me!'

'With reason!' said Giles. 'You have now been on the town for less than a year, my girl, and I have been obliged to repulse no fewer than eight gazetted fortune-hunters!'

'Edwin is not a fortune-hunter!'

'Indeed, Giles, I think him an unexceptionable young man!' interpolated Lady Albinia.

'Let me remind you, ma'am, that you said the same of Winforton!'

'To be sure, I could wish that he were not serving in a Line regiment,' said her ladyship feebly. 'But his birth is perfectly respectable! I own, I should wish dear Letty to make a far more brilliant match, but –'

'Not I! I am going to marry Edwin, and follow the drum!' announced Letty.

Her brother threw her a glance half of amusement, half of exasperation. 'I should be sorry for any penniless lieutenant of Foot who was saddled with you for a wife, my dear!'

'But if he married Letty,' pointed out her ladyship, not entirely felicitously, 'he would not be penniless, Giles!'

'Exactly so!' he said sardonically.

'You are unjust!' Letty cried. 'All you care for is that I should make a splendid marriage, and nothing for my happiness!'

'At present,' he returned, 'I am not anxious to see you make any marriage at all. When you have ceased to imagine yourself to be in love with every man who dangles after you – why, yes! I should wish you to make a good match!'

'Then I wonder you don't make one yourself!' she flashed.

'I dare say there must be a score of eligible females casting out lures to you!'

'You flatter me,' he replied, unmoved.

'Oh, no, it is very true, Giles!' his mother assured him. 'And I wish very much that I could see you creditably established! There is Rothwell's daughter, or –'

'Oh, no, Mama!' Letty struck in, with an angry little titter. 'Giles does not make Earls' daughters the objects of his gallantry! When he marries, he will choose a dab of a girl in an outmoded bonnet, and a black pelisse!'

2

A tinge of colour stole into her brother's lean cheeks, but he said nothing. Lady Albinia, looking very much shocked, exclaimed: 'Dear child, I do not know what you can possibly mean!'

'It is wickedly unjust!' Letty declared, a sob in her throat. 'Giles will have nothing to say to my dearest Edwin because he has neither title nor fortune, but I know very well that if he could but have discovered where she lived *he* would have offered for a Nobody that was never at Almack's or – or anywhere one would look for a lady of quality!'

'Your imagination is as unbridled as your tongue,' Mr Wrexham said curtly.

'But what is this?' demanded Lady Albinia, greatly bewildered.

'You may well ask!' he replied. 'I hope you mean to enlighten us, Letty: who is the Nobody your fancy has marked down as my bride?'

'You know very well that I mean the girl who was knocked down in Bond Street, that day you and I were going to Hookham's Library! You may try to hoax me, but *I* know why you have been so obliging as to escort me to Almack's three times this month, and why you have taken to driving your phaeton in the Park every afternoon! You are trying to find her, because you were so much struck by the *sweetest face you ever beheld* that you lost your wits, and never even discovered what was her name!'

Lady Albinia turned astonished eyes towards her son. He uttered a short laugh. 'One of Letty's high flights, ma'am! The truth is merely that some girl had the misfortune to be knocked down by a curricle and pair, and I rendered her such assistance as lay within my power. Had she come by her deserts, she must have suffered serious injury. Happily, she was merely stunned for a minute. I trust that the incident has served to convince her of the folly of stepping into the road before ascertaining that no vehicle is at that moment approaching.'

Letty, who had listened to this speech with growing indignation, exclaimed: 'How can you, Giles? When you carried her into the Library, and sent me running to a chemist's shop, and told the man in the curricle, in the *rudest* way, that he was unfit even to drive a donkey! Yes, and if the girl would have permitted it you would have conveyed her to her home, and abandoned me in the middle of Bond Street!'

'Had the girl not been accompanied by a servant, I dare say I should have done so,' he replied coolly. 'I collect that this rodomontade is designed to divert my attention from your evident purpose. Understand me, Letty, I will not permit you to go to a Pantheon masquerade under any circumstances whatsoever, least of all in the company of an unknown officer of Foot!' He glanced down at his parent, and added: 'I must say, ma'am, I am amazed that you could sanction so improper a scheme!'

Lady Albinia had recourse to her vinaigrette. 'But, indeed, Giles, you do not perfectly understand how it was to be! The thing is that Mr Ledbury's married sister was to have escorted Letty. She was so civil as to write a letter to me, just as she ought, assuring me that she would take every care of her. There is to be a little party, and Letty is invited to dine at this Mrs Crewe's house before going to the Pantheon. But, of course, if you do not quite like it, I am persuaded she will give up the project!'

'No! No!' said Letty hotly.

'If you have a grain of common-sense, you will!' said her brother. 'Recollect that for two years to come you are in my wardship! Banish this new swain of yours from your thoughts, for if you do not I give you fair warning I shall find the means to compel you!' He paused, looking rather grimly at the stormy countenance upraised to his. After a moment, his own face softened, and he said: 'Come, Letty, don't be a goosecap! Indeed, these masquerades are not at all the thing! Be a good girl, and I will take you instead to the play!'

3

Mr Wrexham, withdrawing, left his sister mutinous, and his mother in a flutter of apprehension. To Letty's diatribe she could find nothing better to say than: 'Yes, indeed, my love, but you know how it is with Giles! I told you how it would be! He will never suffer you to marry a Nobody!'

'I will not be browbeaten by Giles!' said Letty. 'I know very well he means me to marry to oblige him – Rothbury, I daresay! – but I won't do it! I *know* that I shall never love anyone but Edwin!'

Lady Albinia uttered distressful sounds. 'My love, do not say so! He will never let you throw yourself away like that! And I must say I think it was most imprudent of you, Letty, to set up his back with that nonsensical story!'

'Mama, I vow to you that he was so much struck by the girl

that I scarce knew him for my own brother! And he *did* say that she had the sweetest face he ever beheld!'

'Very likely, my love, but you must know that such fancies are common amongst gentlemen, and they do not lead to marriage! If you imagine *that* was in his head, you are a great goose! He has more pride even than his sainted papa, and he, you know – Well, never mind that! But the Wrexhams *always* make good marriages. It has grown to be quite a habit with them!'

Letty said no more, but went away, carrying the domino over her arm.

Mr Wrexham, meanwhile, had left the house. He did not return to it until shortly before seven o'clock, when he was greeted by the staggering tidings that Miss Letty, so far from being in her dressing-room, had driven away in a hackney a few minutes earlier.

'To what address?' asked Mr Wrexham, in a voice of dangerous calm.

Never had the butler been more thankful to be able to disclaim all responsibility for his young mistress's actions. None of the servants had been employed to summon the hackney; and but for the accident of one of the abigails looking out of a window just as Miss Letty was stepping up into the vehicle, no one would have known that she had gone out.

Mr Wrexham went up to Lady Albinia's dressing-room two steps at a time. He found her resting upon a sofa, and, with a total disregard for her nerves, demanded to be told whether she was aware that her daughter had left the house in a manner which he did not scruple to call clandestine.

Her face of shocked dismay was answer enough. Curbing a strong inclination to animadvert severely upon the negligence that had made it possible for Letty to steal from the house, Mr Wrexham curtly requested his parent to furnish him with Mrs Crewe's direction.

'Giles!' protested her ladyship. 'You cannot wrest your sister away from a dinner-party!'

'Oh, yes, I can!' retorted Mr Wrexham.

Lady Albinia, perceiving that he was in a towering rage, sank back against her cushions, and said in a dying voice: 'I can feel a spasm coming on!'

'Furnish me with Mrs Crewe's direction, ma'am, and I will leave you to enjoy it in private!'

'But I don't know it!' wailed her ladyship, almost beyond human aid. 'I never kept her letter, for why should I? And I don't recall the direction, though I am sure it was perfectly respectable, for if it had not been I must have noticed it!'

Controlling himself with a visible effort, Mr Wrexham strode from the room.

He dined alone, the butler informing him that her ladyship had bespoken a bowl of broth in her dressing-room. Since this was his mother's invariable custom, whenever she was confronted by a disagreeable situation, Mr Wrexham was neither surprised nor alarmed. He ate his dinner in frowning silence, and then went upstairs to his room, and rang for his valet. Less than an hour later, clad in the satin knee-breeches and black coat that betokened a gentleman of fashion on his way to an evening party, he left the house, a half-mask in his pocket, and an old black domino, unearthed from the recesses of his wardrobe, over his arm.

4

The Pantheon, which was on the south side of Oxford Street, was a magnificent structure, decorated in a style which rendered it obnoxious to the eye of the fastidious. It comprised a large suite of saloons, and a ballroom, which was a huge rectangular hall, with a painted ceiling, a raised platform for the musicians, and numerous boxes and alcoves. Crystal chandeliers hung from the ceiling, and from every Gothic arch which lined the room; all was gilding and glitter. Originally, it had been patronized by members of the *haut ton*, but when the first building was burnt to the ground, and a new structure erected, the company became so far from select that Mr Wrexham had every excuse for forbidding his sister to be seen there.

Although the hour was early when he arrived there, the ballroom was already full of a motley crowd of persons, some in dominoes, some in historical costume, all masked, and many behaving with the license encouraged by the wearing of disguises. After watching a quadrille for a few minutes, Mr Wrexham decided that his sister had not yet arrived, for although he could see two ladies in pink dominoes one was by far too tall, and the other had pushed back the hood of her domino to show a head of yellow curls. He began to stroll through the saloons, successfully resisting the efforts of two ladies of Covent Garden notoriety to beguile him into dalliance.

It was nearly an hour later, when the revelry was becoming a trifle indecorous, that he suddenly saw Letty. She had her hood drawn over her head, but he caught a glimpse of dusky curls, and recognized her little trim figure. She was waltzing with a large man in a purple domino, and the only circumstance which afforded her brother some slight degree of satisfaction was her obvious lack of pleasure in the exercise. Leaning his broad shoulders against one of the decorated pillars, and folding his arms across his chest, he watched her circle round the room, and very soon realized that her partner (whom he suspected of being slightly foxed) was subjecting her to a form of gallantry which was extremely unwelcome. He thought it would be a salutory lesson to her, and had almost made up his mind not to intervene for a little while, when she suddenly broke away from her partner, and hurried off the floor, hotly pursued. Mr Wrexham, shouldering his way through the loungers at the side of the hall, reached her just as Purple Domino caught her round the waist, saying with a laugh: 'You shan't escape me thus, pretty prude!'

Mr Wrexham, setting a hand on his shoulder, swung him aside. A glance at his sister showed him that she was shaking like a leaf; he was afraid that she might be going to faint, and pushed her into the alcove behind her, saying briefly: 'Sit down!'

At the sound of his voice she jumped under his hand, and gave a gasp.

'Yes, my girl, it is I!' said Mr Wrexham very dryly indeed, and turned to confront Purple Domino.

In a voice which bore out Mr Wrexham's previous estimate of his condition, Purple Domino demanded to know what the devil he meant by it.

'I mean,' said Mr Wrexham, 'that unless you remove yourself within one minute, my fine buck, I shall have the greatest pleasure in supplying you with a little of the home-brewed!'

Purple Domino recoiled instinctively, but recovered, and said in a blustering tone: 'Damme, what right have you to spoil sport?'

'Let me inform you,' said Mr Wrexham, 'that I am this lady's brother!'

'*B-brother?*' echoed Purple Domino, in a dazed voice. 'But I didn't – Curse you, how was I to know?'

He stood staring through the slits of his mask for a moment, in an undecided way, and then, muttering something indistinguishable, took himself off.

Mr Wrexham felt a hand touch his sleeve. He drew it through his arm. It was trembling so much that instead of uttering the blistering words hovering on his tongue, he merely said: 'You see, Letty, I am not quite so gothic as you think me. Come,

I am going to take you home now, and we will forget this military suitor of yours!'

She did not answer, but went meekly with him to the entrance-hall. It was deserted, save for the porter. Mr Wrexham said: 'I sent the carriage home, so I must procure a hack. Go and put on your cloak! There is no need to be in a quake: I am not an ogre!'

5

'No,' said the Pink Domino, in a shaken voice. 'But I – I am not your sister, sir!'

He had turned away, but at this he wheeled about, startled, staring at her. With an impatient movement he ripped off his mask, and it was to be seen that he was suddenly very pale, his eyes fiercely intent upon her face. 'Take off your mask!' he commanded imperatively. 'I know your voice! *Surely* I know your voice?'

She put up her hands to untie the strings of her mask. 'I knew yours,' she said simply. 'You – you are always rescuing me from the consequences of my folly, sir!'

He found himself gazing into the sweetest face he had ever beheld. It was heart-shaped, possessed of a pair of smiling grey eyes, which met his shyly yet frankly, and of a tender, generous mouth. Oblivious of the porter's bored presence, he grasped her hands, ejaculating: '*You!* Oh, my little love, where have you been hiding yourself? I have searched everywhere for you! Such a zany as I was never to have discovered even your name!'

She blushed, and her gaze fell. 'I don't know yours either, sir,' she said, trying to speak lightly.

'I am Giles Wrexham. And you?'

It meant nothing to her; she replied: 'Ruth Welborne. I have not been in hiding, only, when I met you before I was still in mourning for my father, and so, you see, I have not till now gone into society. Did you indeed look for me?'

'Everywhere!' he declared, still grasping her hands. 'I had abandoned hope! Where do you live? Let me not lose you again!'

She gave a little laugh. 'How absurd you are! In Harley Street, with my uncle, who was kind enough to take me into his family when my father died.'

He had never encountered a Welborne; from the direction it seemed probable that her uncle might be a banker, or a merchant, or an Indian nabob. His brain fleetingly acknowledged the possibility, and discarded it as a matter of no consequence. 'But what, in God's name, are you doing at a Pantheon masquerade?' he demanded. 'In *such* company, too! Do you tell me that your uncle brought you here?'

'Oh, no, no!' she said quickly. 'Indeed, I do not think that he or my aunt knew just how it would be, for they do not go into society much.'

'Then how comes it about that you are here?'

She did not seem to resent the question, but it was a moment before she answered it. She said then, with a little difficulty: 'It was a party of Sir Godfrey Claines's contriving. He is the man in the purple domino. A cousin of his, a Mrs Worksop, invited me, and my aunt wished me not to refuse. You see, sir, I – I have not the advantage of fortune, and my aunt has three daughters of her own, the eldest of whom she will bring out next year. It would not be reasonable to suppose that she would desire to be saddled with me under such circumstances.'

'I understand you!' he said, tightly holding her hands.

She had lowered her eyes, but she raised them at that, and said: 'Ah, you are not to be thinking that I have met with unkindness! It is not so! I was bred in the country, and perhaps I am missish in not liking – But I was never more thankful in my life, sir, than when you came to my rescue just now!'

He released her hands at last. 'Go and put on your cloak!' he said, smiling down at her. 'I will take you back to your uncle's house.'

'Mrs Worksop!' she faltered. 'Ought I not —'

'No. She did not take such care of you that you owe her a particle of civility.'

'Your sister! I collect that she too is present. I must not —'

'It is of no consequence,' he interrupted. 'If she is here, it is not under my protection! Come, do as I bid you! Do you think I mean to let you slip through my fingers again?'

6

'Surely I must be dreaming!' Ruth said, as the hack drew to a standstill. 'I thought I should never see you again, and now — ! But how can it be? You do not know me!'

'I am very sure that I do. As for my own mind, I knew that the instant you opened your dear eyes, that day in Bond Street, and looked up into my face.'

'It was so with you too!' she said wonderingly.

He kissed her hand, and let it go. 'It was so. Come, we must get out of this musty coach, and brave your uncle and aunt!'

'Good heavens, you will not tell them — ? They must think you mad! Pray do not — !'

'No, not tonight,' he said reassuringly, assisting her to alight.

'I fear my aunt may be much displeased with me,' she said. 'Should you perhaps leave me now?'

'No. Nor, I fancy, will your aunt be displeased,' he replied.

The master of the house, they were informed by the servant who admitted them, was still at his club, but Mrs Welborne was at home, and in the drawing-room.

They found her deep in the pages of the newest marble-backed novel from the Circulating Library. Taken unawares, she looked up in surprise, and exclaimed: 'Good God, Ruth, what in the world brings you home so soon? I declare, you are the most vexatious –' She stopped short, her gaze travelling past Ruth to Mr Wrexham. One instant she sat with her jaw dropping, then she cast aside her novel and sprang up, a look compound of amazement and delight transfiguring her sharp countenance. 'Oh – ! Surely I cannot be mistaken? Is it not – *Mr Wrexham?*'

He bowed. 'Yes, I am Wrexham, ma'am,' he said. 'I made the acquaintance of Miss Welborne a month and more ago, in Bond Street, as she may have told you.'

Her face was a study. 'In Bond Street! *You* were the gentleman who – ? Good God, Ruth, why did you not inform me? I am sure, sir, that had we but known my husband would have called on you to convey the sense of his obligation!'

Mr Wrexham, inured to flattery, and never famed for his social graces, cut her short, saying in his incisive way: 'It is of no consequence, ma'am. What *is* of consequence is that I have brought Miss Welborne home this evening because I found her where no young lady of quality should be, and being subjected to such embarrassment as, I am persuaded, you would not wish her to be obliged to endure.'

'No, indeed! I am sure, if I had had the least notion –'

'Just so, ma'am. *I* am sure that I need not enlarge upon this topic. May I beg that you will give me leave to call tomorrow to see how Miss Welborne does?'

She was wreathed in smiles. 'We shall be *most* happy, sir!'

'Thank you. I shall hope to have the felicity of finding Mr Welborne at home, for there is something I wish to say to him.'

'He *shall* be at home!' declared Mrs Welborne.

He bowed again, and turned from her to Ruth, who had been listening in bewilderment to her aunt's affability. He held out his hand, and she put hers into it, as though compelled.

He raised it to his lips. 'Have I *your* permission to visit you tomorrow?' he asked, smiling into her wondering eyes.

The smile was reflected in them. 'If you please, sir!' Ruth said, blushing adorably.

Mrs Welborne, much affected, rang for the servant to show Mr Wrexham out of the house. When he had gone, Ruth, looking doubtfully at her aunt, said in her soft voice: 'I hope you are not vexed with me, ma'am? Indeed, I –'

'*Vexed* with you?' cried Mrs Welborne, embracing her with unaccustomed fervour. 'Dearest Ruth, what nonsensical notions you do take into your head! Dear, dear child, I know that when you are rich and fashionable you will not forget your cousins! They say he has never yet attached himself to any female, and you may imagine the caps that have been set at him! Ruth, is it possible – ? Why, you innocent puss, that was *Wrexham of Lyonshall!*'

7

Mr Wrexham, returning to Grosvenor Square just before midnight, learned, with vague surprise, that he was awaited by her ladyship in the drawing-room. He found, in fact, that he was awaited not only by her ladyship, but by his sister, and a well set-up young man in scarlet regimentals, who had a crop of fair, curly hair, a pair of serious blue eyes, set in an open countenance, and a general air of one about to engage in a Forlorn Hope. Both he and Letty rose at Mr Wrexham's entrance. The gentleman eased his black cravat, and was seen to draw a deep breath; the lady burst into tempestuous speech.

'Good heavens, Giles, where can you have been this age? We have been waiting for you these two hours! Giles, this is Edwin!'

'How do you do?' said Mr Wrexham, holding out his hand.

Mr Ledbury's orbs showed a tendency to start from their sockets. He coloured richly, and grasped the outstretched hand. 'How – how do you do?' he stammered. 'I have long been wishful of meeting you, sir!'

'Have you?' said Mr Wrexham abstractedly. He opened his snuff-box, and offered it to his guest. His eyes took in the facings to that scarlet jacket. 'In the 40th are you?'

Mr Ledbury acknowledged it. Almost stunned by the honour done him in being invited to help himself to snuff from Mr Wrexham's own box, he took too large a pinch, and fell into a fit of sneezing. This left the field open to Letty, and she at once said: 'You must know, Giles, that but for my entreaties this visit would have been paid you more than a month ago! No sooner did I divulge to Edwin what had passed between you and me this morning than he declared his unshakeable resolve to wait upon you immediately! We stayed only to dine with his sister.'

'Did you?' said Mr Wrexham. 'I can only offer my apologies for having been absent from home. What do you want with me?'

Letty stared at him. 'Giles, are you quite well?' she gasped.

'I was thinking of something else,' he apologized, a tinge of colour mounting to his cheek. 'Did you say you had been awaiting me for two hours? Were you not at the masquerade, then?'

Mr Ledbury, mastering his paroxysm, said: 'Sir, it is on that head that I was resolved to have speech with you this very night! When I learned that you had taken the scheme in such aversion, nothing, believe me, would have prevailed with me to continue with it! In this determination my sister was stead-fast in upholding me. It was only in response to my earnest representations that she was induced, at the outset, to take part in the scheme.'

'These masquerades are not at all the thing, you know,' said Mr Wrexham.

Mr Ledbury blushed more vividly still. 'Sir, from the circum-stance of my having been employed since the age of fifteen, first in the Peninsula, and later in America, returning thence only just in time to take part in the late conflict at Waterloo, I have never been on the town, as the saying is. Had I suspected that any impropriety would attach to my escorting Miss Wrexham to such a function, I must have been resolute in refusing to lend myself to the project.'

'Letty's notion, was it?' said Mr Wrexham, with what none of his listeners could feel to be more than tepid interest.

His mother and sister gazed at him in uneasy astonishment. Mr Ledbury, emboldened by his mild aspect, plunged into a recital of his ambitions, his present circumstances, and his future expectations. Mr Wrexham, lost in dreams of his own, caught such phrases as 'eldest son', – 'my father's estate in Somerset', and soon interrupted the flow, saying: 'I wish you will not talk so much! It is time you had your company: you had a great deal better exchange into another regiment, but I cannot discuss that with you at this hour!'

Mr Ledbury, transported to find his Letty's brother so much less formidable than he had been led to expect, delivered himself of a rehearsed peroration. In the maximum number of words he conveyed to Mr Wrexham the intelligence that, if it were possible, he would prefer Letty to renounce all claim to her inheritance. This noble speech at last jerked Mr Wrexham out of his abstraction, and caused him to retort with considerable acerbity: 'Happily, it is not possible! I wish you will go away, for I am in no mood for these heroics! Come and talk to me tomorrow morning! You wish to marry my sister: very well, but you must transfer! She will make you the devil of a wife, but that, I thank God, is no concern of mine!'

With these words of encouragement, he inexorably ushered his guest off the premises, barely allowing him time to take a punctilious leave of Lady Albinia, and a fond one of Letty. When he returned to the drawing-room, he found his mother and sister with their heads together, but whatever they were so earnestly discussing remained undisclosed. 'Giles,' said Letty anxiously, 'did you perfectly understand? Edwin has offered for me!'

'I dare say an estimable young man, but he uses too many words,' commented Mr Wrexham. 'Do you think he would like to transfer into a cavalry regiment?'

Alarmed, she laid her hand on his arm. 'Giles, are you sure you are well?'

'Perfectly!' he said, lifting her hand, and gripping it. 'I was never better!'

She cried sharply: 'Giles! You have *found* her!'

'I have found her! The sweetest face I ever beheld, Letty! Mama, I hope you do not mean to succumb to the vapours, for I wish you to make a call of ceremony in Harley Street tomorrow!'

A Husband for Fanny

I

'H IS ATTENTIONS,' SAID THE WIDOW, FIXING A PAIR OF large, rather anxious brown eyes on her cousin's face, 'are becoming most marked, I assure you, Honoria!'

'Fiddle!' said Lady Pednor.

The widow, who had just raised a delicate cup to her lips, started, and spilled some of the morning chocolate into the saucer. A drop fell on her dress. She set the cup and saucer down, and began to rub the mark with her handkerchief, saying despairingly: 'There! Only see what you have made me do! I dare say it will never come out!'

'Very likely it will not,' agreed her hostess, in no way repentant. 'You will be obliged to buy a new dress, and that, let me tell you, Clarissa, will be an excellent thing!'

'I cannot afford a new dress!' said the widow indignantly. 'All very well for you, as rich as you are, to talk in that unfeeling way, but you know –'

'I am not rich,' said Lady Pednor composedly, 'but I can afford a new dress, because I do not squander every penny I possess upon my daughter.'

Mrs Wingham blushed, but replied with spirit: 'You have no daughter!'

'What is more,' continued her ladyship, unheeding, 'I will accompany you to buy the dress, or I dare say you will choose just such another dowdy colour!'

'Purple-bloom, and very suitable!' said Mrs Wingham defiantly.

'Extremely so – for dowagers!'

'I am a dowager.'

'You are a goose,' replied her cousin calmly. 'It would be interesting to know what you spent on that spangled gauze gown Fanny wore at Almack's last night!' She paused, but Mrs Wingham only looked guilty. 'Pray, what is to be the end of all this extravagance, Clarissa? You will be ruined!'

'No, no! I have saved every penny I could spare ever since Fanny was a baby, just for this one season! If only I can see her creditably established, it will have been worth it! And although you may say "fiddle!" if you choose to be so uncivil, it is true about Harleston! From the moment of your bringing him up to me at Almack's that night, I could see that he was instantly struck by my darling's beauty. And never can I be sufficiently obliged to you, Honoria!'

'If I had thought that you would be so foolish, my dear, I never would have presented him,' said Lady Pednor. 'Harleston and Fanny! Good God, he must be forty if he is a day! How old is she? Seventeen? You are out of your senses!'

The widow shook her head. 'I don't wish her to be poor, and –' She broke off, and looked away from her cousin. 'Or to marry a very young man. It doesn't endure, the sort of attachment one forms when one is young, and young men don't make comfortable husbands, Honoria. With such a man as Lord Harleston – in every way so exactly what one would desire for one's child! – she would be very happy and never know care, and – and the disagreeable effects of poverty!'

'My love,' said Lady Pednor, 'because your mama made a bad bargain for you when she married you to Tom Wingham, is not to say that every young man must prove to be a monster of selfishness!'

'I was in love with Tom: it was not all Mama's doing!'

'I dare say. An excessively handsome creature, and he could be perfectly amiable, if events fell out according to his wishes.'

'I have sometimes thought,' said Mrs Wingham wistfully, 'that if only his Uncle Horsham had not married again and had a son, after all those years, and poor Tom had succeeded to the title, as he always expected to do, he would have been quite different!'

'Well, he would have had more money to fling away,' said Lady Pednor dryly. 'That might, of course, have made him more amiable.'

'But that is exactly what I have been saying,' said the widow eagerly. 'It was the poverty that made him often so cross and so disobliging! Heaven knows I do not wish to say unkind things of Tom, but can you wonder at me for – yes, for *scheming*, like the most odious match-maker alive, to provide my Fanny with everything that will make her life all that mine was not?'

'I wish you will stop talking as though you were in your dotage!' said her ladyship irascibly. 'Let me remind you that you are not yet thirty-seven years old! If you would not drape yourself in purple you might well pass for Fanny's sister! As for these precious schemes of yours, Fanny should rather be falling in love with an ineligible young man. In fact, I thought that that was what she had done. Didn't you tell me of some boy in the –th Foot?'

'No, no!' cried the widow. 'At least, I did, but it was only a childish fancy. He has no expectations, and I am persuaded that it was nothing more than the circumstance of his being a neighbour of ours in Buckinghamshire. Why, he cannot afford even to buy his promotion! And since I have brought Fanny to town, and she has met so many gentlemen of *far* greater address than Richard Kenton, I am persuaded she has forgotten all about him. Fanny marry into a Line regiment, pinching and scraping, living in garrison towns, and – No, a thousand times, no!'

'I dare say she would enjoy it very much,' said Lady Pednor.

'I won't have it!' declared the widow. 'Call me worldly, if you will, but only consider! What comparison can there be between Richard Kenton and the Marquis of Harleston? Mind, if Harleston were not the man he is, I would not for one moment countenance his suit. But have you ever, Honoria – tell me candidly – have you ever, I say, met any gentleman more likely to make a female happy? Setting aside his position and his wealth, where will you find such delightful manners, such engaging solicitude, and, oh, such smiling eyes? What could Fanny find in Richard to rival these attributes?'

'His youth,' replied Lady Pednor, with a wry smile. 'Indeed, I hope she may find a dozen things, for I tell you, Clarissa, if she is setting her cap at Harleston –'

'Never! I have not uttered a word to her on this subject, and to suppose that she could do anything so vulgar –'

'So much the better! Not, however, that she would be the first to do so, my love. No man has been more pursued than Harleston; no man has more frequently confounded expectation. They say that he suffered a severe disappointment in youth: be that as it may, it is certain that he has now no thought of marriage. If you had not buried yourself in the country these fifteen years, Clara, you would know that not even such a hardened match-maker as Augusta Daventry would waste one moment's speculation on Harleston.'

The widow began to pull on her gloves. 'Very likely she might not. She has a bevy of daughters, but I fancy there is not one amongst them who would not be cast into the shade by my Fanny.'

'That, I own, is true,' said Lady Pednor fairly. 'Fanny casts them all into the shade.'

Mrs Wingham turned quite pink. Her brown eyes sparkled through a sudden mist of tears. She said, in her pretty, imploring way: 'Oh, Honoria, she *is* beautiful, is she not?'

'She is beautiful; her manners are engaging – and to suppose that you will catch Harleston for her is the greatest piece of nonsense ever I heard,' said her ladyship.

2

Since Lady Pednor's mansion was in Berkeley Square, and the furnished house, hired by Mrs Wingham for the season at shocking cost, in Albemarle Street, the widow had not far to go to reach her own door when she parted from her cousin. Disregarding the solicitations of several chairmen, she stepped out briskly, one hand holding up her demi-train, the other plunged into a feather muff. Her face, framed by the brim of a bonnet with a high crown and three curled ostrich plumes, still wore its faintly anxious expression, for her cousin's words had a little ruffled her spirits. Lady Pednor spoke with all the authority of one who moved habitually in the circle Mrs Wingham had reentered only at the start of the season; and although her kind offices, as much as the Wingham connection (headed by the youthful Lord Horsham, whose birth had put an end to Tom Wingham's expectations), had thrust an almost forgotten widow and her lovely daughter into the heart of the *ton*, there could be no doubt that she was in a better position to pronounce on the Marquis of Harleston's probable intentions than one who had met him for the first time barely two months previously.

This reflection deepened the frown between Mrs Wingham's brows. She had for some time been conscious of a depression on her spirits, which might, she thought, be due to fatigue, or to the prospect of losing the companionship of her child. Her morning visit had done nothing to lift the cloud. Not content with trying to damp her hopes of a brilliant marriage for Fanny, Lady Pednor had, most unnecessarily, recalled Richard Kenton to her mind.

Not that the thought of Richard disturbed her very much. There had certainly been some boy-and-girl nonsense between him and Fanny, but both had behaved very well. Indeed, Richard seemed to realize that he could not support a wife on a lieutenant's pay; and he had manfully agreed with Mrs Wingham that it would be wrong to permit Fanny to enter upon an engagement until she had seen rather more of the world. Nor had Fanny raised more than a faint demur at her mama's plans for a London season. She had always been a biddable daughter, and if she had a will of her own it did not find expression in tantrums or odd humours. Launched into society, she behaved just as she ought, neither losing her head at so much unaccustomed gaiety, nor grieving her mama by appearing not to enjoy herself. She had many admirers, but not quite as many suitors, her want of fortune making her an ineligible choice for those who looked for more than birth and beauty in a bride. Mrs Wingham had foreseen that this would be so. She had been hopeful of achieving a good match for her; not until Lord Harleston had shown how strongly he was attracted towards Albemarle Street had she dreamed of a brilliant one. But his lordship, upon first setting eyes on Fanny, had requested Lady Pednor to present him to Fanny's mama, and, during that evening, at Almack's Assembly Rooms, when he had civilly devoted himself to Mrs Wingham, conversing with her while Fanny went down a country dance with young Mr Bute, she had known that he was the very man who could be depended on to make Fanny happy. When Fanny had joined them, he had solicited her to dance; later, he had called in Albemarle Street, and had begged Mrs Wingham to bring her daughter to a party of his contriving at Vauxhall Gardens. Since that day they had seemed always to be in his company; and if Mrs Wingham had at first doubted the serious nature of his intentions, such doubts were banished by a morning visit from his sister, a gentle lady who certainly called at her brother's desire, and who not only treated the widow with distinguishing kindness, but complimented her on Fanny's beauty, saying, with a smile: 'My brother has told me, ma'am, that you have a very lovely daughter.'

Lady Pednor had not known *that* when she tried to depress her cousin's hopes, reflected Mrs Wingham, mounting the steps to her own front door.

Fanny was going on a picnic expedition to Richmond Park, but her hostess's carriage had not yet arrived in Albemarle Street. Mrs Wingham found her trying to decide whether to wear a green spencer over her muslin dress, or a shawl of Norwich silk. Mrs Wingham thought that the spencer would be the more suitable wear, and enquired who was to be of the party. Fanny, tying a straw bonnet over her dark curls, replied: 'I don't know, Mama, but there are to be two carriages, besides Mr Whitby's curricle, and Eliza said that most of the other gentlemen would ride, so that it must be quite a large party. I think it was very obliging of Mrs Stratton to have invited me, don't you?'

Mrs Wingham agreed to it, but added: 'I hope you will be home in good time, dearest, for I should like you to rest before our own party. And I think you should wear the figured lace. I will lend you my pearls.'

'And *I* think you will wear the pearls yourself, and on no account that horrid turban, which makes you look like some dreadful dowager, and not in the least like my own, pretty Mama!' retorted Fanny, bestowing a butterfly's kiss on the widow's cheek. She then turned away and began to hunt for a pair of gloves. 'We sent out a great many cards, didn't we?' she said. 'I quite forget how many guests are coming!'

'About fifty,' said Mrs Wingham, with a touch of pride.

'Gracious, it will be a regular squeeze! I suppose all our particular friends? The Shanklins, and the Yeovils, and Lord Harleston?'

This was airily said. Mrs Wingham, unable to see her daughter's face, replied calmly: 'Oh yes!'

'Of course!' Fanny said, considering the rival claims of one pair of silk mittens and one pair of French kid gloves. 'Mama?'

'My love!'

'Mama, do you – do you like Lord Harleston?' Fanny asked shyly.

Whatever ambitious schemes Mrs Wingham had in mind, she would have relinquished them all rather than have encouraged her unspoiled daughter to share them. She replied, therefore, in a cool tone: 'Why, yes, very much! Do you?'

A glowing face was turned towards her. 'Oh, Mama, *indeed* I do! I think him quite the nicest person we have met in London. One could tell him almost anything, and be sure that he would understand just how it was,' Fanny said impulsively. She bestowed a brief hug upon the widow. 'Dearest Mama, I am so *glad* you like him!'

Mrs Wingham, returning the embrace, felt tears – thankful tears – sting her eyelids, but was spared the necessity of answering by a scratch on the door, which heralded the entrance of the page-boy, come to inform Miss Wingham that Mrs Stratton's barouche awaited her.

3

Fanny did not return from her picnic in time to indulge in rest, but she was in her best looks that evening. Several persons commented on her radiance; and Lord Harleston, obliging his hostess to recruit her energies with a glass of champagne, said, with his attractive smile: 'You are to be congratulated, ma'am! I do not know when I have seen so engaging a creature as your daughter. Such a bloom of health! Such frank, open manners! I think, too, that she has a disposition that matches her face.'

'Indeed, my lord, she is the dearest girl!' Mrs Wingham said, blushing with gratification and raising her eyes to his. 'I do think – but I might be partial – that she is very pretty. She favours her papa, you know.'

'Does she?' said his lordship, seating himself beside her on the sofa. 'I own that it is her mama I perceive in her countenance.'

'Oh no!' the widow assured him earnestly. 'My husband was an excessively handsome man.'

He bowed. 'Indeed? I think I had not the pleasure of the late Mr Wingham's acquaintance. He would certainly be proud of his daughter, were he alive today.' His eyes had been resting on Fanny, as she chatted, not many paces distant, to a gentleman with very high points to his shirt-collar, but he brought them back to Mrs Wingham's face, adding: 'And also of her mama. It is seldom that one discovers a well-informed mind behind a lovely face, ma'am; and Fanny has told me that she owes her education to you.'

'Why, yes!' admitted Mrs Wingham frankly. 'It has not been within my power to provide Fanny with the governesses and the professors I should have desired for her. If you do not find her deficient in attainments, I think myself complimented indeed!'

'May I say that I believe no governess or professor could have achieved so admirable a result?'

'You are too flattering, my lord!' was all she could find to say, and that in faltering accents.

'No, I never flatter,' he responded, taking the empty glass from her hand. 'I perceive that we are about to be interrupted by Lady Luton. I have something of a very particular nature to say to you, but this is neither the time nor the occasion for it. May I beg of you to indulge me with the favour of a private interview with you, at whatever time may be most agreeable to you?'

Such a tumult of emotion swelled in the widow's breast that she could scarcely find voice enough to utter the words: 'Whenever you wish, my lord! I shall be happy to receive you!'

He rose, as Lady Luton surged down upon them. 'Then, shall we say, at three o'clock tomorrow?'

She inclined her head; he bowed and moved away; and a moment later she had the felicity of seeing his tall, well-knit frame beside Fanny. Fanny was looking up at him, with her sweet smile, and putting out her hand, which he took in his and held for an instant, while he addressed some quizzing remark to her that made her laugh and blush. A queer little pang shot through the widow, seeing them on such comfortable terms. She reflected that her absorption in Fanny had made her stupidly jealous, and resolutely turned her attention to Lady Luton.

4

Having ascertained that her daughter had no engagement on the following afternoon, Mrs Wingham was surprised, when she returned from a shopping expedition in Bond Street, to find that only one cover had been laid for a luncheon of cold meat and fruit. She enquired of the butler, hired, like the house, for the season, whether Miss Fanny had gone out with her maid.

'No, madam, with a military gentleman.'

These fell words caused the widow to feel so strong a

presentiment of disaster that she turned pale, and repeated numbly: 'A military gentleman!'

'A Mr Kenton, madam. Miss Fanny appeared to be well acquainted with him. *Extremely* well acquainted with him, if I may say so, madam!'

Making a creditable effort to maintain her composure, Mrs Wingham said: 'Oh, Mr Kenton is an old friend! I had no notion he was in town. He and Miss Fanny went out together, I think you said?'

'Yes, madam, in a hackney carriage. I understand, to the City, Mr Kenton desiring the coachman to set them down at the Temple.'

This very respectable address did nothing to soothe Mrs Wingham's agitated nerves. The whole locality, from Temple Bar to St Paul's Cathedral, appeared to her to be sinister in the extreme. Amongst the thoughts which jostled one another in her head, the most prominent were Fleet Marriages, Doctors' Commons and Special Licences. She was obliged to sit down, for her knees were trembling. Her butler then proffered a tray on which lay a note, twisted into a little cocked hat.

It was scribbled in pencil, and it was brief:

Dearest Mama, – Forgive me, but I have gone with Richard. You shall know it all, but I have no time now. Pray do not be vexed with me! I am so happy I am sure you cannot be.

Mrs Wingham became aware that she was being asked if she would partake of luncheon or wait for Miss Fanny, and heard her own voice replying with surprising calm: 'I don't think Miss Fanny will be home to luncheon.'

She then drew her chair to the table and managed to swallow a few mouthfuls of chicken, and to sip a glass of wine. A period of quiet reflection, if it did not lighten her heart, at least assuaged the worst of her fears. She could not believe that either Fanny or Richard would for a moment contemplate the impropriety of a clandestine marriage. But that the sight of Richard had revived all Fanny's tenderness for him she could not, in the face of Fanny's note, doubt. What to do she could not think, and in a state of wretched indecision presently went up to her bedroom. After removing her hat, setting a becoming lace cap on her head and tying it under her chin, there seemed to be nothing to do but to await further news of the truants, so she went to sit in the drawing-room, and tried to occupy herself with her needle.

Fortunately, she had not long to wait. Shortly after two o'clock an impetuous step on the stair smote her listening ears, and Fanny herself came into the room, out of breath, her cheeks in a glow, and her eyes sparkling. 'Mama? Oh, Mama, Mama, it is *true*, and you *will* give your consent now, won't you?'

She came running across the room as she spoke and cast herself at her mother's feet, flinging her arms round her, and seeming not to know whether to laugh or cry. Behind her Mr Kenton, very smart in his regimentals, shut the door and remained at a little distance, as though doubtful of his reception. He was a well-set-up young man, with a pleasant countenance and an air of considerable resolution. At the moment, however, he was looking a trifle anxious, and he seemed to find his neckcloth rather too tight.

'Fanny, my dear, pray — !' remonstrated Mrs Wingham. 'I don't know what you are talking about! How do you do, Richard? I am very pleased to see you. Are you on furlough?'

'Mama, we have such news for you! Richard's godmother has died!' interrupted Fanny ecstatically. 'And she has left Richard a great deal of money so that he *can* support a wife after all! He came to tell me at once, and I went with him to the lawyer, and it is *true*!'

Mrs Wingham turned her bewildered eyes towards Mr Kenton. He said bluntly: 'No, it is not a great deal of money, ma'am, but it will enable me to buy my exchange, for you must know that I have been offered the chance of a company in the –th, only I never thought I should be able – . However, I can *now* afford the purchase money, and once I am in the –th, I hope I shan't be obliged to wait upon the chance of Boney's escaping a second time, and starting another kick-up, for my promotion. And I thought, if you would give your consent to our marriage, I would settle what will be left of the legacy on Fanny. It won't be a fortune, but – but it will be *something*!'

'Mama, you will consent?' Fanny said imploringly. 'You said I must see something of the world before I made up my mind, but I have now seen a great deal of the world, and I haven't met anyone I like better than Richard, and I know I never shall. And although it is very amusing to lead a fashionable life, and, *indeed*, I have enjoyed all the parties, I would much prefer to follow the drum with Richard! You *will* consent?'

Mrs Wingham stared down into the radiant face upturned to hers. A dozen objections died on her lips. She said, with a wavering smile:

'Yes, Fanny. If you are quite, quite sure, I suppose I must consent!'

Her daughter's lips were pressed to her cheek, Mr Kenton's to her hand. Seated amongst the ruins of her ambition, with that weight of depression upon her heart, she said: 'And Lord Harleston is coming to visit me at three o'clock!'

'Lord Harleston!' exclaimed Fanny. 'Oh, will you tell him, Mama, that I am going to marry Richard? I should have wished to have told him myself, but the thing is that Richard has leave of absence only for one day, and he must rejoin the regiment immediately. Mama, if I take Maria with me, may I go with him to the coach office? Pray, Mama!'

'Yes – oh yes!' said Mrs Wingham. 'I will tell Lord Harleston.'

5

Thus it was that when one of the biggest but most unobtainable prizes of the Matrimonial Mart was ushered into Mrs Wingham's drawing-room, he found the widow alone and sunk in melancholy. The depression, of which she had been conscious for so many weeks, threatened now to overcome her, and was in no way alleviated by her inability to decide which of the various evils confronting her was at the root of her strong desire to indulge in a hearty bout of tears. The years of economy had been wasted; yet she could not regret the weeks spent in London. Her maternal ambition was utterly dashed; but when she saw the happiness in Fanny's face she could not be sorry. She must soon lose the daughter on whom her every thought had been centred for years; but if by the lifting of a finger she could have kept Fanny, she would have held her hands tightly folded in her lap, as they were when the Marquis walked into the room.

He paused upon the threshold. The one glance she permitted herself to cast at his face showed her that there was an arrested expression in his eyes, a look of swift concern. The pain she was about to inflict on him most poignantly affected her; for a startling moment she found herself blaming Fanny for having wounded one of whom she was all unworthy. She was unable to sustain his steady regard; her eyes fell to the contemplation of the little gold tassels on his Hessian boots. They moved, swinging jauntily as he came towards her. 'Mrs Wingham! Something has occurred to distress you. May I know what it is? If there is anything I may do —'

He was bending solicitously over her, one shapely hand lifting one of hers, and holding it in a sustaining clasp. She said disjointedly: 'Yes — no! It is nothing, my lord! I beg you will not — ! Indeed, it is nothing!'

She drew her hand away as she spoke. He said: 'Shall I leave you? I have come, I believe, at an unfortunate time. Tell me what you wish! I would not for the world add to your distress!'

'Oh no! Do not go! This interview ought not to be − must not be − postponed!'

He looked intently at her, as much anxiety in his eyes as there was in hers. 'I came − I believe you must know for what purpose.'

She bowed her head. 'I do know. I wish − oh, how deeply I wish that you had not come!'

'You wish that I had not come!'

'Because it is useless!' said the widow tragically. 'I can give you no hope, my lord!'

There was a moment's silence. He was looking at once astonished and chagrined, but, after a pause, he said quietly: 'Forgive me! But when I spoke to you last night I was encouraged to think that you would not be averse from hearing me! You have said that you guessed the object of my visit − am I a coxcomb to imagine that my suit was not then disagreeable to you?'

'Oh no, no, no!' she uttered, raising her swimming eyes to his face. 'I should have been most happy − I may say that I most sincerely desired it! But all is now changed! I can only beg of you to say no more!'

'You desired it! In heaven's name, what can possibly have occurred to alter this?' he exclaimed. Trying for a lighter note, he said: 'Has someone traduced my character to you? Or is it that −'

'Oh no, how could anyone − ? My lord, I must tell you that there is Another Man! When I agreed last night to receive you today, I did not know − that is, I thought −' Her voice became suspended; she was obliged to wipe teardrops from her face.

He had stiffened. Another silence fell, broken only by the widow's unhappy sniffs into her handkerchief. At last he said, in a constrained tone: 'I collect − a prior attachment, ma'am?'

She nodded; a sob shook her. He said gently: 'I will say no

more. Pray do not cry, ma'am! You have been very frank, and I thank you for it. Will you accept my best wishes for your future happiness, and believe that –'

'Happiness!' she interrupted. 'I am sure I am the wretchedest creature alive! You are all kindness, my lord: no one could be more sensible than I am of the exquisite forbearance you have shown me! You have every right to blame me for having encouraged you to suppose that your suit might be successful.' Again her voice failed.

'I have no blame for you at all, ma'am. Let us say no more! I will take my leave of you, but before I go will you permit me to discharge an obligation? I may not have the opportunity of speaking to you alone again. It concerns Fanny.'

'Fanny?' she repeated. 'An *obligation*?'

He smiled with a slight effort. 'Why, yes, ma'am! I had hoped to have won the right to speak to you on this subject. Well – I have not won that right, and you may deem it an impertinence that I should still venture, but since Fanny has honoured me with her confidence, and I promised her that I would do what I might, perhaps you will forgive me, and hear me with patience?'

She looked wonderingly at him. 'Of course! That is – What can you possibly mean, my lord?'

'She is, I collect, deeply attached to a young man whom she has known since her childhood. She has told me that you are opposed to the match, ma'am. Perhaps there exists some reason beyond his want of fortune to render his suit ineligible, but if it is not so – if your dislike of it arises only from a very natural desire that Fanny should contract some more brilliant alliance – may I beg of you, with all the earnestness at my command, not to stand between her and what may be her future happiness? Believe me, I do not speak without experience! In my youth I was the victim of such an ambition. I shall not say that one does not recover from an early disappointment – indeed, you know that I at least have done so! – but I am most sincerely fond of Fanny, and I would do much to save her from what I suffered. I have some little influence: I should be glad to exert it in this young man's favour.'

The damp handkerchief had dropped from the widow's clutch to the floor; she sat gazing up at his lordship with so odd an expression in her face that he added quickly: 'You find it strange that Fanny should have confided in me. Do not be hurt by it! I believe it is often the case that a girl will more easily give her confidence to her father than to a most beloved mother. When she spoke, it was in the belief that I might become – But I will say no more on *that* head!'

The widow found her voice at last. 'My lord,' she said, 'do I – do I understand that you are desirous of becoming Fanny's *father*?'

'That is not quite as I should phrase it, perhaps,' he said, with a wry smile.

'Not,' asked the widow anxiously, '*not* – you are quite sure? – Fanny's *husband*?'

He looked thunderstruck. '*Fanny's* husband?' he echoed. '*I*? Good God, no! Why – is it possible that you can have supposed – ?'

'I have never fainted in all my life,' stated Mrs Wingham, in an uncertain voice. 'I very much fear, however –'

'No, no, this is no time for swoons!' he said, seizing her hands. 'You cannot have thought that it was Fanny I loved! Yes, yes, I know what Fanny has been to you, but you cannot have been so absurd!'

'Yes, I was,' averred the widow. 'I could even be so absurd as not to have the remotest guess why I have felt so low ever since I met you, and thought you wished to marry her!'

He knelt beside her chair, still clasping her hands. 'What a fool I was! But I thought my only hope of being in any way acceptable to you was to praise Fanny to you! And, indeed, she is a delightful girl! But all you have said to me today – you were not speaking of *yourself*?'

'Oh no, no! Of Fanny! You see, she and Richard –'

'Never mind Fanny and Richard!' he interrupted. 'Is it still useless for me to persist in my errand to you?'

'Quite ridiculous!' she said, clinging to his hands. 'You have not the least need to *persist* in it! That is, if you do indeed wish to marry such a blind goose as I have been!'

His lordship disengaged his hands, but only that he might take her in his arms. 'I wish it more than for anything else on this earth!' he assured her.

To Have the Honour

I

𝒴OUNG LORD ALLERTON, A LITTLE PALE UNDER HIS TAN, glanced from his mother to his man of business. 'But – good God, why was I never told in what case I stood?'

Mr Thimbleby did not attempt to answer this home question. He perceived that young Lord Allerton's facial resemblance to his deceased father was misleading. There was nothing the late Viscount had desired less than to be told in what case he stood. Three years of campaigning in the Peninsula had apparently engendered in the Fifth Viscount a sense of responsibility which, however welcome it might be in the future to his man of business, seemed at the moment likely to lead to unpleasantness. Mr Thimbleby directed an appealing look towards the widow.

She did not fail him. Regarding her handsome eldest born with an eye of fond pride, she said: 'But when poor Papa died, you had been wounded, dearest! I would not for the world have distressed you!'

The Viscount said impatiently: 'A scratch! I was back in the saddle within a week! Mama, how *could* you keep me in ignorance of our circumstances? Had I had the least notion of the truth I must have returned to England immediately!'

'Exactly so!' nodded his parent. 'And that, dearest Alan, I was determined you should not be obliged to do! Everyone said the war would so soon be over, and I knew how mortified you would be to be forced to sell out before the glorious end! To be sure, I did hope that directly after Toulouse you might have been released, but it was not to be, and it is of no consequence, except that here we are, with all the foreign notables upon us, and I have the greatest dread that your tailor may not have your evening dress ready for you to wear at my ball next week!'

'That, Mama, believe me, is the least of our problems!'

'Very true, my love,' agreed her ladyship. 'Trix has been in despair, but "Depend upon it", I have said from the outset, "even though your brother may patronize Scott, instead of Weston, who always did so well by poor Papa, you may be confident that *no* tailor would fail at such a juncture!"' Her gaze dwelled appreciatively upon his lordship's new coat of olive-green, upon the pantaloons of delicate yellow which clung to his shapely legs, upon the Hessian boots which shone so bravely, and upon the neckcloth which was tied with such nicety, and she heaved a satisfied sigh.

The Viscount turned in desperation to his man of business. 'Thimbleby!' he uttered. 'Be so good as to explain to me why *you* did not think it proper to inform me that my father had left me encumbered with debt.'

Mr Thimbleby cast another imploring glance at the widow. 'Her ladyship having done me the honour to admit me into her confidence, my lord, it seemed to me – that is, I was encouraged to hope…'

'To hope what?'

'My dear son, you must not blame our good Thimbleby!' intervened Lady Allerton. 'Indeed, no one is to be blamed, for if you will but consider you will perceive that our case is not desperate!'

'Desperate! I trust not! But that there is the most urgent need of the strictest economy – even, I fear, of measures as repugnant to me as they must be to you, ma'am, I cannot doubt! I dare not think what my own charges upon the estate have been during these months, when I should have been doing what lies within my power to repair what I do not scruple to call a shockingly wasted fortune!'

'No, no, it is not as bad as *that*!' she assured him. 'My dear Alan, there is *one* circumstance you are forgetting!'

He stared at her with knitted brows. 'Pray, what am I forgetting, ma'am?'

'Hetty!' she said, opening her eyes at him.

'I certainly do not forget my cousin, Mama, but in what way my embarrassments can be thought to concern her I have not the remotest conjecture!' said his lordship. A dreadful thought flashed into his mind; he said quickly: 'You are not trying to tell me, ma'am, that my cousin's fortune has been used to – No, no, impossible! She is still under age, and cannot have been allowed – There was another trustee besides my father, after all! Old Ossett could never have countenanced such a thing!'

'Nothing of the sort!' said her ladyship. 'And I must say, Alan, that I wonder at your supposing that I would entertain such a notion, except, of course, under such circumstances as must render it entirely proper! My own niece! I might almost say my *daughter*, for I am sure she is as dear to me as Trix!'

Mr Thimbleby, who had been unobtrusively engaged in putting up his papers, now judged it to be time to withdraw from a discussion which was not progressing according to hopeful expectation. The Viscount, beyond reminding him rather sharply that he should require his attendance upon the morrow, made no objection to his bowing himself out of the room, but began to pace about the floor, his brow furrowed, and his lips compressed as though to force back unwise speech.

His parent said sympathetically: 'I was afraid you would be a trifle shocked, dearest. It was hazard, of course. I knew no good would come of it when poor Papa forsook faro, at which he had always been so fortunate!'

The Viscount halted, and said with careful self-control: 'Mama, have you realized that to win free from this mountain of debt I must sell some – perhaps all! – of the unentailed property? When I learned that my father had left everything to me, making not the least provision for Timothy or for Trix, I own I was astonished! I see now why he did so, but how I am to provide for them I know not! Ma'am, you have been talking ever since my arrival of the ball you are giving in honour of this Grandduchess of yours, of the drawing-room at which you mean to present my sister, but have you realized that there is no money to pay for these things?'

'Good gracious, Alan, you should realize that if I do not!' exclaimed her ladyship. 'I declare I can scarcely recall when I was last able to pay a bill, and the tiresome thing is that there are now so many of them in that drawer in my desk that I can't open it!'

'For God's sake, Mama, how have you contrived to continue living in this style?' demanded the Viscount.

'Oh, well, my love, upon credit! Everyone has been most obliging!'

'Merciful heavens!' muttered the Viscount. '*What* credit, ma'am?'

'But, Alan, they all guess that you are going to marry dear Hetty, and they know *her* fortune to be immense!'

'O my God!' said the Viscount, and strode over to the window. 'So that's it, is it?'

Lady Allerton regarded his straight back in some dismay. 'It has always been an understood thing!' she faltered.

'Nonsense!'

'But it was my dear brother's wish!'

'It can scarcely have been his wish that his daughter should be married to an impoverished – fortune-hunter!' said the Viscount bitterly. 'And it must be very far from Sir John Ossett's wish!'

'Now there you are out!' said her ladyship triumphantly. 'Sir John will raise not the smallest objection to the match, for he has told me so! He knows it is what my brother intended, and, what is more, he has a great regard for you, my love!'

'I am obliged to him!'

'Alan!' ejaculated her ladyship. 'You – you have not formed an attachment for another?'

'No!'

'No, I was persuaded – Dearest, I thought – Of course, she was very young when you went away, but it did seem to me –'

'Mama,' he interrupted, 'whatever my sentiments, you cannot have supposed it possible that I would offer for my cousin in my present circumstances!'

'But it seems just the moment!' protested his mother. 'Besides, she expects it!'

He wheeled about. '*Expects* it?'

'Yes, I assure you she does! Dearest Hetty! If she could have done it, she would have bestowed her entire fortune on me! I never knew a better-hearted girl, never!'

'Oh, good God, then that is why she is now so shy of me!' said the Viscount. 'My poor little cousin! How *could* you let her think it was her duty to marry me, Mama? It is infamous! Have you kept her shut away from the world in case she should meet a more eligible suitor than ever I can be?'

'No, I have not!' replied Lady Allerton, affronted. 'I brought her out two years ago, and she has had a great many suitors, and has refused them all! She is a very well-behaved girl, and would never dream of marrying to disoblige me!'

'She has been shamefully used!' he said.

2

The object of the Viscount's pity, Miss Henrietta Clitheroe, was at the moment seated in a small saloon at the back of the house, studying, with her young cousin, the latest issue of *La Belle Assemblée*, and endeavouring to convince Miss Allerton that a dress of gauze worn over a damped and transparent petticoat was a toilette scarcely designed to advance her in the good graces of those august members of the *ton* who were pledged to appear at her mama's party given in honour of the Grandduchess Catherine of Oldenburg. This was not a circumstance which weighed with Miss Allerton, who, at seventeen, was thought by the censorious to have been born for the express purpose of driving her mother into her grave by the outrageous nature of her pranks; but she knew that she would never be permitted to wear such a dress, and so allowed herself to be distracted by the picture of a damsel arrayed in white satin embellished with rosebuds and love-knots.

She was just saying, though disconsolately, that she supposed it was quite a pretty dress, when the Viscount came into the room, and, still holding the door, said: 'The latest fashions? Am I very much in the way, or may I have a word with you, cousin?'

The colour flooded Henrietta's cheeks; she stammered: 'Oh no! I mean, to be sure you may, Alan!'

Miss Allerton, unwontedly meek, obeyed the command contained in the jerk of his lordship's head, and tripped out of the room. The Viscount shut the door, and turned to look across the saloon at his cousin. Her colour rose higher still, and she pretended to search for something in the litter of objects on the table.

'Henry...' the Viscount said.

She looked up at that, a little shy smile on her lips. 'Oh,

Alan, no one has called me that since you went away! How nice it sounds!'

He returned the smile, although with an effort. 'Does it? You will always be Henry to me, you know.' He paused; and then said with a good deal of constraint: 'I have been with my mother and with Thimbleby for the past hour. What I have learnt from them has made me feel that I must speak to you immediately.'

'Oh – oh, yes?' said Henrietta.

'Yes. I think I was never more shocked in my life than when I realized –' He broke off, conscious of the awkwardness of his situation. His own colour rose; he said with a rueful laugh: 'The devil! I'm as tongue-tied as a schoolboy! Henry, I only wanted to say – I'm not going to offer for you!'

The flush in Henrietta's cheeks began to ebb. 'Oh!' she said. '*N-not* going to offer for me?'

He came towards her, and took her hands, giving them a reassuring squeeze. 'Of course I am not! How could you think I would do so, you foolish Henry? You have been made to believe that you were in some way promised to me, haven't you? Some absurd talk of what your father desired – of what you owed to my family. Well, you owe us nothing, my dearest cousin! It is rather we who owe you a great debt. You have been our – most beloved sister – ever since you came to live with us. I am ashamed that it should ever have been suggested to you that it is your duty to marry me: it is no such thing! You are free to marry whom you please.'

This did not, at the moment, appear likely to the heiress. She disengaged her hands. 'Am – am I?'

'Indeed you are!' With an attempt at lightness, he added: 'Unless you choose someone quite ineligible! I warn you, I should do what I could to prevent *that*, Henry!'

She managed to smile. 'I should be obliged to elope, then,

should I not? I – I am glad you have been so frank with me. Now we can be comfortable again!'

'My poor girl!' he said quickly. 'If only you had told me what was in the wind – ! There was never a hint in any of your letters. I would have set your mind at rest months ago! No: you could not, of course!'

She turned away, and began to tidy the litter on the table. She said, in a voice that did not sound to her ears quite like her own: 'I own, I had as lief not be married for my fortune!' He returned no answer; after a pause, she added: 'Are your affairs in very bad case, Alan?'

'Not so bad that I shall not be able, with time and good management, to set them to rights, I hope,' he replied. 'I could wish that my mother had not chosen, at this moment, to entertain upon so lavish a scale. I suppose nothing can be done about this party for the Russian woman, but for the rest – the White's Ball, Trix's presentation –'

'Good God, do not tell my aunt she must postpone *that*!' exclaimed Henrietta. 'If she is obliged to wait another year, Trix will very likely run off with a handsome Ensign!' She saw the startled look on his face, and added: 'You don't yet know her, Alan!'

'My dear Henry, at seventeen she can hardly be thinking of marriage, surely!'

'The last man she fell in love with was young Stillington,' said Henrietta thoughtfully. 'To be sure, he was better than that actor she saw in Cheltenham, but still quite ineligible of course. Fortunately, her mind was diverted by the plans for her first season.'

'It is time Trix was broke to bridle!' said his lordship roundly. He then favoured his cousin with a few animadversions upon the conduct of his lively young sister, and left her to her reflections.

These were not for many moments concerned with the almost

inevitable clash between brother and sister. They led Henrietta to the mirror, and caused her to stare long at her own image.

It should have comforted her. Dark ringlets framed a charming countenance in which two speaking eyes of blue became gradually filled with tears that obscured her vision of a short, straight nose, a provocative upper lip, and an elusive dimple. These attributes had apparently failed to captivate the Viscount. The heiress uttered a strangled sob, and dabbed resolutely at her eyes, realizing that she would shortly be obliged to confront Miss Allerton, agog to know whether the date of her wedding had been fixed.

Nor was she mistaken. In a very few minutes, Trix peeped into the room, and, finding her cousin alone, at once demanded to be told what Alan had said to her.

Henrietta replied in the most cheerful of accents: 'I am so much relieved! He does not wish to marry me at all!'

Trix, shocked by these tidings, could only stare at her.

'You may imagine how happy he has made me!' continued Henrietta glibly. 'Had he desired it, I must have thought it my duty to marry him, but he has set my mind at rest on this head, and now I can be easy again!'

'But you have loved him for years!' Trix blurted out.

'Indeed I have!' said Henrietta cordially. 'I am sure I always shall!'

'*Hetty!* When you have been writing to him for ever!'

'Pray, what has that to say to anything? To me, he is the elder brother I never had.'

'Hetty, what a hum! He is *my* brother, and I never wrote to him above twice in my life!'

Before Henrietta could reply suitably to this, they were joined by a willowy young gentleman in whom only the very stupid could have failed to recognize a Pink of the Ton. From the tip of his pomaded head to the soles of his dazzling Hessians, the Honourable Timothy Allerton was beautiful to behold. He was generally supposed to care for nothing but the fashion of his neckcloth, but he showed unmistakable signs of caring for the news which his sister broke to him. '*Not* going to offer for Hetty?' he repeated, aghast. 'Well, upon my soul! Well, what I mean is, might think what's due to the rest of us! Mind, I don't say I'm surprised he don't like it above half, but the thing is he's the head of the family, and he dashed well ought to do it! What's more,' he said, his amiable countenance darkening, 'if he thinks he can make *me* offer for her he'll find he's devilish mistaken! It ain't that I don't like you, Hetty,' he added kindly, 'because I do, but that's coming it a trifle too strong!'

3

If the Viscount had harboured doubts of his mother's veracity, these were speedily dispelled. His cousin, far from having been kept in seclusion, seemed to him to be acquainted with all the eligible bachelors upon the town, and with far too many of those whom he did not hesitate to stigmatize as gazetted fortune-hunters. She dispensed her favours impartially amongst these gentlemen, whirled about town under the chaperonage of various not wholly disinterested matrons, and in general conducted herself with such frivolity that her perturbed aunt said that she had never known her to be in such a flow of spirits. She raised hopes in a dozen breasts, but the only suitor for whom she betrayed the smallest partiality was Sir Matthew Kirkham; and it was absurd to suppose (as Lady Allerton assured Alan) that a girl with as much good sense as Hetty would for an instant entertain the pretensions of a penniless roué, past his first youth, and with at least two unsavoury scandals attached to his name.

Alan could place no such dependence on his cousin's good

sense. It was rarely that he took a dislike to anyone, but he took a quite violent dislike to Sir Matthew, and warned Henrietta to give the fellow no encouragement: an exercise of cousinly privilege which had no other effect than to cause her to wear Sir Matthew's flowers at the Opera House that very evening.

He was brought to realize that however obnoxious Kirkham might appear in the eyes of his fellow-men he possessed considerable charm for the ladies: Trix told him so. Trix listened with interest to his trenchantly expressed opinion of Sir Matthew, and then disgusted him by talking of the fellow's polished manners, and of the distinguishing attentions he had for so long bestowed upon Hetty.

Sir Matthew was not one of the two hundred guests invited to have the honour of being presented to the Tsar's sister. This lady had arrived in England some time before the various Kings, Princes, Generals, and Diplomats who were coming to take part in the grand Peace celebrations, and was putting up at the Pulteney Hotel. She was neither beautiful nor particularly amiable, but she was being much courted, and had already created a mild sensation by being rude to the Prince Regent, and by parading the town in enormous coal-scuttle bonnets, which instantly became the rage. Trix, giggling over the story of her having abruptly left the party at Carlton House just as soon as the expensive orchestra provided for her entertainment had struck up, because (she said) music made her want to vomit, prophesied that her departure from Lady Allerton's ball would be equally speedy; but Lady Allerton, well-acquainted with the Grandduchess, said, No: she only behaved like that when she wished to be disagreeable.

Trix was not to appear at the ball either. The Viscount had told her that with all the will in the world to do so he was unable at present to find the funds which would enable his mama to launch her into society; and Lady Allerton's sense of propriety was too nice to allow of her consenting to let her daughter attend a ball of such importance before she was out.

Trix bore her disappointment surprisingly well, neither arguing with Alan nor reproaching him. Touched by her restraint, he promised her a magnificent début the following spring, if he had to sell every available acre to achieve it. She thanked him, and said that she had made up her mind to help him in his difficulties.

Such unprecedented docility ought to have alarmed Henrietta, but Henrietta was too much occupied with her own affairs to notice it. It was not until the very evening of the ball, when Trix helped her, in the most selfless way, to array herself in all the elegance of primrose satin and pale green gauze, that it occurred to her that this saintly conduct was as suspicious as it was unusual. But Trix, looking the picture of hurt innocence, assured her that she had no intention of perpetrating some shocking practical joke, and she was obliged to be satisfied. Trix embraced her with great fondness, and she went away to join Lady Allerton feeling that she had misjudged her wayward cousin.

In this belief she continued until midnight, when she suffered a rude disillusionment.

4

Mr Allerton, seizing a respite from his conscientious labours on the floor, stood in the doorway of the ballroom, and delicately wiped his brow. The May night was very warm, and although the long windows stood open scarcely a breath of wind stirred the curtains which masked them, and the heat from the hundreds of wax candles burning in the wall-sconces and in the huge crystal chandelier which hung from the ceiling was making not only the flowers wilt, but every gentleman's starched shirt-points as well. But this was a small matter. Mr Allerton, a captious critic, was well-satisfied with the success of the ball. Every domestic detail had been perfectly arranged; his mother did him the greatest credit in a robe of sapphire satin lavishly trimmed with broad lace; his cousin was in quite her best looks; and even his brother, although dressed by a military tailor, did not disgrace him. The Grandduchess was in high good humour; besides the flower of the *ton*, two of the Royal Dukes were lending lustre to the evening; and, to set the final *cachet* upon a brilliant function, the great Mr Brummell himself was present.

These agreeable reflections were interrupted. A hand grasped Mr Allerton's wrist, and his cousin's voice said urgently in his ear: 'Timothy, come quickly to my aunt's dressing-room! I must speak to you alone!'

A horrible premonition that the champagne had run out and the ice melted away seized Mr Allerton. But the news which Henrietta had to impart to him had nothing to do with domestic arrangements. She was clutching in one hand a sheet of writing-paper, with part of the wafer that had sealed it still sticking to its edge, and this she dumbly proffered. Mr Allerton took it, and mechanically lifted his quizzing-glass to his eye. 'What the deuce − ?' he demanded. 'Lord, I can't read this scrawl! What is it?'

'Trix!' she uttered, in a strangled voice.

'Well, that settles it,' he said, giving the letter back to her. 'Never been able to make head or tail of her writing! You'd better tell me what it is.'

'Timothy, it is the most terrible thing! She has eloped with Jack Boynton!'

'What?' gasped Timothy. 'No, hang it, Hetty! Must be bamming you!'

'No, no, it is the truth! She is not in the house, and she left this note for me. Dawson has this instant given it to me!'

'Well, I'm dashed!' said Timothy. *'Jack Boynton?* Y'know, Hetty, I wouldn't have thought it of him!'

Too well accustomed to Mr Allerton's mental processes to be exasperated, Henrietta replied: 'No, indeed! She must have persuaded him to do it: he is so very young! I never dreamed – Good God, I thought that affair had ended months ago! How could she have been so sly? But I might have guessed how it would be! If I had not been so selfishly taken up with my own troub – I mean, *pleasures*! – it could never have happened! Timothy, I must act immediately, and you must help me!'

He blinked at her. 'Dash it, can't do anything in the middle of m'mother's party!'

'We can, and we must! They have fled to Gretna Green, and they must be overtaken!'

'Gretna Green?' echoed Mr Allerton, revolted. 'No, really, Hetty! Can't have!'

'She makes no secret of it. Besides, where else could they be married, two children under age? She supposed, of course, that I should not receive her letter until too late, but Dawson, good, faithful soul, thought it right to give it to me as soon as she might, and it is not too late! You and I may slip away, and it can't signify to anyone if our absence is noticed. I have thought it all out, and I have the greatest hope of overtaking them before morning! I am persuaded that boy cannot have scraped together enough money to pay for the hire of more than a pair of horses. You and I may hire four, and change them at every stage. The moon is at the full; we shall come up with them before they have gone thirty miles beyond London! Then we may bring Trix home, and no one need know what happened, not even my poor aunt, for I can trust Dawson to keep the secret, and ten to one my aunt won't leave her room until noon tomorrow!'

'Seems to me we'd do better to tell Alan,' objected Timothy.

'Upon no consideration! The Grandduchess is still here, and

Sussex too! He at least cannot leave the house! Besides, Trix trusts me not to betray her to him, and however dreadfully she may have behaved I *could* not do so! He would be so angry! Oh, dear, it is all his fault for having postponed her coming-out! I warned him how it would be! Timothy, *you* must know where we can hire a post-chaise and four good horses!'

He admitted it, but entered a caveat. 'Thing is, dare say you're right about Boynton, but I ain't got the ready to pay for a chaise and four either!'

'No, but I have! I drew quite a large sum only yesterday, and I will give it to you,' said Henrietta. 'I will fetch my cloak, and instruct Dawson in what she must say if she should be questioned, and then we may be off. Do not tell Helmsley to call up a hackney! We will creep out by the door into the yard, and find one for ourselves directly!'

'But, Hetty!' protested Mr Allerton. 'Can't go driving about the countryside in evening-dress! Must change!'

But long acquaintance with her cousin had made Henrietta too familiar with the exigencies of his toilet to allow him this indulgence. Assuring him that his swallow-tailed coat and satin knee-breeches would be hidden by a driving-cloak, she so admonished and hustled him that within a very few minutes he found himself being smuggled out of the house by way of the back stairs and a door leading from the nether regions into the stable-yard.

5

'No,' said Mr Allerton, some five hours later. 'I won't tell 'em to drive on to the Norman Cross inn! And it ain't a bit of use arguing with me, Hetty, because I'm not going to go another mile on a dashed wild-goose chase, and so I tell you! If you want to go on jolting over a devilish bad road, asking questions at every pike of a set of gapeseeds who wouldn't be able to tell you whether Cinderella had driven by in a dashed great pumpkin, let alone Trix in a chaise, you do it! We've come a cool seventy miles, and never had so much as a whiff of Trix, and I want my breakfast! What's more, when I've had it I'm going back to town! She's hoaxing you; told you so at the outset!'

Miss Clitheroe, who had been ushered by an astonished waiter into one of the private parlours of the Talbot Inn, in Stilton, untied the strings of her cloak and pushed back its hood from her dishevelled curls. Pressing her hands to her tired eyes, she said wretchedly: 'She would not do such a thing! I know she plays shocking pranks, but she would never do this, only for mischief!'

'If I know Trix,' said Timothy, 'very likely told you she was off to Gretna Green to set you on a false scent!'

Henrietta stared at him in dismay. 'You mean she may have fled in quite another direction? Timothy, that would be worse than anything! It may be days before we can discover her whereabouts, and where, in heaven's name, will they find a clergyman to marry them?'

'Exactly so!' said Timothy. He added ghoulishly: 'Won't be a case of taking her home. Have to get 'em married in a hurry to save scandal.'

'No, no, I will not believe it!' cried Henrietta. 'They are ahead of us still! We must go on!'

Mr Allerton's reply was brief and unequivocal, but when he perceived the real distress in his cousin's face he relented suffi-ciently to promise that when he had eaten breakfast he would make enquiries at each of the other three posting-houses in the town. With this Henrietta was obliged to be content. The waiter set breakfast before them, listened with polite incredulity to the story, hastily manufactured by Timothy, to account for their appearance in Stilton at eight o'clock in the morning in full dress, of the moribund relative to whose bedside they had been summoned, and withdrew, shaking his head over the reprehensible habits of the Quality.

Mr Allerton then applied himself to a substantial repast. Henrietta, unable to do more than drink a cup of coffee, and nibble a slice of bread and butter, eyed him in growing impatience, but knew better than to expostulate. He finished at last, and, with a kindly recommendation to her not to expect any good outcome, went off to call at the Bell, the Angel, and the Woolpack.

She was left to await his return with what patience she could muster. The time lagged unbearably; when half an hour had passed she could no longer sit still, but got up, and began to pace about the room, trying to think what were best to be done if he failed to obtain news of the fugitives in Stilton.

The sound of a vehicle approaching at a smart pace, and pulling up outside the inn, made her run to the window. The sight that met her eyes was so unexpected and so unwelcome that she caught her breath on a gasp of dismay. Leaning from his own sporting curricle to interrogate one of the ostlers was her cousin Alan, and one glance at his face was enough to inform her that he was quite as angry as she had known he must be, if ever his sister's escapade came to his ears. As she stared out at him, he sprang down from the curricle, and came striding to the door into the inn.

She retreated from the window, wondering how much Dawson had disclosed to him, and what she should say to mollify him. She could almost wish now that the eloping couple had fled beyond recall, for it seemed to her that young Mr Boynton would be fortunate to escape with his bare life if the Viscount caught him.

The Viscount came in, and cast a swift, searching look round the room. Unlike his brother, he had found time to change his ball-dress for a riding-habit, over which he wore a caped greatcoat with large buttons of mother-of-pearl. He was looking extremely handsome, and singularly unyielding. After that one glance round the parlour, his attention became fixed on his cousin, his pleasant gray eyes so full of wrath that she took an involuntary step backward. Stripping off his gloves, he said furiously: 'How *dared* you do this, Henry? How *could* you?'

It had not occurred to her that any part of his anger would be directed against her. She said pleadingly: 'I suppose it was improper, but it seemed to be the only thing I could do!'

'*Improper?*' he exclaimed. 'So that's what you call it, is it? The most damnable escapade!'

'Alan! No, no! Imprudent I may have been, but what other course was open to me? I would not for the world tell my aunt, and I dared not say a word of it to you, because –'

'That at least I believe!' he interrupted. 'You knew well I would never permit it! You were right, my girl, very right! Where is the fellow?'

'I don't know. Oh, Alan, pray don't be so out of reason cross with me! Indeed I meant it for the best! *Alan!*'

The Viscount, who had most ungently grasped her shoulders, shook her. 'Don't lie to me! Where is he?'

'I tell you I don't know! And if I did I would not tell you while you are in such a rage!' said Henrietta, with spirit.

'We'll see that!' said the Viscount grimly. 'I'll settle with him when I've settled with you! Had you chosen an honest man I would have stood aside, whatever it cost me, but this fellow – ! No, by God! If you are determined to marry a fortune-hunter, Henry, let him be me! At least I *love* you!'

Shock bereft her of the power of speech; she could only gaze up into his face. He dragged her into his arms, and kissed her with such savagery that she uttered an inarticulate protest.

To this he paid no heed at all, but demanded sternly: 'Do you understand me, Henry? Give you up to Kirkham I will not!'

'Oh, Alan, don't give me up to anyone!' begged Henrietta, laughing and crying together. 'Oh, dear, how *odious* you are! Of all the infamous notions to – Alan, let me go! Someone is coming!'

The door opened. 'Told you no good would come of it,' said Mr Allerton, with gloomy satisfaction. 'Not a trace of 'em to be –' He broke off, staring at his brother. 'Well, upon my word!' he said, mildly surprised.

'What the devil are *you* doing here?' exclaimed the Viscount.

'Came with Hetty,' explained Timothy. 'Said it was a stupid thing to do, but she would have it we should overtake 'em.'

'Came with Hetty? Overtake – ?' repeated the Viscount. 'In heaven's name, what are you talking about?'

Mr Allerton raised his quizzing-glass. 'You been in the sun, old fellow?' he asked solicitously.

'Timothy, he doesn't know!' Henrietta said. '*That* is not what brought him here! Alan, a dreadful thing has happened. Trix has eloped! I can't think what made you suppose that *I* had! Timothy and I came in pursuit, and oh, I was so hopeful of catching them, but we can discover no trace of them!'

'Quite true,' corroborated Timothy, observing that the tidings had apparently stunned his brother. 'Eloped with Jack Boynton. At least, that's what she said.'

'Are you mad?' demanded the Viscount. 'Trix is at home!'

'Alas, Alan, she is not!' said Henrietta. 'She slipped out in the middle of the party, leaving a letter, which her maid gave me at midnight. She wrote that she had gone with Boynton to Gretna Green, but I very much fear that she was deceiving me, and that is not her destination.'

The Viscount, who had listened to this with an arrested expression on his face, drew an audible breath. 'Most certainly she was deceiving you!' he said, in an odd tone. 'I see! The – little – cunning – *devil*!'

'He *is* cut, Hetty!' said Timothy.

A rueful smile was quivering at the corners of the Viscount's mouth. He paid no heed to this brotherly remark, but said: 'Let me tell you, my love, that an hour after you had left Grosvenor Square, I also received a billet from Trix!'

'You?' said Henrietta incredulously.

'Yes, I! It summoned me with the utmost urgency to join her in Mama's dressing-room. There she disclosed to me that *you* had slipped out of the house, to elope to the Border with Kirkham. She said that you had bound her to secrecy, but that her conscience misgave her, and she felt it to be her duty to betray you to me.'

'*Oh!*' gasped Henrietta. 'The little *wretch*! She – she deserves to be *flogged*!'

'Well, yes, I suppose she does,' admitted the Viscount. 'You cannot, however, expect *me* to flog her, for she has put me deep in her debt! Besides, you must own her strategy has been masterly!'

'Abominable!' scolded Henrietta, trying not to laugh.

'Told you she was hoaxing you,' said Timothy. 'Good notion, as it chances. What I mean is, if you *are* going to marry Hetty, Alan, we shall be all right and tight. The thing that's worrying me is that you must have left home before the ball was over. Dashed improper, y'know! That dishfaced Grandduchess! Half the *ton* invited to have the honour of meeting her, and you walk off in the middle of the party!'

'Well,' said the Viscount impenitently, 'they *had* the honour of meeting her, and *I* have the honour of asking Henry to be my wife, and so we may all be satisfied!' He held out his hands as he spoke, and Henrietta put hers into them.

'Yes, I dare say,' said Mr Allerton, 'but it ain't the thing.

What's more,' he added severely, 'it ain't the thing to kiss Hetty in a dashed inn parlour, and with me watching you, either!'

Night at the Inn

I

THERE WERE ONLY THREE PERSONS PARTAKING OF DINNER at the inn, for it was neither a posting-house, nor a hostelry much patronized by stage-coaches. The man in the moleskin waistcoat, who sat on one of the settles flanking the fireplace in the coffee-room, gave no information about himself; the young lady and gentleman on the other side were more forthcoming.

The lady had been set down at the Pelican after dusk by a cross-country coach. Her baggage was as modest as her appearance, the one consisting of a bandbox and a corded trunk; the other of brown curls smoothed neatly under a bonnet, a round cashmere gown made high to the neck and boasting neither frills nor lace, serviceable half-boots, and tan gloves, and a drab pelisse. Only two things belied the air of primness she seemed so carefully to cultivate: the jaunty bow which tied her bonnet under one ear, and the twinkle in her eye, which was as sudden as it was refreshing.

The gentleman was her senior by several years: an open-faced, pleasant young man whose habit proclaimed the man of business. He wore a decent suit of clothes, with a waistcoat that betrayed slight sartorial ambition; his linen was well-laundered, and the points of his shirt-collar starched; but he had tied his neckcloth with more regard for propriety than fashion, and he displayed none of the trinkets that proclaimed the dandy. However, the watch he consulted was a handsome gold repeater, and he wore upon one finger a signet-ring, with his monogram engraved, so that it was reasonable to suppose him to be a man of some substance.

He was fresh from Lisbon, he told the landlord, as he set down his two valises in the tap-room, and had landed at Portsmouth that very day. Tomorrow he was going to board a coach which would carry him within walking-distance of his paternal home: a rare surprise for his parents that would be, for they had not the least expectation of seeing him! He had been out of England for three years: it seemed like a dream to be back again.

The landlord, a burly, rubicund man with a smiling countenance, entered into the exile's excitement with indulgent good humour. Young master was no doubt come home on leave from the Peninsula? Not wounded, he did hope? No, oh, no! Young master had not the good fortune to be a soldier. He was employed in a counting-house, and had no expectation of getting his transfer from Lisbon for years. But – with offhand pride – he had suddenly been informed that there was a place for him at headquarters in the City, and had jumped aboard the first packet. No time to warn his parents: he would take them by surprise, and wouldn't they gape and bless themselves at the sight of him, by Jupiter! He had meant to have put up at the Swan, in the centre of the town, but such a press of custom had they that they had been obliged to turn him away. The same at the George: he hoped he was going to be more fortunate at the Pelican?

The landlord, gently edging him into the coffee-room, reassured him: he should have a good bedchamber, and the sheets well aired, a hot brick placed in the bed, and a fire lit in the grate. The gentleman from Lisbon said: 'Thank the Lord for that! I have had my fill of tramping from inn to inn, I can tell you! What's more, I'm devilish sharp-set! What's for dinner?'

He was promised a dish of mutton and haricot beans, with soup to go before it, and a dish of broccoli to accompany it. He rubbed his hands together, saying boyishly: 'Mutton! Real English mutton! That's the dandy! That's what I've been longing for any time these three years! Bustle about, man! – I could eat the whole carcase!'

By this time he had been coaxed into the coffee-room, a low-pitched apartment, with shuttered windows, one long table, and an old-fashioned hearth flanked by high-backed settles. On one of these, toasting her feet, sat the young lady; on the other, his countenance obscured by the journal he was perusing, was the man in the moleskin waistcoat. He paid no heed to the newcomer; but the lady tucked her toes under the settle, and assumed an attitude of stiff propriety.

The gentleman from Lisbon trod over to the fire, and stood before it, warming his hands. After a slight pause he observed with a shy smile that these November evenings were chilly.

The lady agreed to it, but volunteered no further remark. The gentleman, anxious that all the world should have a share in his joy, said that he was quite a stranger to England. He added hopefully that his name was John Cranbrook.

The lady subjected him to a speculative, if slightly surreptitious, scrutiny. Apparently she was satisfied, for she relaxed her decorous pose, and said that hers was Mary Gateshead.

He seemed much gratified by this confidence, and bowed politely, and said how do you do? This civility encouraged Miss Gateshead to invite him to sit down, which he instantly did, noticing as he did so that a pair of narrow eyes had appeared above the sheets of the journal on the opposite settle, and were fixed upon him. But as soon as his own encountered them they disappeared again, and all he could see, in fat black print, was an advertisement for Pears' Soap, and another adjuring him to consider the benefits to be derived from using Russia Oil regularly on the hair.

Searching his mind for something with which to inaugurate a conversation, Mr Cranbrook asked Miss Gateshead whether she too had found the Swan and the George full.

She replied simply: 'Oh, no! I could not afford the prices they charge at the big inns! I am a governess.'

'Are you?' said Mr Cranbrook, with equal simplicity. 'I am a clerk in Nathan Spennymore's Counting-house. In the ordinary way I can't afford 'em either, but I'm very plump in the pocket just now!' He patted his breast as he spoke, and laughed, his eyes dancing with such pride and pleasure that Miss Gateshead warmed to him, and invited him to tell her how this delightful state of affairs had come about.

He was nothing loth, and while the man in the moleskin waistcoat read his paper, and the landlord laid the covers on the table, he told her how he had been sent out to Lisbon three years ago, and what it was like there – very well in its way, but a man would rather choose to be at home! – and how an unexpected stroke of good fortune had befallen him, and he was to occupy a superior place in the London house. He didn't know why he should have been chosen, but Miss Gateshead might imagine how he had jumped at the chance!

Miss Gateshead suggested that the promotion might be a reward for good service, which made Mr Cranbrook blush vividly, and say that he was sure it was no such thing. In haste to change the subject, he enquired after her prospects and destination. Miss Gateshead was the eldest daughter of a curate with a numerous progeny, and she was bound for her first situation. Very eligible, she assured him! A large house, not ten miles from this place; and Mrs Stockton, her employer, had graciously promised to send the gig to the Pelican to fetch her in the morning.

'I should have thought she might have sent a closed carriage in this weather,' said John bluntly.

'Oh, no! Not for the governess!' Miss Gateshead said, shocked.

'It may rain!' he pointed out.

She laughed. 'Pooh, I shan't melt in a shower of rain!'

'You might take a chill,' insisted John severely. 'I don't think Mrs Stockton can be at all an amiable person!'

'Oh, do not say so! I am in such a quake already, in case I do not give satisfaction!' said Miss Gateshead. 'And there are nine children – only fancy! – so that I might be employed there for years!'

She seemed to regard this prospect with satisfaction, but Mr Cranbrook had no hesitation in favouring her with his own quite contrary views on such a fate.

The landlord came in, bearing the leg of mutton, which he set down on a massive sideboard. His wife, a decent-looking, stout woman in a mob-cap, arranged various removes on the table, bobbed a curtsy to Miss Gateshead, and asked if she would care for a glass of porter, or some tea.

Miss Gateshead accepted the offer of tea, and, after a moment's hesitation, untied the strings of her bonnet, and laid this demure creation down on the settle. Her curls, unconfined, showed a tendency to become a trifle wayward, but, rather to John's disappointment, she rigorously smoothed them into decorum.

The man in the moleskin waistcoat folded his journal, and bore it to the table, propping it up against a tarnished cruet, and continuing laboriously to peruse it. His attitude indicated that he preferred his own company, so his fellow-guests abandoned any ideas they might have had of including him in their chat, and took their places at the other end of the board. The landlady dumped a pot of tea at Miss Gateshead's elbow, flanking it with a chipped jug of milk, and a cup and saucer; and John bespoke a pint of ale, informing Miss Gateshead, with his ingenuous grin, that home-brewed was one of the things he had chiefly missed in Portugal.

'And what for you, sir?' asked Mrs Fyton, addressing herself to the man at the bottom of the table.

'Mr Waggleswick'll take a heavy-wet as usual,' said her spouse, sharpening the carving-knife.

It was at this point that John, suppressing an involuntary chuckle, discovered the twinkle in Miss Gateshead's eye. They exchanged looks brimful of merriment, each perfectly understanding that the other found the name of Waggleswick exquisitely humorous.

The soup, ladled from a large tureen, was nameless and savourless, but Miss Gateshead and Mr Cranbrook, busily engaged in disclosing to one another their circumstances, family histories, tastes, dislikes, and aspirations, drank it without complaint. Mr Waggleswick seemed even to like it, for he called for a second helping. The mutton which followed the soup was underdone and tough, and the side-dish of broccoli would have been improved by straining. Mr Cranbrook grimaced at Miss Gateshead, and remarked during one of the landlord's absences from the room that the quality of the dinner made him fearful of the condition of the bedchambers.

'I don't think they can enjoy much custom here,' said Miss Gateshead wisely. 'It is the most rambling old place, but no one seems to be staying here but ourselves, and you can *lose* yourself in the passages! In fact, I did,' she added, sawing her way through the meat on her plate. 'I have not dared to look at the sheets, but I have the most old-fashioned bed, and I asked them not to make up the fire again because it was smoking so dreadfully. And what is more I haven't seen a chambermaid, and you can see there is no waiter, so I am sure they don't expect guests.'

'Well, I don't think you should be putting up at a place little better than a hedge-tavern!' said John.

'Mrs Stockton wrote that it was cheap, and the landlady would take care of me,' she explained. 'Indeed, both she and the landlord have been most obliging, and if only the sheets are clean I am sure I shall have nothing to regret.'

Some cheese succeeded the mutton, but as it looked more than a little fly-blown the two young persons left Mr Waggleswick to the sole enjoyment of it, and retired again to the settle by the fire. The room being indifferently lit by a single lamp suspended above the table Mr Waggleswick elected to remain in his place with his absorbing journal. When he had finished his repast he noisily picked his teeth for some time, but at last pushed back his chair, and took himself off.

Miss Gateshead, who had been covertly observing him, whispered: 'What a strange-looking man! I don't like him above half, do you?'

'Well, he is not precisely handsome, I own!' John replied, grinning.

'His nose is crooked!'

'Broken. I dare say he is a pugilist.'

'How horrid! I am glad I am not alone with him here!'

That made him laugh. 'Why, we can't accuse him of forcing his attentions on us, I am sure!'

'Oh, no! But there is something about him which I cannot like. Did you notice how he watched you?'

'Watched me? He barely raised his eyes above the newspaper!'

'He did when he thought you were not looking at him. I know he was listening to every word we said, too. I have the oddest feeling that he may even be listening now!'

'I would wager a large sum he is consuming another of his heavy-wets in the tap rather!' replied John.

The door opened as he spoke, and Miss Gateshead's nervous start was infectious enough to make him look round sharply. But it was only the landlady who came into the room, with a tray, on which she began to pile the plates and cutlery. She remarked that it was a foggy night, so that she had tightly closed the shutters in the bedrooms.

'Get a lot of fog hereabouts, we do,' she said, wiping a spoon on her apron, and casting it into a drawer in the sideboard. 'Like a blanket it'll be before morning, but it'll clear off. I come from Norfolk myself, but a body gets used to anything. It's the clay.'

'Who is our fellow-guest?' asked John.

'Mr Wagglewick? He's an agent of some sort: I don't rightly know. Travels all over, by what he tells me. We've had him here two-three times before. He's not much to look at, but he don't give no trouble. I'll bring your candles in presently. Your room is at the end of the passage, sir: turn to the right at the top of the stairs, and you'll come to it. Fyton took your bags up.'

2

Wagglewick did not return to the coffee-room, and as no other visitors, other than the local inhabitants, who crowded into the tap-room across the passage, came to the Pelican, Miss Gateshead and Mr Cranbrook were left to sit on either side of the fire, chatting cosily together. Miss Gateshead was most interested to hear about Portugal, and as John, like so many young travellers, had filled a fat sketch-book with his impressions of an unknown countryside, it was not long before she had persuaded him to fetch down from his room this treasure.

The landlord was busy in the tap, and Mrs Fyton was nowhere to be seen, so John went upstairs unescorted, trusting to the landlady's directions.

Another of the hanging oil-lamps lit the staircase, and rather feebly cast a certain amount of light a little way along the passage above, but beyond its radius all was in darkness. For a moment John hesitated, half-inclined to go back for a candle, but as his eyes grew more accustomed to the murk he thought that he could probably grope his way along the corridor to the room at the end of it. He did this, not entirely without mishap, since he tripped down one irrelevant step in the passage, and up two others, slightly ricking his ankle in the process, and uttering an exasperated oath. However, he reached the end of the passage, and found that there was a door confronting him. He opened it, and peeped in, and saw, by the light of a fire burning in the high barred grate, his two valises, standing in the centre of the room. As he knelt before them, tugging at the strap round the larger of them, he glanced cursorily round the apartment. It was of a respectable size, and boasted a very large bed, hung with ancient curtains, and bearing upon it a quilt so thick as to present more the appearance of a feather-mattress than of a coverlet. The rest of the furniture was commonplace and old-fashioned, and comprised several chairs, a dressing-table, a wash-stand, a huge mahogany wardrobe, a table by the bed, and a wall-cupboard on the same side of the room as the fireplace. A pair of dingy blinds imperfectly concealed the warped shutters bolted across the window. Some attempt to embellish the room had been made, for a singularly hideous china group stood in the middle of the mantelpiece, and a religious engraving hung above it. Mr Cranbrook hoped that Miss Gateshead's room might be less gloomy: for himself he cared little for his surroundings, but he could imagine that a lady might find such an apartment comfortless, and even rather daunting.

The sketch-book was easily found, and he went off with it, shutting the door of the room behind him. He remembered the treacherous steps in the corridor, and went more carefully, putting out a hand to feel his way by touching the wall. It encountered not the wall, but something warm and furry.

He snatched it back, his eyes straining in the darkness, his heart suddenly hammering. Whatever he had touched was living and silent, and quite motionless. 'Who's that?' he said quickly, an absurd, nameless dread knocking in his chest.

There was a slight pause, as though of hesitation, and then a voice said in a grumbling tone: 'Why can't you take care where you're a-going, young master?'

Mr Cranbrook recognized the voice, which he had heard speaking to the landlord, and knew that what he had touched was a moleskin waistcoat. 'What are you doing here?' he demanded, relieved, yet suspicious.

'What's that to you?' retorted Waggleswick. 'I suppose a cove can go to his room without axing *your* leave!'

'I didn't mean – But why were you spying on me?'

'Spying on you? That's a loud one! What would I want to do that for?' said Waggleswick scornfully.

John could think of no reason, and was silent. He heard a movement, and guessed that Waggleswick was walking away from him. A moment later a door opened farther down the passage, and the glow of firelight within the room silhouetted Waggleswick's figure for a brief instant before he went in, and shut the door behind him.

John hesitated, on the brink of retracing his steps to lock his own door. Then he recollected that he carried his money on his person, and had packed nothing of value in his valises, and he shrugged, and proceeded on his way.

Miss Gateshead was seated where he had left her. She greeted him with a smile that held some relief, and confided to him that she hated foggy nights.

'There's not much fog in the house,' he replied reassuringly.

'No, but it muffles all the noises, and makes one think the

world outside dead!' she said. She perceived that he did not quite appreciate this, and coloured. 'It is only a foolish fancy, of course! I don't think I like this house. A rat has been gnawing in the wainscoting in that corner, and a few minutes ago I heard the stairs creak, and quite thought it must be you. Do you believe in ghosts?'

'No, certainly not,' said John firmly, resolving to make no mention of his encounter with Mr Waggleswick.

'Well, I didn't think I did,' confessed Miss Gateshead, 'but I have the horridest feeling all the time that there is someone just behind me!'

Mr Cranbrook did not feel quite comfortable about the Pelican himself, but since it was plainly his part to comfort Miss Gateshead he adopted a bracing tone, saying that she was perhaps tired after her journey, and was suffering from an irritation of the nerves. She accepted this explanation meekly, and came to sit at the table, so that she could more clearly see Mr Cranbrook's Peninsular sketches.

Shortly after ten o'clock the landlady came in with two tallow candles, stuck into pewter holders. She offered to escort Miss Gateshead up to bed, and since John thought he might as well go to bed too as sit on a settle beside a dying fire, he said that he would also go upstairs. He and Miss Gateshead had reached an excellent understanding by this time, and although nothing so blunt had passed between them as a declaration on Mr Cranbrook's part that he meant to follow up this chance acquaintanceship with a view to extending it rather considerably, his intention was as patent as it was unavowed. Nor did Miss Gateshead make any attempt to discourage him in his resolve. She was even much inclined to think there was a good deal to be said for his vehemently expressed opinion that the life of a governess would not at all suit her.

They took up their candles, and followed Mrs Fyton upstairs.

The noise had died down in the tap; Mrs Fyton said that they kept early hours in these parts, besides that folks were anxious to get home before the fog came down really thick. The light of the candle she carried threw wavering, grotesque shadows on the walls, and disclosed, upstairs, two other passages, leading off at right-angles from the one which ran the length of the house.

'You know your way, sir,' said Mrs Fyton, nodding a chaperon's dismissal to John. 'Come along, miss!'

John knew an impulse to accompany Miss Gateshead at least to her door. He thought she was looking scared, and guessed that this was probably the first time she had ever been alone in a strange inn. However, Mrs Fyton seemed a motherly woman, who might be trusted to look after a young lady, so he said good night, and contented himself with lingering at the head of the stairs until he had seen which door it was that led into Miss Gateshead's room. It lay at the far end of the house to his, with Waggleswick's between them; an arrangement John did not much like – though what evil intentions a middle-aged man of business putting up at an unfrequented inn could harbour in his breast he was unable to imagine. He went on to his own room, leaving the door ajar behind him. His valises were just as he had left them, and until he heard the landlady go down the stairs again he occupied himself in unpacking such articles as he would require for the night. When Mrs Fyton's footsteps had died away, he picked up his candle, and went softly along the passage, and scratched on Miss Gateshead's door.

'Who is it?'

Her voice sounded frightened; he said reassuringly: 'Only me – Cranbrook! I wanted to be sure you are quite comfortable: I won't come in.'

Apparently Miss Gateshead had no dread of this new acquaintance at least. There was a step within the room, the door was opened, and she stood on the threshold, whispering: 'I am so glad you have come! I have discovered that there is no key in this lock, and I know I shan't sleep a wink! Did you see that dreadful creature as we came up the stairs?'

'Waggleswick?' he said sharply, looking down the passage. 'No! Where was he?'

'In the corridor that leads to the back stairs. I caught a glimpse of him, but he stepped out of sight on the instant. I *told* you he was spying on us!'

'It's impossible! Why should he?' Mr Cranbrook said, in a lowered tone. 'Shall I go down and ask Mrs Fyton for a key to your door?'

'I am persuaded it would not be the least avail. I dare say it has been lost for years, for this is the most ramshackle, neglected place I ever was in! The dust under my bed – ! Oh, I do wish Mrs Stockton would have fetched me tonight!'

'So do I – at least, no, I don't, for if she had I should not have met you,' said John honestly. 'But it is very uncomfortable for you, and I don't like *that*! Mind, I don't believe that fellow Waggleswick means any harm: ten to one it is all curiosity! but put a chair under your door-handle, if you are afraid.'

This suggestion found favour. Miss Gateshead wondered that she should not have thought of it for herself, thanked him, and once more bade him good night.

He went back to his own room, pausing at the entrance to the corridor that led to the back stairs, and peering down it. He could see no one, nor did any sound, other than those issuing from the tap downstairs, come to his ears.

3

He had a book packed in his valise, which he had meant to read in the chair by his fire, but this was reduced to glowing embers, and when he would have put more coal on it he found that there was no scuttle in the room. It hardly seemed worth while to ring for it, so he undressed, and got into bed, setting the candle on the table beside him, and thrusting his watch and his pocket-book under the pillow. The bed was a feather one, and though rather smothering, not uncomfortable. He opened his book, and began to read, occasionally raising his head to listen intently. His room was situated too far from the tap for him to be able to hear the murmur of voices there. He heard nothing at all, not even the stir of a mouse.

This dense stillness began presently to make him feel uneasy. It was not very late, and it would have been natural had some sounds broken the silence. In any inn one expected to hear noises: the voices of other guests; footsteps; the slam of a door; the clatter of crockery; or the rumble of wheels in the court-yard. The Pelican, of course, had no courtyard, and obviously did not enjoy much custom; but it did seem odd that he had seen no servant in the house other than the tapster. One would have thought that there would have been at least a waiter, and a chambermaid. He wondered who would clean the boots he had put outside his door, and whether anyone would bring him any shaving-water in the morning.

The silence was so profound that when a coal dropped in the grate it made him start. He was neither a nervous nor an imaginative young man, and the realization that Miss Gateshead had communicated to him some of her alarm vexed him. More than once he found himself lowering his book to glance round the room; and the creak of the chair in which he had sat to pull off his boots actually made him sit up in bed to make sure that he was alone.

When the candle was burnt down to a stub he began to be sleepy; and after finding that the printed words before his eyes were running one into the other, he closed the book, and snuffed the candle. A faint glow showed that the fire still lived. He turned on his side, the feather-bed billowing about him, and in less than ten minutes was asleep.

He awoke he knew not how much later, but so suddenly and with such a certainty that something had roused him that he was alert on the instant, and listening intently. His first thought was that Miss Gateshead must have called to him, but not a sound reached his ears. The glow from the hearth had disappeared; the room was in darkness.

He raised himself on his elbow. As he crouched thus, his ears straining, his eyes trying unavailingly to pierce the night, the conviction that he was not alone took such strong possession of his mind that the sweat broke out on his body. He stretched out his hand, and groped cautiously on the table for the tinder-box. It brushed against the candlestick, which made a tiny sound as it was shifted on the table, and in that moment it seemed to John that something moved in the room. He said breathlessly: 'Who's there?'

As he spoke, his fingers closed over the tinder-box. He sat up with a jerk, felt the bed move as something cannoned into it, and, even as he flung up his hands to grapple his unknown visitant, was thrust roughly down again on to his pillows, a hand clamped over his mouth, and another gripping his throat in a strangling hold. He struggled madly, trying to wrench away the clutch on his windpipe. His hands brushed against something warm and furry; a voice breathed in his ear: 'Dub your mummer!'

He tore at the unyielding hands, writhing, and trying to kick his feet free of the bedclothes, the bed creaking under his frenzied efforts. The grip on his throat tightened till the blood roared in his ears, and he felt his senses slipping from him. 'Still! *Still!*' hissed Wagglewick. 'One squeak out of you, and I'll land you a facer as'll put you to sleep for a se'ennight! Bow Street, clodpole! – *Bow Street!*'

He stopped struggling, partly from surprise at these last words, partly because the breath was choked out of him. The hand on his throat slightly relaxed its grip. He drew a sobbing breath, and distinctly heard the creak of boards under a stealthy footfall. It seemed to come from the direction of the wall-cupboard beside the fireplace.

'For God's sake, lay you still!' Mr Waggleswick's breath was hot in his ear.

He was free, and heard the stir of the bed-curtains, as though Waggleswick had shrunk behind them. He lay perfectly still, rigid and sweating. If Waggleswick were indeed a Bow Street Runner, he ought undoubtedly to obey his instructions; if he were not, it did not seem as though he would have much compunction in silencing those who defied him in a manner highly unpleasant to them. The darkness seemed to press on his eyeballs; he had difficulty still in breathing, but his senses were quite acute, and he caught the sound of a key softly, slowly turning in a lock. This unquestionably came from the direction of the cupboard; a faint lightening of the gloom gradually appeared as the door of the cupboard opened, as though a very dim light had been concealed there. It was obscured by a monstrous shadow, and then dwindled, as the door was pushed to again.

A loose floor-board cracked; John's fists clenched unconsciously, but a warning hand coming from out of the curtains and pressing his shoulder kept him otherwise motionless.

Someone was coming inch by inch towards the bed: someone who knew the disposition of the furniture so exactly that he made no blunder. The heavy coverlet stirred over John's limbs, and, as his hands came up instinctively, smothering folds were over his face, pressed down and down over nose and mouth. He grabbed at this new assailant's wrists, but before his fingers could close on them the pressure abruptly left his face, and he heard a sudden scuffle, a strangled, startled oath, and the quick shifting of stockinged feet on the floor.

He flung the quilt off, groping for the tinder-box, which he had dropped on the bed.

'The glim! light the glim!' panted Waggleswick.

A chair went over with a crash; something was knocked flying from the dressing-table, as the two men swayed and struggled about the room. John's desperate fingers found the tinder-box, and as with trembling fingers he contrived to strike a light from it, a heavy thud shook the room.

The tiny flame flared up; the landlord and Waggleswick were writhing and heaving together on the floor, silent but murderous.

John lit the candle, and tumbled out of bed, hurrying to Waggleswick's aid. The treatment he had suffered during the last few minutes had considerably shaken him, and he felt rather dizzy, nor did a wild kick from one of Fyton's plunging legs do anything to improve his condition. The landlord was immensely strong, and for several minutes he made it impossible for the two other men to overpower him. He and Waggleswick rolled on the floor, locked together, but at last John managed to grab one of his arms, as he was attempting to gouge out Waggleswick's eye, and to twist it with all his might. Waggleswick, who happened at that moment to be uppermost, was thus enabled to drive home a shattering blow to the jaw. This half stunned the landlord, and before he could recover Waggleswick had vigorously banged his head on the floor. This deprived him of his wits for several minutes, and by the time he was at all able to continue the struggle a pair of handcuffs had been locked round his wrists.

'Bide, and watch him!' commanded Waggleswick, out of breath, much abraded, but still surprisingly active. 'Take my barker and don't stand no gammon!' With that, he thrust a pistol into Mr Cranbrook's hand, and dived into the cupboard, adding over his shoulder: 'Hit him over the head with the butt, if he don't stay still! I don't want him shot: he's one for the Nubbing Cheat, he is!'

John found that his knees were shaking. He sat down, and curtly bade the landlord, who seemed to be trying to get up, to stay where he was. He had only just recovered his breath when a glimmer of light shone through the cupboard door, growing brighter as footsteps approached. Mr Waggleswick came back into the room with a lamp.

'All's bowman!' he announced, taking his gun away from John. 'Caught both the bites red-handed. *She's* as bad as he is, and worse! Get up, hang-gallows!'

He endorsed this command with a kick, and the landlord heaved himself to his feet. A settled, dogged expression had descended on to his face; he did not speak, but when John met his eyes he saw that there was so malevolent a look in them that it was almost impossible to believe he could be the same man as the comfortable, smiling host of a few hours earlier.

John shuddered, and turned away to pick up his breeches. When he had pulled these on over his nightshirt, and had thrust his feet into a pair of shoes, Waggleswick invited him to come down and see what had awaited him in the wash-house below his room.

'Jem and me'll lock the cull and his moll in the cellar till morning,' he said. 'Taken me a rare time to snabble you, my buck, ain't it? You'll pay for it! Get down them dancers, and don't you go for to forget that this little pop o' mine is mighty liable to go off! *Mighty* liable it is!'

He motioned the landlord to go before him into the cupboard, grinning at John's face of horror. 'Didn't suspicion what there was behind these here doors, did you?' he said.

'I never tried to open them. Good God, *a stairway*?'

'Down to the wash-house. Took me three visits to get a sight of them, too! Ah, and you'd have gone down 'em feet first if I hadn't have been here, master, like a good few other young chubs! To think I been here four times, and never a blow come worth the biting until you walked in tonight, with your pocket-book full o' flimseys, and your talk of no one suspicioning you was in England! Axing your pardon, you was a regular noddy, wasn't you, sir?'

Mr Cranbrook agreed to it humbly, and brought up the rear of the little procession that wound its way down a steep, twisting stair to a stone-flagged wash-house, where a huge copper was steaming in one corner, and the tapster was standing over Mrs Fyton, loudly protesting her innocence of evil intent in a chair in the middle of the room.

'My assistant – junior, o' course, but a fly cove!' said Waggleswick, jerking a thumb at the tapster. 'All right, Jem: we'll stow 'em away under hatches now!'

John, whose revolted gaze had alighted on a chopper, lying on a stout, scrubbed table, was looking a little pale. He was left to his own reflections while the prisoners were driven down to the cellar; and his half-incredulous and wholly nause-ated inspection of the wash-house made it unnecessary for Waggleswick to inform him, as he did upon his return with Jem, that it had been the Fytons' practice to chop up the bodies of their victims, and to boil down the remains in the copper. 'Though I don't rightly know what they done with the heads,' added Mr Waggleswick thoughtfully.

John had heard tales reminiscent of this gruesome disclosure, but he had imagined that they belonged to an age long past.

'Lor' no, sir!' said Waggleswick indulgently. 'There's plenty of willains alive today! We've had this ken in our eye I dunno how long, but that Fyton he was a cunning one!'

'Ah!' nodded Jem, signifying portentous assent.

'You might have told me!' John said hotly.

'Well,' said Waggleswick, scratching his chin, 'I might, o' course, but you was in the nature of a honey-fall, sir, and I wasn't so werry sure as you'd be agreeable to laying in your bed awaiting for Fyton to come an' murder you unbeknownst if I was to tell you what my lay was.'

A horrible thought crossed John's mind. 'Miss Gateshead!'

'*She's* all right and tight! She was knowed to be putting up here, and Fyton never ran no silly risks.'

''Adn't got no 'addock stuffed with beans neither,' interpolated Jem, somewhat incomprehensibly.

Waggleswick said severely: 'Don't talk that cant to flash coves as don't understand it, sap-head! What he means, sir, is she hadn't no full purse, like you told us all *you* had!'

'Not but what Fyton might ha' done a bit in the body-snatching line,' suggested Jem.

Mr Cranbrook shuddered.

'Well, he ain't snatched *her* body,' pointed out Mr Waggleswick.

John looked at him. 'She must not know of this! It is ghastly!'

Waggleswick scratched his chin again. 'I dunno as she need. She won't be wanted as a witness – like you will, sir!'

'Yes, of course: I know that! I am very willing. Has that monster disposed of many travellers in this frightful way?'

'There's no saying,' replied Waggleswick. 'Not above two or three since we got wind of it in Bow Street.'

'And before? It is horrible to think of!'

'Ah!' agreed Jem. 'Dear knows 'ow many went into that there copper afore us Runners come down 'ere!'

On this macabre thought, Mr Cranbrook retired again to his interrupted repose, if not to enjoy much slumber, at least to employ his time profitably in thinking out what plausible tale he would concoct for Miss Gateshead's benefit in the morning.

4

They met in the coffee-room, still shuttered and unaired. Miss Gateshead was unbarring the shutters when John came into the room, and her comments on the lack of orderly management in the inn were pungent and to the point.

'I tugged and tugged at the bell, and who do you think brought me a can of hot water at last?' she said. 'The tapster!'

'It is too bad! But the thing is that they were cast into a pucker by the landlady's being taken ill in the night,' explained John glibly. 'Should you mind putting on your bonnet, and stepping out with me to partake of breakfast at one of the other inns?'

'Not at all!' replied Miss Gateshead promptly. 'I am very sorry for the landlady, but she almost deserves to be taken ill for keeping her house in such a shocking state! I will fetch my bonnet and pelisse directly.' She paused, coloured slightly, and said in a shamefaced voice: 'I am afraid you must have thought me very foolish last night! Indeed, I cannot imagine what can have possessed me to be so nonsensical! I never slept better in my life! Is it not odd what absurd fancies one can take into one's head when one is a little tired?'

'Most odd!' agreed Mr Cranbrook, barely repressing a shiver.

The Duel

I

$\mathcal{I}$T AMUSED HIM, ENTERING HIS HOUSE SO UNEXPECTEDLY early in the evening, to know that he had disconcerted Criddon, his porter. He suspected Criddon of having slipped out to dally with a serving-maid at the top of some area steps. The rogue was out of breath, as though, having perceived his master sauntering up the flag-way in the light of the oil street lamps, he had scurried back into the house more swiftly than befitted a man of his bulk. As he took the silk-lined cloak, the curly-brimmer beaver, and the tall cane, he wore a faint air of injury. No doubt he felt ill-used because his master, leaving the ball hours before his carriage had been ordered to call for him, had chosen to walk home, instead of looking in at Watier's, according to his more usual custom.

He told Criddon he might go to bed, and strolled to the side table, where a letter, delivered during the evening, awaited him. As he broke the wafer and spread open the sheet, his butler came up from the nether regions, but he waved him away, as irritated by his presence as he would have been angered by his absence. He threw the letter aside and opened the door into the dining-room. The room was in darkness, a circumstance which almost caused him to summon back the butler. It was his pleasure that lights should burn in every room which he might conceivably wish to enter in his great house, and well did his servants know it. But he did not call to Radstock, for his nostrils had caught the acrid smell of candles newly blown out, and he was indefinably aware that he was not alone in the room. Some of the boredom left his face: a turn-up with a housebreaker might relieve the monotony of his existence, and would certainly surprise the housebreaker, who would no doubt consider a seeming dandy in satin knee-breeches and a long-tailed coat easy game. He stepped back into the hall, and picked up the heavy chandelier from the side table there. Carrying this into the dining-room, he stood for a moment on the threshold, looking keenly round. The flames of half a dozen candles flickered, and showed him only the furniture, and the wavering shadows it threw. He glanced towards the windows and it seemed to him that one of the brocade curtains bulged slightly. He set the chandelier down, trod silently to the window, and flung the curtains back.

As he did so, he sprang out of range, and brought his hands up in two purposeful fists. They dropped to his sides. No housebreaker met his astonished gaze, but a girl, shrinking back against the window, the hood of her cloak fallen away from a tangle of silken curls, her frightened face, in which two dark eyes dilated, upturned to his.

For a moment he wondered if Criddon had hidden his doxy in the dining-room; then his critical glance informed him that the girl's cloak was of velvet, and her gown of sprigged muslin the demure but expensive raiment of the débutante. His astonishment grew. He was so eligible a bachelor that he was accustomed to being pursued, and could recognize and evade every snare set in his path. But this seemed to go beyond all bounds. Anger came into his eyes; he thought he must have been mistaken in his assessment of the girl's quality, and that a fair Cyprian had invaded his house.

Then she spoke, and her words confirmed him in his first impression. 'Oh, I *beg* your pardon! P-pray forgive me, sir!' she said, in a pretty, conscience-stricken voice.

Anger gave way to amusement. 'What, ma'am, may I ask, are you doing in my house?' he demanded.

She hung her head. 'Indeed, you must think it most odd in me!'

'I do.'

'The door was open, so – so I ran in,' she explained. 'You see, there – there was a man following me!'

'If you must walk through the streets of London at this hour, I should hope your footman was following you!'

'Oh no! No one knows I am not in my bed! My mission is most secret! And I never meant to walk, but the hackney carried me to the wrong house – at least, I fear I gave the coachman the wrong direction, and he had driven away before I was made aware of my mistake. The servant told me that it was only a step, so I thought I might walk, only there was an *odious* man – ! I ran as fast as I could into this street, and – and your door stood open. Indeed, I meant only to hide in the hall until that creature was gone, but then your porter came in, and I was obliged to run into this room, because how could I explain? When I told that other servant where I wished to go, he – he –' She broke off, lifting her hand to a burning cheek. 'And then you came in, so I slipped behind the curtain.'

It occurred to him, while she offered this explanation of her presence in his house, that although she was agitated she was not at all shy, and seemed not to be much afraid of him. He said: 'You intrigue me greatly. Where, in fact, *do* you wish to go?'

'I wish – I have a particular desire – to go to Lord Rotherfield's house,' she replied.

The amusement left his face. He looked frowningly at her, a hint of contempt in his rather hard eyes. He said in a dry tone: 'No doubt to call upon his lordship?'

She put up her chin. 'If you will be so obliging as to direct me to Lord Rotherfield's house, which I believe to be in this street, sir, I need no longer trespass upon your hospitality!'

'It is the last house in London to which I would direct you. I will rather escort you back to your own house, wherever that may be.'

'No, no, I must see Lord Rotherfield!' she cried.

'He is not a proper person for you to visit, my good girl. Moreover, it is unlikely that you would find him at home at this hour.'

'Then I must wait for him,' she declared. 'I am persuaded he will not be so very late tonight, for he is going to fight a duel in the morning!'

He stared at her, his eyes narrowed. 'Indeed?'

'Yes! – with my brother!' she said, a catch in her voice. 'I must – I *must* prevent him!'

'Is it possible,' he demanded, 'that you imagine you can persuade Rotherfield to draw back from an engagement? You do not know him! Who sent you on this fantastic errand? Who can have exposed you to such a risk?'

'Oh, no one, no one! I discovered what Charlie meant to do by the luckiest accident, and surely Lord Rotherfield cannot be so *very* bad? I know he is said to be heartless and excessively dangerous, but he cannot be such a monster as to shoot poor Charlie when I have explained to him how young Charlie is, and how it would utterly prostrate Mama, who is an invalid, and suffers from the most shocking palpitations!'

He moved away from the window, and pulled a chair out from the table. 'Come and sit down!' he said curtly.

'But, sir –'

'Do as I bid you!'

She came reluctantly to the chair and sat down on the edge of it, looking up at him in a little trepidation.

He drew his snuff-box from his pocket and flicked it open. 'You, I apprehend, are Miss Saltwood,' he stated.

'Well, I am Dorothea Saltwood,' she amended. 'My sister Augusta is Miss Saltwood, because no one has offered for her yet. And that is why I am not yet out, though I am turned nineteen! But how did you know my name is Saltwood?'

He raised a pinch of snuff to one nostril. 'I was present, ma'am, when your brother insulted Rotherfield.'

She seemed grieved. 'At that horrid gaming-hell?'

'On the contrary! At an exclusive club, to which few of us, I fancy, know how Lord Saltwood gained admission.'

She flushed. 'He prevailed upon that stupid creature, Torryburn, to take him there. I dare say he should not have done so, but Lord Rotherfield need not have give him *such* a set-down! You will own it was the unkindest thing!'

'Certainly,' he said. 'Pray do not think that I have the smallest desire to defend Rotherfield! But in justice to his lordship I must tell you that your brother offered him an insupportable insult. His lordship has many faults – indeed, I sometimes think I dislike him more than anyone of my acquaintance! – but I assure you that in all matters of play he is scrupulous. Forgive me if I venture to suggest, ma'am, that your brother will be the better for a sharp lesson, to teach him, in future, not to accuse a gentleman of using loaded dice!'

'Indeed, I know it was very bad, but if he meets Lord Rotherfield he won't have a future!'

'This is high Cheltenham tragedy with a vengeance!' he replied, amused. 'Rotherfield will scarcely proceed to such extremes as you dread, my dear child!'

'They say he never misses!' she uttered, her cheeks blanched.

'Then he will hit Saltwood precisely where he means to.'

'They must not, and they *shall* not meet!' she said earnestly. 'I am persuaded that if I can only tell Lord Rotherfield how it is with Charlie, he cannot be so cruel as to persist in this affair!'

'You would be better advised to prevail upon your brother to apologize for his conduct.'

'Yes,' she agreed mournfully. 'That is what Bernard said, but the thing is that Lord Rotherfield is so deadly a shot that Charlie would never, never do that, because everyone would think he was afraid to meet him!'

'And who, may I ask, is Bernard?'

'Mr Wadworth. We have known him for ever, and he is one of Charlie's seconds. It was he who told me about it. I made him do so. I promised I would not disclose to Charlie that he had breathed a word to me, so what can I do but throw myself upon Lord Rotherfield's mercy?'

'Lord Rotherfield, as you are aware, has no mercy. You would, moreover, be doing Mr Wadworth a vast disservice if you were to betray to anyone the impropriety of his conduct in speaking one word to you on this subject.'

'Oh, dear, I would not injure him for the world, poor Bernard! But I have told *you* already, sir!'

'Your confidence is quite safe in my keeping.'

She smiled engagingly up at him. 'Indeed, I know it must be! You are so very kind! But I am determined to see Lord Rotherfield.'

'And I am determined that you shall return to your home. Rotherfield's is no house for you to visit in this style. Good God, if it should become known that you had done so – !'

She got up, clasping her hands. 'Yes, but it is *desperate*! If anything were to happen to Charlie, it would kill Mama! I assure you, it is of no consequence what becomes of me! Augusta says I am bound to ruin myself, because I have no notion how I should go on, so I might as well ruin myself now as later, don't you think?'

'I do not!' he replied, laughing. 'Oh, don't look so much distressed, you absurd child! Will you trust me to see that no harm comes to your tiresome brother?'

She stared at him, sudden hope in her eyes. 'You, sir? Oh, will *you* see Lord Rotherfield, and explain to him that it was only that poor Charlie has been so sadly indulged, because my father died when he was a little boy, and Mama would not let him go to school, or permit anyone to cross him, and he has only just come to town, and he does not know how to guard his temper, or –'

He interrupted this tumbled speech, possessing himself of one agitated little hand, and kissing it lightly. 'Rest assured I will not allow Lord Rotherfield to hurt poor Charlie at all!'

'Will he listen to you?' she asked doubtfully. 'Augusta's particular friend, Miss Stanstead, says he is a very proud, disagreeable man, and cares nothing for anyone's opinion.'

'Very true, but I have it in my power to compel him to do what I wish. You may safely trust in me.'

She heaved a relieved sigh, and again the enchanting smile trembled on her lips. 'Oh yes! I do, sir! It is the oddest thing, for, to own the truth, I was a little afraid when you pulled back the curtain. You looked at me in *such* a way! But that was quite my own fault, and I saw in a trice that there was not the smallest need for me to be afraid. You are so very kind! I don't know how I may thank you.'

'Forget that I looked at you in *such* a way, and I shall be satisfied. I am going to take you home now. I think you said that no one knew you had left the house. Have you the means to enter it again without being seen by the servants?' She nodded, a gleam of mischief in her big eyes. The amusement in his deepened. 'Abominable girl! Lady Saltwood has my sincere sympathy!'

'I know I have behaved shockingly,' she said contritely. 'But what was I to do? And you must own that it has come about for the best, sir! For I *have* saved Charlie, and I know you will never tell anyone what a scrape I have been in. I hope – I hope you don't truthfully think me abominable?'

'If I were to tell you what I truthfully think, *I* should be abominable. Come! I must convey you home, my little one.'

2

Never did a young gentleman embarking on his first affair of honour receive less encouragement from his seconds than Lord Saltwood received from Sir Francis Upchurch and Mr Wadworth. Sir Francis, being inarticulate, did little more than shake his head, but Mr Wadworth, presuming upon an acquaintance with his principal which dated from the cradle, did not hesitate to speak his mind. 'Made a dashed cake of yourself!' he said.

'Worse!' said Sir Francis, contributing his mite.

'Much worse!' corroborated Mr Wadworth. 'Devilish bad *ton*, Charlie! You were foxed, of course.'

'I wasn't. At least, not very much.'

'Drunk as a wheelbarrow. I don't say you showed it, but you must have been!'

'Stands to reason!' said Sir Francis.

'No right to bully Torryburn into taking you to the Corinthian Club in the first place. Above your touch, my boy! Told you so, when you asked me to take you. No right to have stayed there after Rotherfield gave you that set-down.'

Lord Saltwood ground his teeth. 'He need not have said *that*!'

'No, I dare say he need not. Got a nasty tongue. But that don't signify. You'd no right to accuse him of using Fulhams!'

Sir Francis shuddered, and closed his eyes for an anguished moment.

'Ought to have begged his pardon then and there,' pursued Mr Wadworth relentlessly. 'Instead of that, dashed well forced a quarrel on him!'

'If he hadn't told a waiter – a *waiter*! – to show me out – !'

'Ought to have called for the porter,' agreed Sir Francis. He then perceived that this amiable response had failed to please his fiery young friend, and begged pardon. A powerful thought assailed him. He turned his eyes towards Mr Wadworth, and said suddenly: 'You know what, Bernie? He shouldn't have accepted Charlie's challenge. Must know he ain't been on the town above six months!'

'The point is he *did* accept it,' said Mr Wadworth. 'But it ain't too late. Charlie dashed well ought to apologize.'

'I *will* not!' said Lord Saltwood tensely.

'You were in the wrong,' insisted Mr Wadworth.

'I know it, and I mean to fire in the air. That will show that I acknowledge my fault, but was not afraid to meet Rotherfield!'

This noble utterance caused Sir Francis to drop with a clatter the cane whose amber knob he had been meditatively sucking, and Mr Wadworth to stare at his principal as though he feared for his reason. 'Delope?' he gasped. 'Against Rotherfield? You must be queer in your attic! Why, man, you'd be cold meat! Now, you listen to me, Charlie! If you won't beg the fellow's pardon, you'll come up the instant you see the handkerchief drop, and shoot to kill, or I'm dashed if I'll have anything more to do with it!'

'Awkward business, if he killed him,' objected Sir Francis. 'Might have to leave the country.'

'He won't kill him,' said Mr Wadworth shortly.

He said no more, but it was plain to Saltwood that his seconds thought poorly of his chances of being able to hit his opponent at a range of twenty-five yards. He was by no means a contemptible shot, but he suspected that it might be easier to hit a small wafer at Manton's Galleries than a large man at Paddington Green.

Mr Wadworth called for him in a tilbury very early in the morning. He did not find it necessary to throw stones up at his lordship's window, for his lordship had not slept well, and was already dressed. He stole downstairs, and let himself out of the house, bidding Mr Wadworth good morning with very creditable composure. Mr Wadworth nodded, and cast a knowledgeable eye over him. 'No bright buttons on your coat?' he asked.

The question did nothing to allay the slightly sick feeling at the pit of Saltwood's stomach. Mr Wadworth followed it up with a reminder to him to turn up his collar, and to be careful to present the narrowest possible target to his adversary. Lord Saltwood, climbing into the tilbury, answered with spurious cheerfulness: 'I must suppose it can make little difference to such a shot as they say Rotherfield is.'

'Oh, well – ! No sense in taking needless risks,' said Mr Wadworth awkwardly.

After that, conversation became desultory. They were the first to arrive on the ground, but they were soon joined by Sir Francis, and a man in a sober-hued coat, who chatted about the weather. Saltwood realized that this insensate person must be the doctor, gritted his teeth, and hoped that Rotherfield would not be late. It seemed to him that he had strayed into nightmare. He felt cold, sick, and ashamed; and it said much for the underlying steel in his spoilt and wayward nature that it did not enter his head that he might even now escape from a terrifying encounter by apologizing to Rotherfield for conduct which he knew to have been disgraceful.

Rotherfield arrived even as the church clocks were striking the hour. He was driving himself in his sporting curricle, one of his friends seated beside him, the other following him in a high-perch phaeton. He appeared to be quite nonchalant, and it was obvious that he had dressed with all his usual care. The points of his shirt stood up stiffly above an intricate neckcloth; his dark locks were arranged with casual nicety; there was not a speck upon the gleaming black leather of his Hessian boots. He sprang down from the curricle and cast his drab driving-coat into it. The seconds met, and conferred, and presently led their principals to their positions, and gave into their hands the long-barrelled duelling-pistols, primed and cocked.

Across what seemed to be an immeasureable stretch of turf, Saltwood stared at Rotherfield. That cold, handsome face might have been carved in stone; it looked merciless, faintly mocking.

The doctor turned his back; Saltwood drew in his breath, and grasped his pistol firmly. One of Rotherfield's seconds was holding the handkerchief high in the air. It fell, and Saltwood jerked up his arm and fired.

He had been so sure that Rotherfield would hit him that it seemed to him that he must have been hit. He recalled having been told that the bullet had a numbing effect, and cast an instinctive glance down his person. But there did not seem to be any blood, and he was certainly still standing on his feet. Then he heard someone ejaculate: 'Good God! *Rotherfield!*' and, looking in bewilderment across the grass, he saw that Mr Mayfield was beside Rotherfield, an arm flung round him, and that the doctor was hurrying towards them. Then Mr Wadworth removed his own pistol from his hand, and said in a stupefied voice: 'He *missed!*'

Young Lord Saltwood, realizing that he had hit the finest pistol-shot in town and was himself untouched, was for a moment in danger of collapsing in a swoon. Recovering, he pushed Mr Wadworth away, and strode impetuously up to the group gathered round Rotherfield. He reached it in time to hear that detested voice say: 'The cub shoots better than I bargained for! Oh, go to the devil, Ned! It's nothing – a graze!'

'My lord!' uttered Saltwood. 'I wish to offer you my apology for –'

'Not now, not now!' interrupted the doctor testily.

Saltwood found himself waved aside. He tried once more to present Rotherfield with an apology, and was then led firmly away by his seconds.

3

'Most extraordinary thing I ever saw!' Mr Wadworth told Dorothea, when dragged by her into the small saloon, and bidden disclose the whole to her. 'Mind, now! Not a word to Charlie! Rotherfield missed!'

Her eyes widened. 'Fired in the air?'

'No, no! Couldn't expect him to do that! Dash it, Dolly, when a man does that he's owning he was at fault! Don't mind telling you I felt as sick as a horse. He was looking devilish grim. Queer smile on his face, too. I didn't like it above half. I'll swear he took careful aim. Fired a good second before Charlie did. Couldn't have missed him by more than a hair's breadth! Charlie got him in the shoulder: don't think it's serious. Thing is, shouldn't be surprised if it's done Charlie good. Tried to beg Rotherfield's pardon on the ground, and he's called once in Mount Street since then. Not admitted: butler said his lordship was not receiving visitors. Given Charlie a fright: he'll be more the thing now. But don't you breathe a word, Dolly!'

She assured him she would not mention the matter. An attempt to discover from him who, besides Lord Rotherfield, resided in Mount Street could not have been said to have advanced the object she had in mind. Mr Wadworth was able to recite the names of several persons living in that street; but when asked to identify a gentleman who apparently resembled a demigod rather than an ordinary mortal, he said without hesitation that he had never beheld anyone remotely corresponding to Miss Saltwood's description. He began then to show signs of suspicion, so Dorothea was obliged to abandon her enquiries and to cast round in her mind for some other means of discovering the name of her brother's unknown preserver. None presented itself; nor, when she walked down Mount Street with her maid, was she able to recognize the house in which she had taken refuge. A wistful fancy that the unknown gentleman might perhaps write to tell her that he had kept his word was never very strong, and by the end of the week had vanished entirely. She could only hope that she would one day meet him, and be able to thank him for his kind offices. In the meantime, she found herself to be sadly out of spirits, and behaved with such listless propriety that even Augusta, who had frequently expressed the wish that something should occur to tame her sister's wildness, asked her if she were feeling well. Lady Saltwood feared that she was going into a decline, and herself succumbed immediately to a severe nervous spasm.

Before any such extreme measures for the restoration to health of the younger Miss Saltwood as bringing her out that very season had been more than fleetingly contemplated by her mama and angrily vetoed by her sister, her disorder was happily arrested. Eight days after Saltwood's duel, on an afternoon in June, the butler sought out Dorothea, who was reading aloud to her afflicted parent, and contrived to get her out of the drawing-room without arousing any suspicion in Lady Saltwood's mind that she was wanted by anyone more dangerous than the dressmaker. But once outside the drawing-room Porlock placed a sealed billet in Dorothea's hand, saying with the air of a conspirator that the gentleman was in the Red Saloon.

The billet was quite short, and it was written in the third person. '*One who had the pleasure of rendering a trifling service to Miss Dorothea Saltwood begs the honour of a few words with her.*'

'Oh!' gasped Dorothea, all her listlessness vanished. 'Porlock, pray do not tell Mama or my sister! *Pray* do not!'

'Certainly not, miss!' he responded, with a readiness not wholly due to the very handsome sum already bestowed upon him downstairs. He watched his young mistress speed down the stairs, and thought with pleasure that when Miss Augusta discovered what kind of an out-and-outer was courting her sister she would very likely go off in an apoplexy. The gentleman in the Red Saloon, to his experienced eye, was a bang-up Corinthian, a Nonpareil, a very Tulip of Fashion.

Dorothea, coming impetuously into the saloon, exclaimed on the threshold: 'Oh, I am so very glad to see you, sir! I have wished so much to thank you, and I have not known how to do so, for I never asked you your name! I don't know how I came to be such a goose!'

He came towards her, and took her outstretched hand in his left one, bowing over it. She perceived that he was quite as handsome as she had remembered, and that his right arm lay in a sling. She said in quick concern: 'How comes this about? Have you broke your arm, sir?'

'No, no!' he replied, retaining her hand. 'A slight accident to my shoulder merely! It is of no consequence. I trust that all went well that evening, and that your absence had not been discovered?'

'No, and I have not mentioned it to anyone!' she assured him. 'I am so very much obliged to you! I cannot imagine how you contrived to prevail upon that man not to hit Charlie! Bernard told me that Charlie hit *him*, and I must say I am sorry, because it was quite my fault, and although he is so odious I did not wish him to be hurt precisely!'

'To own the truth, he had little expectation of being hurt,' he said, with a smile. He released her hand, and seemed to hesitate. 'Lord Rotherfield, Miss Saltwood, does not wish to appear odious in your eyes, believe me!'

'Is he a friend of yours?' she asked. 'Pray forgive me! I am sure he cannot be so very bad if that is so!'

'I fear he has been quite my worst friend,' he said ruefully. 'Forgive me, my child! *I* am Lord Rotherfield!'

She stood quite still, staring at him, at first pale, and then with a flush in her cheeks and tears sparkling in her eyes. '*You* are Lord Rotherfield?' she repeated. 'And I said *such* things about you, and you let me, and were so very kind, and allowed yourself to be wounded – Oh, I am sure you must be the best person in the world!'

'I am certainly not that, though I hope I am not the worst. Will you forgive me for having deceived you?'

She put out her hand, and again he took it, and held it. 'How can you talk so? I am quite ashamed! I wonder you did not turn me out of doors! How *good* you are! How truly noble!'

'Ah, how can *you* talk so?' he said quickly. 'Do not! I do not think I had ever, before that evening, wished to please anyone but myself. You came to me – enchanting and abominable child that you are! – and I wanted more than anything in life to please you. I am neither good nor noble – though I am not as black as I was painted to you. I assure you, I had never the least intention of wounding your brother mortally.'

'Oh *no*! Had I known it was you I should never have thought that!'

He raised her hand to his lips. The slight fingers seemed to tremble, and then to clasp his. He looked up, but before he could speak Lord Saltwood walked into the room.

Lord Saltwood stopped dead on the threshold, his eyes starting from their sockets. He stared in a dazed way, opened his mouth, shut it again, and swallowed convulsively.

'How do you do?' said Rotherfield, with cool civility. 'You must forgive me for having been unable to receive you when you called at my house the other day.'

'I came — I wished — I wrote you a letter!' stammered Saltwood, acutely uncomfortable.

'Certainly you did, and I have come to acknowledge it. I am much obliged to you, and beg you will think no more of the incident.'

'C-came to see *me*?' gasped Saltwood.

'Yes, for I understand you to be the head of your family, and I have a request to make of you. I trust that our late unfortunate contretemps may not have made the granting of it wholly repugnant to you.'

'No, no! I mean — anything in my power, of course! I shall be very happy — ! If you would care to step into the book-room, my lord — ?'

'Thank you.' Rotherfield turned, and smiled down into Dorothea's anxious eyes. 'I must take my leave of you now, but I trust Lady Saltwood will permit me to call on her tomorrow.'

'Yes, indeed, I am persuaded — that is, I do hope she will!' said Dorothea naïvely.

There was a laugh in his eye, but he bowed formally and went out with Saltwood, leaving her beset by a great many agitating emotions, foremost amongst which was a dread that Lady Saltwood would, in the failing state of her health, feel herself to be unequal to the strain of receiving his lordship. When, presently, Saltwood went up to the drawing-room, looking as though he had sustained a severe shock, Dorothea was seized by a conviction that her escapade had been disclosed to him, and she fled to the sanctuary of her bedchamber, and indulged in a hearty bout of tears. From this abyss of woe she was jerked by the unmistakable sounds of Augusta in strong hysterics. Hastily drying her cheeks, she ran down the stairs to render whatever assistance might be needed, and to support her parent through this ordeal. To her amazement, she found Lady Saltwood, whom she had left languishing on the sofa, not only upon her feet, but looking remarkably well. To her still greater amazement, the invalid folded her in the fondest of embraces, and said: 'Dearest, dearest child! I declare I don't know if I am on my head or my heels! *Rotherfield!* A countess! You sly little puss, never to have told me that you had met him! And not even out yet! You must be presented at once: *that* I am determined upon! He is coming to visit me tomorrow. Thank heaven you are just Augusta's size! You must wear the pomona silk dress Celestine has just made for her: I knew how it would be, the instant I brought you out! I was never so happy in my life!'

Quite bewildered, Dorothea said: 'Presented? Wear Augusta's new dress? Mama, *why?*'

'My innocent treasure!' exclaimed Lady Saltwood. 'Tell me, my love, for you must know I am scarcely acquainted with him, do you – do you *like* Lord Rotherfield?'

'Oh, Mama!' said Dorothea impulsively. 'He is exactly like Sir Charles Grandison, and Lord Orville, only far, far better!'

'Dearest Dorothea!' sighed her ladyship ecstatically. 'Charlie, do not stand there staring! Go and throw a jug of water over Augusta this instant! This is *not* the moment for hysterics!'

Hazard

T HE GIRL STOOD UNDER THE LIGHT OF THE GUTTERING candles, still as a statue, her hands clasped in front of her, and no colour in her cheeks. She was dressed in a simple muslin gown with blue ribbons, and wore no ornament save the fillet threaded through her gold hair. She did not look at her half-brother, nor at any one of the five other men who were gathered round the table in the centre of the over-heated room. But she knew who was present; she had seen them all in the one swift glance she had cast at them under her lashes as she had entered the room. There was Lord Amberfield, sprawling over the table with his head pillowed on his arm; Mr Marmaduke Shapley, not so drunk as Amberfield, leaning on his chair and giggling; Sir Thomas Fort, a little blear-eyed, very purple in the face; Mr Lionel Winter, idiotically smiling; and Carlington Carlington with his black curls in disorder, and his exquisite cravat crumpled, his lean cheeks hectically flushed, and a reckless look in his bright eyes.

And there was Half-brother Ralph, in answer to whose peremptory summons she had got up out of her bed, and dressed herself, and come down to this stuffy room in the chill small hours. He was lounging back in his chair, still grasping the dice-box in one hand, while the other sought to refill his empty glass. Some of the wine slopped over on to the baize cloth that covered the table; Sir Ralph cursed it, and thrust the bottle on towards his left-hand neighbour. 'Fill up, Lionel! Fill up!' he said, hiccuping. 'Now, my lord – now Carlington! You want to play on, hey? But I'm done-up, d'ye see? Only one thing left to stake, and that's m'sister!' A fit of insane laughter shook him; he made a gesture towards the girl, who stood motionless still, her gaze fixed on a point above Carlington's handsome head. 'I'll set her for my last stake, gen'lemen. Who'll cover?'

Mr Winter said: 'Tha's – tha's Miss Helen,' and nodded wisely.

'Damme, Morland, this – this is not right!' said Sir Thomas, getting on to his feet. 'Miss Morland – very obedient servant, ma'am! Amberfield – my lord! ladies present!'

He lurched towards the sleeping Viscount, and shook him by one shoulder. Lord Amberfield moaned, and muttered: 'Pockets to let: all my vowels in – in Carlington's hands.'

'Freddy, my boy, I'm saying it's not right. Can't stake a lady.'

Lord Amberfield said: 'Can't stake anything. Nothing to stake. Going to sleep.'

Mr Marmaduke Shapley clasped his head in his hands, as though to steady it, and said rather indistinctly: 'It's the wine. Confound you, Ralph, you're drunk!'

Sir Ralph gave a boisterous laugh, and rattled the dice in the box. 'Who'll cover?' he demanded. 'What d'ye say, Lionel? Will you have my jade of a sister to wife?'

Mr Winter rose to his feet, and stood precariously balancing on his heels. 'Sir,' he said, looking owlishly at his host, 'shall take leave to tell you – no one will cover prepost'rous stake!'

Sir Ralph's wicked eyes went past him to where Carlington sat, gazing at the girl under frowning, night-black brows. By the Marquis' left arm, stretched negligently before him on the table, scraps of paper were littered, vowels for the money he had won. There were rouleaus of guineas at his elbow, and more guineas spilled under his hand. Through Sir Ralph's blurred mind drifted a thought that he had never seen the young Marquis in so wild a humour before. He leaned forward, and said mockingly: 'Will you cover, my lord, or do you refuse the bet?'

Carlington's eyes turned slowly towards him. They were not glazed but unnaturally bright. 'I – refuse?' he said.

'There's the true elbow-shaker!' crowed Sir Ralph. 'Cover, Carlington! What's the jade worth?'

Mr Winter laid hold of his chair-back, and with difficulty enunciated four words: 'My lord, you're d-drunk!'

'Drunk or sober, no man shall set me a stake I won't cover,' Carlington answered. His long fingers closed over the heap of vowels, crushing them into a ball. He thrust them forward, and his rouleaus with them.

'Good God, Charles!' cried Sir Thomas, catching at his wrist. 'There's a matter of twenty thousand pounds there! Have sense, man, have sense!'

Carlington shook him off. 'A main, Morland, call a main!' he said.

'Seven!' Sir Ralph responded, and cast the dice on to the table.

Carlington laughed, and dived a hand into his pocket for his snuff-box, and flicked it open.

'Five to seven!' announced Mr Shapley, peering at the dice.

The girl's fixed gaze had wavered as the dice rattled in the box, and she had shot a swift glance downwards at the chance, as it lay on the table. Her brother gathered up the dice, shook them together and again threw them.

They rolled across the table, and settled into five and ace.

'Cinque-ace!' called Mr Shapley, constituting himself groom-porter. 'Any bets, gentlemen? any bets?'

No one answered; the Marquis took snuff.

The dice were shaken a third time, and cast. 'Quatre-trey!' called out Mr Shapley. 'Carlington, you've – you've the d-devil's own luck!'

The girl's eyes remained fixed for a moment on the four and the three lying on the green cloth; then she raised them, and looked across the table at Carlington.

The Marquis leaped up, and achieved a bow. 'Ma'am, I have won your hand in fair play!' he said, and stretched out his own imperatively.

Sir Ralph was staring at the dice, his lower lip pouting, and some of the high colour fading from his cheeks. Without a glance at him Miss Morland walked round the table, and curtsied, and laid her hand in Carlington's.

His fingers closed on it; he swung it gently to and fro, and said recklessly: 'It's time we were going. Will you come, my golden girl?'

Miss Morland spoke for the first time, in a composed, matter-of-fact voice. 'Certainly I will come, sir,' she said.

Carlington's eyes danced. 'I'm drunk, you know,' he offered. 'Yes,' she said.

He shook with laughter. 'By God, I like your spirit! Come, then!'

Sir Thomas started forward, lurched heavily against the table, and caught at it to steady himself. 'Damme, you're mad! Ralph, this won't do — bet's off — joke's a joke — gone far enough!'

'Play or pay!' the Marquis retorted, a smile not quite pleasant curling his lips.

Sir Ralph raised his eyes, and looked sullenly towards his sister. She returned his gaze thoughtfully, dispassionately, and transferred her attention to Carlington. 'I think,' she said tranquilly, 'I had better go and fetch a cloak if we are leaving now, sir.'

The Marquis escorted her to the door, and opened it, and set a shout ringing for his carriage. Miss Morland passed out of the hot room into the hall, and went across it to the stairs.

When she came down again some minutes later, cloaked, and with a chip hat on her head, and a bandbox in her hand, her brother had joined the Marquis in the hall, and was standing leaning against the lintel of the front door, scowling. The Marquis had put on a high-waisted driving-coat of drab cloth with row upon row of capes, and buttons of mother-of-pearl as large as crown-pieces. He had a curly-brimmed beaver, and a pair of York tan gloves in one hand, and his ebony cane in the other, and he flourished another bow at Miss Morland as she trod unhurriedly across the hall towards him.

'If you go, by God, you shan't return!' Sir Ralph said.

Miss Morland laid her hand on Carlington's proffered arm. 'I shall never return,' she said.

'I mean it!' Sir Ralph threatened.

'And I,' she replied. 'I have been in your ward three years. Do you think I would not sooner die than return to this house?'

He flushed, and addressed the Marquis. 'You're crazy to take her!'

'Crazy or drunk, what odds?' said Carlington, and opened the front door.

Sir Ralph caught at his coat. 'Where are you going?' he asked.

Carlington's wild laugh broke from him. 'Gretna!' he answered, and flung his arm about Miss Morland's waist, and swept her out of the house into the misty dawn.

His post-chaise and four was waiting, drawn up by the steps of the house, with the postilions shivering in their saddles, and one of Sir Ralph's servants holding the chaise door open.

The sharp morning air had an inevitable effect on the Marquis. He reeled, and had to catch at the footman's shoulder to steady himself. He was able, however, to flourish another bow in Miss Morland's direction, and to hand her up into the chaise.

Sir Ralph's house being situated at Hadley Green, and the Marquis having driven out from London to attend his card-party, the postilions had faced the chaise southwards. Upon receiving their master's order to drive to Gretna Green they were at first a great deal too astonished to do more than blink at him, but as, assisted by the footman, he began to climb up into the chaise, the boy astride one of the leaders ventured to point out that Gretna Green was some three hundred miles off, and his lordship totally unprepared for a long journey. The Marquis, however, merely reiterated: 'Gretna!' and entered the chaise, and sank down on to the seat beside Miss Morland.

The postilions were quite aware that their master was extremely drunk, but they knew him well enough to be sure that however much he might, in the morning, regret having ordered them to drive north he would blame them less for obeying him than for disregarding his instructions, and carrying him safely home. No sooner were the steps folded up than they wheeled the chaise, and set off in the direction of the Great North Road.

The Marquis let his hat slide on to the floor, and rested his handsome head back against the blue velvet squabs. Turning it a little he smiled sweetly upon his companion, and said, still with a surprising clarity of diction: 'I've a notion I shall regret this, but I'm badly foxed, my dear – badly foxed.'

'Yes,' said Miss Morland. 'I know. It doesn't signify. I am quite accustomed to it.'

That was the sum of their discourse. The Marquis closed his eyes, and went to sleep. Miss Morland sat quite still beside him, only occasionally clasping and unclasping her hands in her lap.

Potter's Bar, Bell Bar, Hatfield were all passed. Miss Morland paid for the tickets at the turnpikes with some loose coins found in the sleeping Viscount's pockets. A little more than two miles out of Hatfield the chaise passed through the hamlet of Stanborough, and began the long rise of Digswell Hill. At the Brickwall pike the postilion mounted on one of the wheelers informed Miss Morland that if his lordship desired to press on horses must be changed at Welwyn. An attempt to rouse the Marquis was unavailing; he only groaned, and seemed to sink deeper into slumber. Miss Morland, who had had time to reflect upon the rashness of this flight, to which sheer anger had prompted her, hesitated for a moment, and then desired the postilions to drive to a respectable posting-house in Welwyn, where they might put up for what was left of the night.

In a little while the chaise had drawn up at the White Hart; the landlord had been awakened, and a couple of drowsy ostlers, still in their nightcaps, had lifted the Marquis out of the coach, and carried him up to a bedchamber on the first floor.

No one seemed to feel very much surprise at this strange arrival in the small hours of the morning. The Marquis, who was well-known to the landlord, was obviously drunk, and this circumstance provided a perfectly reasonable explanation for both his and Miss Morland's presence. 'Though I must say,' remarked the landlord, as he once more rejoined his sleepy wife, 'I didn't know he was one of them hard topers – not Carlington. Wild, of course, very wild.'

The Marquis did not wake until past nine o'clock. His first sensations were those of supreme discomfort. His head ached, and his mouth was parched. He lay for some time with closed eyes, but presently, as fuller consciousness returned to him, he became aware of being almost completely clad. He opened his eyes, stared filmily upon his strange surroundings, and with a groan sat up in bed, clasping his temples between his hands. He found that with the exception of his neckcloth and his shining Hessians he was indeed fully clad, the kind hands that had relieved him of boots and cravat having failed in their endeavour to extricate him from the perfectly fitting coat of Mr Weston's cutting.

After another dazed look round the room, the Marquis reached for the bell-pull, and tugged at it vigorously.

The summons was answered by the landlord in person.

Carlington, still clasping his aching head, looked at him with acute misgiving and pronounced: 'I've seen your rascally face before. Where am I?'

The landlord smiled ingratiatingly, and replied: 'To be sure, my lord, your lordship is in the very best room at the White Hart.'

'Which White Hart?' demanded the Marquis irritably. 'I know of fifty at least!'

'Why, at Welwyn, my lord!'

'Welwyn!' ejaculated Carlington, letting his hands fall. 'What the devil am I doing in Welwyn?'

This question the landlord, who had had an illuminating conversation with the two postilions, thought it prudent to leave unanswered. He coughed, and said vaguely that he was sure he couldn't say. He waited for his noble client's memory to assert itself, but the Marquis, with another groan, merely sank back upon his pillows, and closed his eyes again. The landlord gave another cough, and said: 'The lady has ordered breakfast in a private parlour, my lord.'

The Marquis' eyes opened at that. 'Lady? What lady?' he said sharply.

'The – the lady who accompanies your lordship,' replied the landlord.

'My God!' said the Marquis, and clasped his head in his hands again. There was a pause. 'Oh, my God, what have I done?' said the Marquis. 'Where is she?'

'The lady, my lord, spent the night in the bedchamber adjacent to this, and awaits your lordship in the parlour. Your lordship – er – does not appear to have any trunk or cloak-bag.'

'I know that, curse you!' said the Marquis, casting off the coverlet, and setting his stockinged feet to the ground. 'Damnation take this head of mine! Help me out of this coat, fool!'

The landlord extricated him from it, not without difficulty, and suggested that his lordship might like to be shaved. 'For I have a very reliable lad, my lord, and should be honoured to lend your lordship my own razors.'

The Marquis had poured a jugful of hot water into the wash-basin. 'Send him up, man, send him up!' he said. He dipped his head into the basin, but raised it again to say: 'My compliments to the lady, and I shall do myself the honour of joining her in half an hour.'

Downstairs in the private parlour Miss Morland had ordered breakfast for half-past nine. When the Marquis at last appeared she was drinking a cup of coffee, and looking as neat and as fresh as though she had had her maid with her, and several trunks of clothes.

The Marquis had been shaved, had had the creases pressed out of his coat, and had contrived to arrange his starched but crumpled cravat in decent folds, but he did not look very fresh. He was pale, and the reckless look had gone from his face, leaving it worried, and rather stern. He came into the parlour, and shut the door behind him, and paused with his hand still on the knob, looking across at Miss Morland with a mixture of remorse and bewilderment in his fine eyes.

Miss Morland's colour rose, but she said calmly: 'Good morning, sir. A very fine day, is it not?'

'I have not noticed whether it is fine or not,' replied Carlington. 'I have to beg your pardon, ma'am. I have no very clear recollection of what occurred last night. I was drunk.'

'Yes,' said Miss Morland, a slice of bread and butter halfway to her mouth. 'You explained that at the time. May I give you some coffee?'

He came to the table, and stood looking down at her in even greater bewilderment. 'Miss Morland, drunk I may have been, but was I so drunk that I forced you to accompany me to this place?'

'I came with you quite willingly,' she assured him.

He grasped the back of the chair before him. 'In God's name, what induced you to commit so imprudent an action?'

'You won me,' she explained. 'I was the stake set by my brother.'

'I remember,' he said. 'I must have been mad, and he −' He broke off. 'Good heavens, ma'am, that you should have been subjected to such an indignity!'

'It was not very pleasant,' she agreed. 'It seemed to me preferable to go away with you than to remain under that roof another hour.' She paused, and raised her eyes to his face. 'You have always treated me with a courtesy my brother does not accord me. Besides,' she added, 'you assured me that your intentions were honourable.'

'My intentions!' he exclaimed.

'Certainly, sir,' said Miss Morland, casting down her eyes to hide the gleam of mischief in them. 'You informed my brother that you would take me to Gretna Green. We are on our way there now.'

The Marquis pulled the chair out from the table, and sank down into it. 'Gretna Green!' he said. 'My dear girl, you don't know − This is appalling!'

Miss Morland winced a little, but said in a considering voice: 'A little irregular, perhaps. But if I do not mind that I am sure you need not. You have a reputation for doing odd things, after all.'

He brought his open hand down on the table. 'If I have, the more reason for you to have refused to come with me on this insane journey! Were you mad, Miss Morland?'

'Oh, by no means!' she replied, cutting her bread and butter into thin strips. 'Of course, it is not precisely what I should have chosen, but you offered me a way of escape from a house in which I was determined not to spend another night.'

'You must have relatives − someone to whom −'

'Unfortunately I have no one,' said Miss Morland composedly.

The Marquis leaned his head in his hand, and said: 'My poor girl, you do not appear to realize the scandal this escapade will give rise to! I must get you to some place where you will be safe from it.'

Miss Morland bit into one of her strips of bread and butter. 'As your wife, sir, I shall expect you to protect me from slanderous tongues,' she said blandly.

The Marquis raised his head, and said with a groan: 'Helen, the notice of my engagement is in today's *Gazette!*'

There was just a moment's silence. The faintest tremor shook Miss Morland's hand, and she grew rather white. But when she spoke it was in a voice of mild interest. 'Dear me, then what can have possessed you to accept my brother's stake?'

He looked at her with a queer hungriness in his eyes, and answered: 'I have told you that I was drunk. Drunk, I only knew what I wanted, not what I must not do.' He got up, and began to walk about the room. 'No use talking of that. We are in the devil of a fix, my girl.'

'May I ask,' enquired Miss Morland, 'who is the lady to whom you are so lately become engaged?'

'Miss Fanny Wyse,' he answered. 'It is a long-standing arrangement. I can't, with honour, draw back from it. That accursed notice in the *Gazette* – It is impossible for me to repudiate it.'

She regarded him rather inscrutably. 'Are you attached to Miss Wyse, sir?'

'It is not that!' he said impatiently. 'Our parents made this match for us when we were in our cradles. It has been an understood thing. Yesterday I made a formal offer for Miss Wyse's hand, and she accepted me.'

'I suppose,' remarked Miss Morland thoughtfully, 'that your excesses last night were in the nature of a celebration?'

He gave an ugly little laugh. 'My excesses, ma'am, were an all too brief escape from reality!'

Miss Morland looked meditatively at the coffee-pot. 'If you do not care for Miss Wyse, my lord, why did you offer for her?'

'You don't understand!' he said. 'She has been brought up to think herself destined to become my wife! I could do no less than offer for her.'

'Oh!' said Miss Morland. 'Is she very fond of you?'

He flushed slightly. 'It is not for me to say. I believe – I think she wishes to marry me.' A somewhat sardonic smile crossed his lips; he added: 'And God help both of us if ever this adventure should come to her ears!'

Miss Morland poured herself out some more coffee. 'Do you mean to abandon me, sir?' she asked.

'Certainly not,' replied his lordship. 'I shall put you in charge of a respectable female, and compel your brother to make provision for you.'

She raised her brows. 'But you told my brother you would marry me,' she pointed out.

He paused in his striding to and fro, and said: 'I can't marry you! God knows I would, but I can't elope with you the very day my engagement to Fanny is published!'

She smiled at that, but not very mirthfully, and got up from the table. 'Calm yourself, my lord. I have only been – punishing you a little. I came away with you because I was a great deal too angry to consider what I was about. What I really wish you to do is to convey me to London where I shall take refuge with my old governess.' She picked up her hat, and added: 'I think – I am sure – that she will be very willing to engage me to teach music and perhaps painting in her school.'

He strode over to the window, and with his back to her said: 'A Queen's Square boarding-school! Helen, Helen –' He broke off, biting his lips, and staring with unseeing eyes at a chaise that had just drawn up outside the inn. The chaise door opened, a young lady looked out, and the Marquis recoiled from the window with a startled oath.

Miss Morland was tying the strings of her cloak, and merely looked an enquiry.

'Fanny!' the Marquis ejaculated. 'Good God, what's to be done?'

Miss Morland blinked at him. 'Surely you must be mistaken!'

'Mistaken! Do you think I don't know my promised wife?' demanded his lordship savagely. 'I tell you it is she! Someone must have sent her word – that meddling fool, Fort, I dare say!'

'But surely Miss Wyse would not pursue you?' said Miss Morland, rather aghast.

'Wouldn't she?' said Carlington grimly. 'You don't know her! If she does not have hysterical spasms we may count ourselves fortunate!' He looked round the room, saw a door at the opposite end of it, and hurried across to open it. A roomy cupboard was disclosed. 'Go in there, my dear,' commanded Carlington. 'I must get hold of that landlord, and warn him to keep his mouth shut.' With which he thrust Miss Morland into the cupboard, closed the door on her, and went quickly towards the other leading into the coffee-room.

He was not, however, in time to warn the landlord. As he stepped out of the parlour that worthy was escorting Miss Wyse into the coffee-room.

Carlington, realizing that it would be useless now to deny his extraordinary elopement, greeted his betrothed with biting civility. 'Good morning, Fanny,' he said. 'An unexpected pleasure!'

Miss Wyse was a plump little lady, just nineteen years old, with huge, soulful brown eyes, and a riot of dark curls. When she saw Carlington she let fall a very pretty muff of taffeta, and clasped her hands to her bosom. 'You!' she gasped, with a strong suggestion of loathing in her voice. 'Carlington!'

The Marquis grasped her wrist in a somewhat cavalier fashion, and said angrily: 'Let me have no vapours, if you please! Come into the parlour!'

Miss Wyse uttered a throbbing moan. 'How *could* you, Granville? Oh, I wish I were dead!'

The Marquis fairly dragged her into the parlour, and shut the door upon the landlord's scarcely-veiled curiosity. 'You do not waste much time, Fanny,' he said. 'Is this a sample of what I am to expect in the future? The very day our engagement is announced!'

'Do not speak to me!' shuddered Miss Wyse, who seemed to have a leaning towards the dramatic. 'I am so mortified, so –'

'I know, I know!' he interrupted. 'But you would have done better to have stayed at home.'

Miss Wyse, who had tottered to the nearest chair, sprang up again at this, and said: 'No! Never! Do you hear me, Carlington? Never!'

'I hear you,' he replied. 'So, I imagine, can everyone else in the place. There is a great deal I must say to you, but this is not the moment. My whole object now is to avert a scandal. Explanations – oh yes, they will be hard enough to make! – can come later.'

'I don't care a fig for scandal!' declared Miss Wyse stormily. 'People may say what they please: it is nothing to me! But that I should find you here – that you should have – Oh, it is cruel of you, Carlington!'

'I'm sorry, Fanny,' he said. 'You'll find the truth hard to believe, but I promise you you shall hear the truth from me. I beg of you, be calm! I will myself escort you back to town –'

'Do not touch me!' said Miss Wyse, retreating. 'You shan't take me back! I won't go with you!'

'Don't be such a little fool!' said the Marquis, exasperated. 'I warn you, this is no moment to play-act to me! I shall take you home, and there shall be no scandal, but help you to create a scene I will not!'

Miss Wyse burst into tears. 'I dare say you're very angry with me,' she sobbed, 'and I know I have behaved badly, but indeed, indeed I couldn't help it! I meant to be sensible – really, I did Carlington! – but I couldn't bear it! Oh, you don't understand! You've no s-sensibility at all!'

Rather pale, he answered: 'Don't distress yourself, Fanny. Upon my soul, there is no need! This escapade means nothing: I will engage to give you no cause for complaint when we are married.'

'I can't!' said Miss Wyse desperately. 'You shan't escort me home!'

He regarded her with a kind of weary patience. 'Then perhaps you will tell me what you do mean to do?' he said.

Miss Wyse lowered her handkerchief and looked boldly across at him. 'I'm going to Gretna Green!' she announced. 'And nothing you can say will stop me!'

'Have you taken leave of your senses?' he demanded. 'There's no question of going to Gretna! And if there were what in the name of heaven could possess you to go there?'

'I'm going to be married there!' said Miss Wyse in a rapt voice.

'Oh no, you are not!' replied the Marquis forcibly. 'Though it is just like you to do your best to turn everything to dramatic account! If you go to Gretna, you'll go alone!'

Miss Wyse gave a shriek at this. 'Good God, what do you mean to do?' she cried, running forward, and clasping her hands about his arm. 'Granville, I implore you, have mercy!'

The Marquis disengaged himself, looking down at her in the liveliest astonishment. Even supposing her to be on the verge of a fit of strong hysterics her behaviour seemed to him inexplicable. He was just about to inquire the reason for her last outburst when the door into the coffee-room was thrust open, and a young man in a bottle-green coat strode into the parlour, and checked on the threshold, staring in a challenging way at Carlington.

His bearing, though not his dress, proclaimed the soldier. He was about five-and-twenty years old, with a fresh, pleasant countenance, and a curly crop of brown hair brushed into the Brutus style made fashionable by Mr Brummell.

Carlington, turning his head to observe the newcomer, said somewhat irascibly: 'This, my good sir, is a private room!'

Miss Wyse released Carlington's arm, and sped towards the intruder, upon whose manly bosom she seemed more than half inclined to swoon. 'Henry!' she cried. 'This is Carlington himself!'

Henry said in a grave, rather conscious voice: 'I apprehended that it could be none other. I beg of you, however, not to be alarmed. My lord, I must request the favour of a few words with you alone.'

'Oh no, he will kill you!' quavered Miss Wyse, grasping the lapels of his coat.

The Marquis put a hand to his brow. 'Who the devil are you?' he demanded.

'I do not expect my name to be known to your lordship, but it is Dobell – Henry Dobell, Captain in the –th Foot, and at present on furlough from the Peninsula. I am aware that my action must appear to you desperate; of the impropriety of it I am, alas, miserably aware. Yet, my lord, I believe that when it is explained any man of sensibility must inevitably –'

The Marquis checked this flow of eloquence with an upflung hand. 'Captain Dobell, have you ever been badly foxed?' he said sternly.

'Foxed, sir?' repeated the Captain, quite taken aback.

'Yes, foxed!' snapped the Marquis.

The Captain gave a cough, and replied: 'Well, sir, well – ! I must suppose that every man at some time or another –'

'*Have* you?' interrupted the Marquis.

'Yes, sir, I have!'

'Then you must know what it is to have a head like mine this morning, and I beg you'll spare me any more long-winded speeches, and tell me in plain words what you're doing here!' said Carlington.

Miss Wyse, finding herself out of the picture, thought it proper at this moment to interject: 'I love him!'

'You need not hang upon his neck if you do,' replied the Marquis unsympathetically. 'Is he a relative of yours whom you have dragged into this affair?'

'Relative! No!' said Miss Wyse, affronted. 'He is the man I love!'

'The man you –?' The Marquis stopped short. 'Good God, is this an elopement?' he demanded.

'But – but you know it is!' stammered Miss Wyse.

The Marquis, who had almost reeled under the shock, recovered himself, and came towards them. 'No, no, I'd not the least idea of it!' he said. 'I thought – well, it's no matter what I thought. You must allow me to offer you my most sincere felicitations! Are you on your way to Gretna Green? Let me advise you to lose no time! In fact, I think you should set forward again at once. You may be pursued, you know.'

'But did *you* not come in pursuit of us, sir?' asked the astonished Captain.

'No, no, nothing of the sort!' replied the Marquis, grasping his hand, and wringing it fervently. 'You have nothing in the world to fear from me, my dear fellow. I wish you every imaginable happiness!'

'Every imaginable happiness?' cried Miss Wyse indignantly. 'Have you forgot that I am engaged to you, Carlington?'

'You will be much happier with Henry,' the Marquis assured her.

'The advertisement will be in today's *Gazette*!'

'Don't let that weigh with you! Is a mere advertisement to stand in the path of true love?' said the Marquis. 'I'll repudiate it immediately. Leave everything to me!'

'Don't you *want* to marry me?' gasped Miss Wyse.

'Not in the – Not when your heart is given to another!' said his lordship, with aplomb.

'But Mama said – and your Mama too – and everybody – that I must accept you because you were desperately in love with me, and it had been understood for so many years! Only when I had done it I knew all at once I couldn't bear it, and I sent for Henry, and –'

'Very right and proper,' approved his lordship. 'I could wish, of course, that you had sent for Henry before I wrote the advertisement for the *Gazette*, but never mind that now. The thing is for you to waste no time upon this journey.'

The Captain, who had been gazing upon his lordship in a bemused way, said in a much-moved voice: 'Sir, your generosity does you honour! An explanation of conduct which you must deem treacherous indeed is due to you.'

'No, no, pray don't explain anything to me!' begged the Marquis. 'My head is none too clear, you know. Let me take you out to your chaise!'

The Captain, finding himself propelled towards the door, hung back, and said: 'We stopped here to partake of breakfast, sir!'

'Not to be thought of!' said Carlington firmly. 'At any moment you may be overtaken, and Fanny wrested from your arms. You must make all possible speed to Gretna.'

The mere thought of being wrested from the Captain's arms caused Miss Wyse to add her entreaties to his lordship's. Captain Dobell, still faintly protesting, was swept out of the inn, informed that this was no time to be thinking of food and drink, and pushed up into his chaise. He made a second attempt to explain his elopement to Carlington, but at a sign from the Marquis the post-boys whipped up their horses, and the chaise bowled off down the street, with the Captain hanging out of the window and shouting a final message to the Marquis, the only words of which to reach him were 'everlasting gratitude' and 'eternally obliged'.

The Marquis turned back into the inn, and strode across the coffee-room to the parlour. Miss Morland had emerged from the cupboard, and was standing by the table, trying hard not to laugh. The Marquis said: 'Did you hear, Helen?'

She nodded. 'Yes. I couldn't help hearing,' she answered, a slight quaver in her otherwise solemn voice.

'We must go back to London at once,' said the Marquis.

'Yes,' agreed Miss Morland.

'For one thing,' said the Marquis, 'I want a change of clothes and for another this Gretna scheme was a piece of nonsense. I am not going to be married in company with that pair. We must have a special licence.'

'But we are not going to be married,' said Miss Morland. 'It was all a jest. I was mad – I never meant to come with you!'

'You had to come with me,' retorted the Marquis. 'I won you and you're mine.'

Miss Morland was trembling a little. 'But –'

'I have been in love with you for months, and you know it!' said the Marquis.

'Oh!' said Miss Morland on the oddest little sob. 'I did think sometimes that you were not – not indifferent to me, but indeed, indeed this is impossible!'

'Is it?' said the Marquis grimly. 'We'll see!'

It seemed to Miss Morland that he swooped on her. Certainly she had no time to escape. She was nipped into a crushing embrace, and kissed so hard and so often that she had no breath left to expostulate. The Marquis did at last stop kissing her, but he showed not the least inclination to let her go, but looked down into her eyes, and said in an awe-inspiring voice: 'Well? Are you going to marry me?'

Miss Morland, quite cowed by such treatment, meekly nodded her head.

Snowdrift

A THIN COVERING OF SNOW ALREADY LAY ON THE GROUND
when the Bath and Bristol Light Post Coach set out from
Holborn at two o'clock in the afternoon of a bleak December
day. Only two hardy gentlemen ventured to ride on the roof;
and the inside passengers consisted only of a pessimistic man in
a muffler, a stout lady with several bandboxes, a thickset young
man with small eyes, and a jowl, a scarlet-coated young lady
and a raw-boned countrywoman, who appeared to be her maid.

The scarlet-coated lady and the young man sat opposite each
other, and occasionally exchanged glances of acute dislike. Upon
their initial encounter in the yard of the White Horse Inn, the
gentleman had uttered: '*You* going to Bath? Much good may
it do you!' and the lady had retorted: '*You* travelling upon the
stage, Joseph? I had thought you would have gone post!'

'I am not one to waste my substance,' had pronounced the
gentleman heavily.

Since then they had indulged in no conversation.

The coach was making bad time. At Maidenhead Thicket
the snowflakes were swirling dizzily, and the temperature had
dropped to an uncomfortably low degree. The young man
wrapped himself in a rug; the young lady hummed a defiant
tune: she had not provided herself with a rug.

Slower and slower went the coach. At Reading the fat woman got down, and her place was taken by a farmer, who said that he disremembered when there had been such another hard winter, and prophesied that the roads would be six foot under snow by Christmas. The pessimist said that he had known at the outset that they would never reach their destination.

The coach laboured on, but past Theale actually picked up its pace a little, and for perhaps ten minutes encouraged the passengers to suppose that the weather was clearing. Then the snow began to fall more thickly still, the coachman lost his bearings, and the whole equipage lurched off the road into a deep drift.

It was thrown on to its side with some violence. The two outside passengers were hurled over the hedge into a field, and those inside landed in a heap on the near-side door.

The thickset young man was first to extricate himself, and to force open the off-side door. He scrambled through it, rudely thrusting the pessimist out of the way, floundered into deep snow, and fell upon his face, a circumstance which afforded the pessimist a sour pleasure.

The farmer and the young lady were too much occupied with the abigail, who had fallen awkwardly, to notice this interlude. The abigail said in a faint voice: 'I've broke my leg, Miss Sophy.'

'Oh, Sarah, do not say so!' besought her mistress.

'Well, it's just what she has done,' said the farmer frankly. 'We'll have to get her out of this, missie.' He hauled himself up to look out through the open door, and shouted: 'Hi, you! Come and lend a hand with the poor wench here! Lively, now!'

Thus adjured, the thickset young man came back to the coach, asking rather ungraciously what was wanted. He seemed disinclined to lend his aid, and the scarlet-coated young lady, who had been trying unavailingly to move her henchwoman into an easier position, raised a flushed face in which two large gray eyes sparkled with wrath, and uttered: 'You are the most odious wretch alive, Joseph! Help to lift Sarah out this instant, or I shall tell my grandfather how disobliging you have been!'

'You may tell him what you choose – *if* you reach Bath, which you are not now very likely to do, my dear cousin!' retorted Joseph.

'You hold your gab, and do what I tell you!' interposed the farmer. 'Jump out first, missie: you'll only be in my way here!'

Miss Trent, pausing only to pick up her cousin's abandoned rug, allowed herself to be hoisted through the door. Joseph received her from the farmer, and lost no time in setting her down. Her feet sank above the ankles in the snow, but the pessimistic man helped her to reach the road. By the time she had spread the rug out on the snow Sarah had been extricated from the coach, and the coachman was helping the guard to unharness one of the leaders.

Sarah was laid on the rug; Miss Trent, her bonnet fast whitening under the gathering flakes, knelt beside her; and the coachman informed the assembled company that there was no need for anyone to worry, since the guard would ride on at once to Woolhampton, and get some kind of a vehicle to fetch them all in.

This speech greatly incensed the pessimistic man, who demanded to be told when the next coach to Bath was due. The coachman said: 'Lor' bless you, sir, we'll be snowbound a week, I dessay! Nothing won't get beyond Reading, not if this weather holds!'

There was a general outcry at this; Miss Trent exclaimed: 'Snowbound a week! But I *must* reach Bath tomorrow!'

'Can one hire a chaise in Woolhampton?' asked Joseph suddenly.

'Well, you *might* be able to,' acknowledged the coachman.

'I'll ride in with the guard!' Joseph decided.

Miss Trent started. Stretching up a hand, she grasped a fold of his coat, saying sharply: 'Joseph, if you mean to go on by chaise you'll take me with you?'

'No, by God!' he retorted. '*I* didn't ask you to come to Bath, and *I* shan't help you to get there! You may hire a chaise for yourself!'

'You know I haven't enough money!' she said, in a low, trembling voice.

'Well, it's no concern of mine,' he said sulkily. 'A pretty fool I should be to take you along with me! Besides, you can't go without your woman.'

Miss Trent's eyes were bright with tears, but she would not let them fall. She said passionately: 'I'll get to Bath if I have to *trudge* there, Joseph – and then we shall see!'

He responded to this merely with a jeering laugh, and moved away to confer with the guard. Miss Trent made no further attempt to detain him, and in a very few minutes he had ridden off with the guard in the direction of Woolhampton.

With the departure of the guard a new and more fearful mood descended upon the coachman. He became obsessed by the idea that highwaymen would descend upon the wrecked coach, grasped his blunderbuss nervously, started at shadows, and ended by firing the weapon at the mere sound of muffled hoofbeats.

The sound of horses plunging and snorting was almost immediately followed by the appearance round the bend in the road of a curricle and pair, which drew up alongside the coach. A wrathful voice demanded: 'What in hell's name do you mean by firing at me you fat-witted, cow-handed ensign-bearer?'

The coachman, reassured by this form of address, lowered his weapon, and said that he was sure he begged pardon. The gentleman in the curricle, having by this time taken in the group by the wayside, briefly commanded the groom beside him to go to the horses' heads, and himself jumped down from the curricle, and approached Miss Trent, still kneeling beside her stricken attendant. 'Can I be of assistance, ma'am?' he asked. 'How is she hurt?'

'I very much fear that she has broken her leg,' Miss Trent replied worriedly. 'She is my maid, and I am a wretch to have brought her!'

The gentleman, whose momentary outburst of wrath had swiftly given place to an air of languor which seemed habitual, said calmly: 'Then I had better take you both up, and convey you to the nearest town.'

Miss Trent said impulsively: 'Would you do that, sir? I should be so very grateful! Not only on poor Sarah's account, but on my own! I *must* reach the next town quickly!'

'In that case,' responded the gentleman, rather amused, 'let us waste not a moment. I'll drive you into Newbury.'

The farmer and the pessimistic man, both applauding this scheme, at once volunteered to extricate Miss Trent's baggage from the boot, and to strap it on to the back of the curricle; Sarah was soon lifted up into the carriage, and made as comfortable as possible; and the groom, resigning himself to a most uneasy drive, perched on the baggage behind.

Miss Trent, squeezed between Sarah and her very tall and broad-shouldered rescuer, bade farewell to her old travelling companions, and looked buoyantly towards the future.

This seemed, at the moment, to consist only of snowflakes. The light, moreover, was beginning to fail, so that she would not have been surprised had the curricle, like the coach, plunged off the road into a drift. But its driver seemed to be very sure of his ability to keep the track, and drove his pair along at a steady pace, his eyes, between narrowed lids, fixed on the road ahead.

'How well you drive!' remarked Miss Trent, with a sort of impulsive candour, as engaging as it was naïve.

A slight smile touched his lips. 'Thank you!'

'I do trust we shall reach Newbury,' confided Miss Trent.

'For one thing, I must have poor Sarah attended to, and for another, I *must* get to Bath!'

'I collect that it is of importance to you to reach Bath immediately?'

'Of vital importance!' asserted Miss Trent.

'You might be able to hire a chaise,' he suggested. 'I fear there will be no stage-coaches running for some days.'

'That,' said Miss Trent bitterly, 'is what my cousin means to do! *He* can afford it, and he knows very well I cannot, and he won't take me along with him. He is an odious man!'

'He sounds quite abominable,' agreed the gentleman gravely. 'Is he one of the unfortunates we were obliged to leave by the wayside?'

'Oh, no! He rode off with the guard to Woolhampton. Trying to steal a march on me, of course!' She added, on an explanatory note: 'He has eyes like a pig's, and his name is Joseph.'

'How shocking! One scarcely knows whether to feel pity or disgust.'

Miss Trent knew no such uncertainty. 'He is a hateful wretch!' she declared.

'In that case it is unthinkable that he should be permitted to steal a march on you. May I know your name? Mine is Arden.'

'Yes, of course! I should have told you before,' she said. 'I am Sophia Trent. Do you live near here? I have come all the way from Norfolk!'

Never before had Sir Julian Arden announced his identity with so little effect! Indeed, it was seldom that he was put to the trouble of announcing it at all. Not only was he the acknowledged leader of Fashion, a crack shot, and a nonpareil amongst whips: he was quite the most eligible bachelor in Society as well. He had been toadied all his life; every eccentricity was forgiven him; every door flew open at his approach. Mothers of likely daughters had laid siege to him for the past ten years; while

the efforts of damsels of marriageable age to engage his interest
were as ingenious as they were unavailing. He was so bored that
nothing kept his interest alive for more than a fleeting moment.
Very little, indeed, had the power to rouse his interest at all. But
Miss Trent had achieved this feat quite unconsciously. His name
meant nothing to her.

He permitted himself one swift glance down at her before
resuming his steady scrutiny of the road ahead. There was not
a shadow of guile in the big eyes, which met his in a friendly
smile. Miss Trent was merely awaiting an answer. He said: 'No,
I live for the most part in London.'

'But you did not come from London today, in this weather!'

'You see,' he said apologetically, 'someone laid me odds I
would not venture on it.'

'And you set out, in an open carriage, for such a reason as
that! I beg your pardon, but it seems quite nonsensical!'

He appeared to be much struck by this view of the matter.
'Do you know, ma'am, I believe you are right?'

'I *think*,' said Miss Trent severely, 'that you are quizzing me.
Is your destination Newbury?'

'My present destination, yes. We shall forget my original one.
I daresay I should have been very much bored there.'

'But your friends will wonder what has become of you!'

'It need not concern us, however.'

This indifferent answer made her blink, but she forbore
to press the matter, and chatted away on a number of unexceptionable topics. She held Sarah in one arm, and appeared
to be more concerned for the maid's comfort than her own,
assuring Sir Julian that she thought the whole episode a
famous adventure.

'You see, my home is quite in the country,' she explained,
'and nothing exciting ever seems to happen, except when
Bertram broke his leg, and Ned was thrown over the donkey's

head into the horse-pond. Thieves did once steal three of my stepfather's best hens, but we knew nothing about it until the next day, so it was not precisely exciting.'

Entranced by this artless confidence, Sir Julian at once enquired into the identities of Bertram and Ned. He discovered that they were two of Miss Trent's three half-brothers, and that her stepfather was the incumbent of a parish in Norfolk. She had two young half-sisters as well, and very little prompting was needed to induce her to expatiate on their many engaging qualities. In this way the journey to Newbury was largely beguiled, and when Sir Julian turned his horses in under the archway of the great Pelican Inn, a mile short of the town, Miss Trent exclaimed that she had not thought it possible they could have arrived so soon.

A number of ostlers and waiters came hurrying to serve the newcomer, and in a very short while Sarah had been carried up to a bedchamber, a groom sent off to summon the nearest surgeon to her aid, and a private parlour bespoken for Miss Trent.

She came down to it presently, and found her protector warming himself before a leaping fire. He had shed his hat, and his many-caped greatcoat, and Miss Trent, who had already formed a very good opinion of his person, now perceived that he was decidedly handsome. He was dressed in a coat of blue superfine, which more experienced eyes than Miss Trent's would have recognized as coming from the hands of a master; his buckskins were of impeccable cut; and his cravat was tied in the intricate style that had long baffled all imitators.

Sir Julian was also pleased with what he saw. Now that she had removed her bonnet, and he beheld her in the full candlelight, he perceived that Miss Trent's hair grew in profuse ringlets, and that her eyes were even bigger than he had supposed them to be. He liked the frank way they lifted to his, and found it refreshing, to say the least of it, to encounter a lady who was neither arch nor simpering, and who had obviously not the smallest notion of enslaving him.

She let him lead her to a chair by the fire, and said: 'I have made up my mind to it that the most important thing is for me to reach Bath, sir. I did think at first that I ought not to spend the money I have put by for my fare back to Norwich, but I now feel this would be foolish. So I shall hire a chaise to take me on. Do you think I shall be able to go tonight? I know the coaches travel by night, and the mails too.'

'Nothing travels at night in such weather as this, ma'am. It has been snowing here, I discover, for three days. However, local opinion seems to be that a change is coming, so we must hope that the snow may have ceased to fall by tomorrow.'

'Oh!' said Miss Trent, dashed. She hesitated, and then asked shyly: 'How much will it cost me, do you think, sir, to stay here tonight?'

'As to that,' he replied, 'I have informed the landlord that you are a young relative of mine, travelling in my charge. I think he will expect me to pay your shot, don't you?'

'No!' said Miss Trent, with decision.

'I meant, I need hardly say, a loan!' explained Sir Julian.

Miss Trent, her mind relieved, thanked him, and adjured him to keep a strict account of any sums he might incur on her behalf. He promised most gravely to do so, and an understanding being thus reached Miss Trent was able to relax, and to sip the Madeira he had given her. 'Then all that remains to be done,' she said, 'is to hire a chaise in the morning, for the landlady says she will take care of Sarah for me, so I may be easy on that head.'

'You may be easy on both heads,' Sir Julian said. 'I propose to escort you to Bath tomorrow myself, whatever the weather.'

Miss Trent was too unsophisticated to conceal her pleasure at this prospect. 'Will you indeed?' she cried, warm gratitude in her eyes. 'I do think you are the kindest person I have ever met, sir! But ought you not rather to join your friends?'

'Certainly not,' he replied. 'A very dull set of people! My whole desire is to revisit Bath.'

At this moment the waiter came in to announce the arrival of a surgeon, and Miss Trent went off to lead this practitioner up to the sufferer. When she returned to the parlour, the table had been laid, and dinner awaited her. She made an excellent repast. She said that Sarah must not travel for a few days, but that she was much easier now the limb had been set. 'So there is nothing for it but to leave her here, poor thing!' she said. 'She says she will do very well, but I feel the veriest *brute*! But if my cousin were to get to Bath before me there is no saying what might happen! He would serve me a back-handed turn if he could!'

'But what has engendered this violent antipathy between you, ma'am?' asked Sir Julian, a good deal amused.

'We both want the same thing,' said Miss Trent darkly, 'and he is afraid that I shall get it! But I have detested him all my life.'

She did not stay in the parlour for long after the covers had been removed, but retired early to bed, leaving her protector still ignorant of what her business in Bath could be.

Local prophecy turned out to be exact. It stopped snowing during the night, and although the landscape was thickly shrouded next morning, the sky had lost its leaden hue, and the sun showed some faint signs of breaking through the clouds. Miss Trent came down to breakfast in a mood of high hope. 'I believe it will turn out to be a beautiful day, sir!' she announced. 'And if you will really be so obliging as to escort me to Bath, we may go in your curricle!'

'It would be far too cold for you,' he said.

'No, indeed, I should like it of all things,' she insisted. 'And only think what a deal of expense you may save!'

Sir Julian, who had never in his life considered such a sordid matter, agreed to it meekly, and went out into the yard after breakfast to give orders to his groom.

It was while he was engaged in the stables that Mr Joseph Selsey arrived at the Pelican, having plodded all the way on foot from Woolhampton, carrying his valise. It was perhaps not surprising that he should be in an evil humour, but the head groom made no allowance for this circumstance. Peremptory persons looking suspiciously like provincial merchants would get no extraordinary attention from the Pelican's supercilious servants. No post-chaise, stated the groom, would leave the inn that day. It was not until Mr Selsey had dragged the landlord into the dispute that he was able to hire, not a chaise, but a saddle-horse.

He was obliged to be satisfied, and to trust that he might be able to exchange the horse for a chaise in Hungerford. He then called for hot coffee to be brought him whilst the horse was being saddled, and in crossing the hall of the inn came upon Miss Trent, issuing from the parlour.

He stopped short, staring at her. 'So this is where I find you?' he ejaculated. 'Fine doings, miss! Very pretty behaviour, upon my word!'

'Why, what is wrong?' she demanded.

'Of course *you* would not know!' he said, with one of his jeering laughs. 'But it is all of a piece! By anything I ever heard, your mother was just such another, always ready to run off with any man who offered!'

'How *dare* you?' cried Miss Trent, her eyes blazing.

Sir Julian, who had come in from the yard in time to overhear this passage of arms, here interposed, saying in his languid way: 'Ah, so this is your cousin Joseph, is it? Dear me, yes! Come with me, sir!'

'Why should I?' demanded Mr Selsey, taken aback.

'That you shall see,' said Sir Julian, leading the way out into the yard.

Mr Selsey followed him in some bewilderment, and Miss Trent, running back into the parlour to peep above the blind, had the felicity of seeing her objectionable relative dropped sprawling in the snow by a blow from Sir Julian's famous right.

Mr Selsey picked himself up and bored in furiously. Sir Julian side-stepped neatly and dropped him again. This time Mr Selsey remained on the ground, nursing his jaw.

'And let that be a lesson to you not, in future, to insult a lady!' said Sir Julian calmly.

Mr Selsey, uneasily measuring the size and style of his opponent, said sulkily: 'I didn't mean – that is, I didn't know –'

'You know now,' said Sir Julian, and turned, and went back into the inn.

He was met by Miss Trent, her face aglow with admiration. '*Thank you!*' she said. 'I have been wanting to do that all my life!'

'What, did you see it, then?' he asked, startled.

'Yes, through the window. I clapped my hands! I wonder you did not hear me!'

He flung back his head and laughed. 'You incorrigible child, you should be in a swoon, or indulging in a fit of the vapours!'

'Pooh, as though I had not seen Bertram and Ned at fisticuffs a score of times! When do we set forward?'

'In about half an hour, if you can be ready then.'

'Should we not go at once? I am sure Joseph will be off now without waiting for his coffee!'

'Very likely, but you have no need to be uneasy: we shall overtake him soon enough.'

They overtook him even sooner than Sir Julian had expected. Only fifteen miles from Newbury, where the road passed between the great trees of Savernake Forest, a solitary figure came into view, leading a very lame nag.

'It's Joseph!' exclaimed Miss Trent. '*Poor* Joseph!' she added piously.

'Humbug!' retorted Sir Julian, a note in his voice no other lady had as yet been privileged to hear.

She laughed. Mr Selsey, upon hearing the muffled beat of horses' hooves, wheeled about, and, although he must have perceived who was driving the curricle, placed himself in its way, and waved his arms. Sir Julian drew up, and sat looking down at him with a sardonic lift to his brows.

'Sir,' said Mr Selsey in a voice of deep chagrin, 'I find myself forced to request you to take me up as far as to the next town!'

'But you cannot leave the poor horse!' said Miss Trent. 'Besides, it belongs to the Pelican!'

'No, it does not!' said her cousin angrily. 'It belongs to a rascally thief! He took my horse and my purse, and left me with this jade!'

'A highwayman? Oh, what an adventure!' cried Miss Trent.

Mr Selsey ground his teeth.

'You have only three or four miles to walk before you reach Marlborough,' said Sir Julian helpfully. 'Stand away from my horses' heads!'

'But I have no money!' shouted Mr Selsey.

Sir Julian's pair began to move forward. Miss Trent said quickly: 'No, no, we can't leave him in such a case! It would be too shabby!'

Sir Julian glanced curiously down at her earnest little face. 'Do you wish him to reach Bath?'

'Yes!' said Miss Trent resolutely.

'Very well. I will leave word with the landlord of the Castle Inn, sir, and he will provide you with a conveyance,' said Sir Julian, and drove on.

Mr Selsey, by no means content, bawled after the curricle: 'And you stole my rug, you hussy!'

'Oh, dear!' said Miss Trent, dismayed. 'It is quite true, I did! We ought to have taken him up, perhaps!'

'Nonsense! A walk will do him good.'

'Yes, but if his purse has been taken he won't be able to hire a chaise, even if you do bespeak one!' objected Miss Trent.

'Have no fear! I will arrange the whole, since you wish it.'

'I think you have the most extravagant notions!' said Miss Trent severely. 'And, pray, how am I ever to repay you?'

'Very easily.'

'No, how?'

'By satisfying my curiosity and telling me why we are racing Joseph to Bath!'

'Did I not do so?' she cried, astonished. 'I quite thought I had explained it to you! I have the greatest hope that I may win a fortune!'

'Then in that case you will be able to pay your debts, and you have nothing to worry about,' said Sir Julian, only the merest quiver in his voice betraying him.

'Yes, but I shan't win it quite immediately,' she said. 'Not until my grandfather dies, and although he seems to think that will be soon, there is no telling, after all!'

'Very true. Are we going to call upon your grandfather?'

'Yes, and I fear he will prove to be very disagreeable.'

'Are *all* your relatives disagreeable persons, Miss Trent?' he enquired.

'Certainly not! Mama, and my stepfather, and the children are the dearest creatures!' she replied. 'In fact, it is for them that I am going to Bath. If only my grandfather likes me better than Joseph, the boys may go to Eton, and Clara have lessons upon the pianoforte, and Mama another servant, and Papa – But this cannot interest you, sir!'

'On the contrary. And is Joseph also bent on winning this fortune?'

'Yes, and he does not need it in the least! You see, the case is that my grandfather quarrelled with both his daughters – my mama, and Joseph's mama – because they married men he did not like. Mama says he was determined they should make splendid matches, and they did not. Mama ran away with my papa to Gretna Green – only fancy! He died when I was a baby, and I believe that he was not a very *steady* person. He was related to Lord Cleveland, and in the 1st Foot, only his family cast him off. So, I think, did the 1st Foot,' she added reflectively. 'Mama says he was very wild.'

'Most of that family are,' interpolated Sir Julian.

'Oh, are they? I have never known them. Papa left poor Mama in sad straits, and if it had not been for my stepfather I don't know what would have become of her. He married her, you see, and they are most happy! But Papa has a very small stipend, and there are five children, besides me, so that when my grandfather suddenly wrote to say that he felt his end to be approaching, and since he must leave his fortune to someone, I might go to spend Christmas with him, and perhaps he would leave it to me, it seemed as though it was my duty to go! And then I found that he must have sent for Joseph too, but I do think that he may like me better than Joseph, don't you, sir?'

'Miss Trent,' said Sir Julian, 'unless your grandfather is mad, you need have no doubts on that head!'

'Yes, but *I* think he is!' said Miss Trent candidly.

'Who is he? What is his name?'

'Kennet, and he lives in Laura Place."

'Good God, not the Miser of Bath?'

'Oh, are you acquainted with him, sir?'

'Only by reputation! Bath used to be full of tales of his oddities. I fear it is you who will not like him!'

'No, but in such a cause one must stifle one's feelings!' said Miss Trent.

He agreed to it with becoming gravity, and for some miles

entered in the fullest manner into all her plans for the advancement of her family.

The journey was a long one, and the weather inclement enough to have daunted most females, but Miss Trent remained cheerful throughout. Sir Julian, who had been sure, twenty-four hours earlier, that he had run through every emotion life could hold for him, realized by the time the outskirts of Bath were reached that he had fallen in love for the first time since his salad days.

It was dark when the curricle drew up before a house in Laura Place, and the street lamps had been lit. 'Tired?' Sir Julian said gently.

'A very little,' owned Miss Trent. 'But you must be quite dead with fatigue, sir!'

'I have never enjoyed a day more.'

Miss Trent said shyly: 'I – I have not either!'

'In that case,' said Sir Julian, 'let us go in and beard your grandfather!'

'You too, sir?' she asked doubtfully.

'Certainly. I must ask his permission to pay my addresses to you.'

'To – to – ? Oh!' said Miss Trent in a faint voice.

'Yes, may I do so?'

Miss Trent swallowed. 'I have the most lowering feeling that I ought to say it is too sudden, or – or something of that nature,' she confided.

'Say what is in your heart! Would it displease you to receive my addresses?'

'Well, no, it – it wouldn't *displease* me – precisely!' confessed Miss Trent, blushing in the darkness.

'Then let us instantly seek out your grandfather!' he said gaily.

They were admitted into the house by an aged retainer who reluctantly showed them into a bleak parlour on the ground floor. He left them with a single candle. Miss Trent said: 'It is not very – very welcoming, do you think?'

'Most quelling!' said Sir Julian.

In a few minutes the door opened again to admit a buxom lady of uncertain years and improbable golden ringlets. She said without preamble: 'Are you Mr Kennet's Sophia? He's that forgetful he must have forgotten to write! However, if you want to see him you may! Step upstairs with me, dearie! Don't tell me this is Joseph you have brought with you!'

'Who – who are you?' gasped Miss Trent, utterly taken aback.

The lady bridled. 'The name's Flint,' she said. 'But I'm changing it. I *was* your grandpa's housekeeper.'

'Oh!' said Miss Trent. 'Then will you have the goodness to take me to my grandfather, if you please?'

Mrs Flint sniffed, but turned to lead the way up one pair of stairs. She opened a door giving on to a large parlour, and said: 'Here's your granddaughter, Mr K.!'

From a winged arm-chair by the fire a desiccated old gentleman peered at Miss Trent. 'Well, it's no use her coming here, because I've altered my mind,' he said. 'Maria's girl, hey? Damme if you don't look like her!'

Mrs Flint, who had taken up a position beside his chair, said with a simper: 'Me and Mr K. is going to be married.'

'It'll be cheaper,' explained Mr Kennet simply.

Miss Trent sank nervelessly into the nearest chair. Mr Kennet was meanwhile subjecting Sir Julian to a severe scrutiny. 'A fine buck you've turned out to be!' he pronounced. 'What's your name? Joseph?'

'No,' said Sir Julian. 'My name is Julian Arden.'

Both Mr Kennet and his prospective bride stared very hard at him. 'Mr K., if it isn't Beau Arden himself!' palpitated the lady.

'Are you the son of Percy Arden, who was up at Oxford with me?' demanded Mr Kennet. 'Sir Julian Arden?'

'I am,' said Sir Julian.

'What do you want?' asked the old gentleman suspiciously.

'To marry your granddaughter,' replied Sir Julian coolly.

This intelligence produced an instant change in Mr Kennet's attitude. He rubbed his dry hands together and ejaculated: 'That's good! That's the girl! Come and give me a kiss, Sophy! I'm proud of you, and I'm sorry I said you was like your mother! Damme if I don't do something handsome by you!'

Miss Trent, submitting unwilling to his embrace, was feeling too dazed by the shocks of the past few minutes to speak, but at this her eyes lit with a faint hope.

'I will!' said Mr Kennet, with the air of one reaching a painful decision. 'You shall have your grandmother's pearls!'

'When we're dead and gone, Mr K.,' interpolated the future Mrs Kennet firmly.

'Yes,' agreed Mr Kennet, perceiving the wisdom of this. 'And I'll give her my poor Charlotte's garnet brooch for a bride gift, what's more! I can't lay my hand on it at the moment, but I'll send it. Where are you putting up, my dear?'

Sir Julian, perceiving that Miss Trent was quite stunned, took her hand in a comforting hold, and said: 'She will be staying at the Christopher, sir. And now I think we must take our leave of you.'

Mr Kennet brightened still more at finding that he was not expected to entertain his grandchild and her betrothed to dinner, and said that if she liked she might come to visit him again before she left Bath. 'But I won't have your cousin Joseph coming to batten on me!' he added, suddenly querulous.

'Which leads one to wonder,' remarked Sir Julian, when he had extricated Miss Trent from the house, 'what is to become of Joseph!'

'What is to become of *me*?' said Miss Trent, wringing her hands.

'You are going to marry me.'

'Yes – I mean – But poor Mama! Bertram! Dear Ned! I have no *right* to be so happy when I have failed so miserably!'

He lifted her up into the curricle. 'My little love, you have not so far given my circumstances a thought, but I must inform you that I am accounted to be extremely wealthy. Bertram, and Ned, and Tom shall go to Eton, and Oxford, and anywhere else you may choose; and Clara shall have her lessons on the pianoforte; and your mama shall have a dozen maids; and –'

'Good God, you cannot be as rich as that!' cried Miss Trent, quite frightened.

'Much richer!' he averred, mounting on to the box beside her.

'But you must not marry *me*!' she said, in great distress. 'There must be dozens of *eligible* females whom you should rather marry!'

'I am not the Grand Turk!' he protested.

'No, no, but you know I have no expectations!'

'I know nothing of the sort,' he said, possessing himself of her hand, and kissing it. 'You are to inherit your grandmother's pearls! But if I were you,' he added, gathering up the reins, 'I would not build too much upon that garnet brooch, my love!'

Full Moon

L ORD STAVELY PREPARED TO DESCEND FROM HIS CHAISE.
'We will stop here,' he announced.

It was certainly a charming inn. It stood at the end of the
broad village street, with two great elms behind it and roses
rambling over its old red brick frontage. It was not, of course,
a posting house, which did not incline the two postilions in its
favour. One of them said: 'If we was to drive on for another
mile or two, we'd likely find a decent house for your honour
to bait at.'

'My dear good fellow,' replied his lordship, 'you have no
more notion of where we are than I have. Here we will stop. I
like the place.'

The village seemed asleep in the moonlight, not a soul stirring. But the sound of carriage wheels brought the landlord out
of the inn, all anxiety to oblige. Lord Stavely, alighting from
the chaise, said: 'Arcadia, I presume. Tell me, what is the time?'

The landlord, slightly taken aback, said that it lacked but ten
minutes to the hour.

'But what hour?' asked his lordship.

'Why, nine o'clock, sir!'

'How shocking! Am I anywhere in the neighbourhood of
Melbury Place?'

'Melbury Place?' repeated the landlord. 'Yes, that you are, sir; it lies only a matter of ten miles from here, though the road's tricky, as you might say.'

'After the experiences of today, I should probably use a more forceful epithet. I imagine it will take me nearly an hour to reach the place. Obviously it behoves me to dine here. Or am I too late for dinner?'

The landlord was not one to turn away distinguished custom from his door. This gentleman, with his high crowned beaver hat, his driving coat of many capes, worn negligently open over a neat blue coat, a cut Venetian waistcoat, and the palest of fawn pantaloons, was plainly a member of the Quality. He assured Lord Stavely that, if he would step into the coffee-room, dinner should be served him in a very few minutes. A qualm then attacked him, and he faltered: 'I'm sorry I can't show your honour to a private parlour, but there's only Mr Tom in the coffee-room, after all.'

'Then if Mr Tom does not take exception to me, I shall do very well,' said his lordship. 'I wonder if I should remain here for the night? Shall I endear myself on my host by presenting myself at past eleven o'clock at night?'

'They do keep very early hours up at the Place, by what I hear, sir,' offered the landlord hopefully. 'Was the Squire expecting of you, sir?'

'He was, and I trust still is. Your manner leads me to fear that he will not be pleased by my tardy arrival?'

'Well, sir, begging your pardon, Squire is that pernickety in his ways, and – in a manner of speaking – a testy gentleman – not meaning any disrespect, I'm sure!'

'In fact, I shall *not* endear myself to him by arriving famished on his doorstep at dead of night. Very well. I'll put up here, then.'

The landlord, mentally resolving to have the best sheets

instantly put on the bed in the larger of his two guest chambers, ushered his lordship into the coffee-room.

It had only one occupant, a young gentleman who sat in the window embrasure, with a bottle of brandy on the ledge beside him, and a glass in his hand. The landlord, casting a rather worried glance at the bottle, murmured that Mr Tom would not object to a gentleman's dining in the coffee-room. Mr Tom blinked at Lord Stavely, and inclined his head with dignity. He then resumed his scrutiny of the moon-washed street.

His lordship returned the civility by a slight bow, and a smile hovering about his mouth, but made no attempt to lure Mr Tom into conversation. It was apparent to him that care sat upon the young gentleman's brow. It would have been apparent to someone far less acute than Lord Stavely that Mr Tom was, very properly, drowning his troubles in brandy. He might have been any age between nineteen and twenty-five; he was certainly not older. Leanings towards dandyism were betrayed by the intricate but not entirely successful arrange-ment of his cravat, and by the inordinate height of his shirt collar, whose starched points reached almost to his cheek-bones. But there was little of the dandy in his sturdy figure and fresh-complexioned countenance. He looked like the son of a country gentleman, which, indeed, he was, and as though he would be very much at home in the hunting-field, or with a gun over his shoulder.

In a short time the landlord laid a simple but very tolerable meal before his new guest, and himself waited upon him. Lord Stavely pronounced the fare to be excellent, commended the burgundy, and tactfully declined the only port offered him on the score that he did not wish to encourage a tendency to the gout. He did not look as though he suffered from gout, or any other ailment; in fact, he looked as healthy as any other man of thirty-five; but the landlord did not question his words. He merely swept away the covers and set a bottle of old cognac before him.

For some minutes past Lord Stavely had been aware that the young gentleman in the window was subjecting him to an intent scrutiny. He knew well what was engaging this fixed attention, and when the landlord had withdrawn, he said gently: 'I call it the Nonchalent. It is not very difficult, once you acquire the knack of it.'

'Eh?' said the young gentleman, starting.

'My cravat,' explained Lord Stavely, smiling.

The young gentleman coloured and stammered that he begged pardon.

'Not at all,' said his lordship. 'I'll show you how to tie it, if you like.'

'Will you?' exclaimed the young gentleman eagerly. 'I tie mine in an Osbaldeston, but I don't like it above half.'

Lord Stavely waved one hand invitingly towards a chair at the table. 'Won't you join me?'

'Well – thank you!' The young gentleman got up and crossed the floor circumspectly. He brought his glass and the bottle with him, and set both down on the table. 'My name,' he announced carefully, 'is Hatherleigh.'

'Mine is Stavely,' returned his lordship.

They exchanged bows. Only a purist would have said that Mr Hatherleigh was drunk. He could, by taking only reasonable pains, walk and speak with dignity, and if his potations had had the effect of divorcing his brain a little from the normal, at least it was perfectly clear on all important matters. When Lord Stavely, for instance, touching lightly on the country through which he had driven, said that he should suppose it to be good hunting country, young Hatherleigh was able to expatiate on the subject with enthusiasm and really remarkable coherence. The cloud lifted from his brow, his eyes brightened, and he became quite animated. Then the cloud descended again abruptly, and he fetched a sigh, and said gloomily: 'But that is all at an end! I dare say I may think myself lucky if ever I get a leg across a good hunter again.'

'As bad as that?' said his lordship sympathetically.

Mr Hatherleigh nodded, and poured himself out some more brandy. 'I'm eloping with an heiress,' he announced dejectedly.

If Lord Stavely was startled by this intelligence, he managed to conceal his emotions most creditably. His lip did quiver a little, but he said in the politest way: 'Indeed?'

'Yes,' said Mr Hatherleigh, fortifying himself with a deep drink. 'Gretna Green,' he added.

'Forgive me,' said his lordship, 'but do you feel this to be a wise step to take?'

'No, of course I don't!' said Mr Hatherleigh. 'But what is a fellow to do? I can't draw back now! You must see that!'

'I expect it would be very difficult,' agreed Lord Stavely. 'When one has persuaded an heiress to elope with one —'

'No such thing!' interrupted Mr Hatherleigh. 'I dare say I may have said it would be rare sport to do it, if only to kick up a dust, but I never thought Annabella would think I really meant it! But that is Annabella all over. In fact, I think she's devilish like her father! Let her but once take a notion into her head, and there's no persuading her to listen to reason! Mind, though,' he added, bending a sudden, minatory scowl upon his auditor, 'you are not to be thinking that I wish to back out! I have loved Annabella for years. In fact, I swore a blood-oath to marry her when we were children. But that isn't to say that I want to drive off to the Border with her — and just now, too!'

'The moment is not quite convenient?'

Mr Hatherleigh shook his head. 'My uncle has invited me to Yorkshire for the grouse shooting!' he said bitterly. 'Only think what a splendid time I could have had! I have never tried my hand at grouse, you know, but I am accounted a pretty fair shot.'

'You could not, I suppose, postpone the elopement until after the shooting season?' suggested his lordship.

'No, because if we waited there would be no sense in eloping at all, because very likely Annabella will be tied up to the old fogy her father means her to marry. Besides, the moon's at the full now.'

'I see. And who is this old fogy? Is he *very* old?'

'I don't know, but I should think he must be, wouldn't you, if he's a friend of Sir Walter?'

His lordship paused in the act of raising his glass to his lips. 'Sir Walter?'

'Sir Walter Abingdon. He is Annabella's father.'

'Oh!' said his lordship, sipping his brandy. 'I collect that he does not look with favour on your suit?'

'No, and my father does not either. He says we are too young, and should not suit. So very likely I shall be cut off with a shilling, and be obliged to enter a counting-house, or some such thing, for Sir Walter will certainly cut Annabella off. But of course females never consider anything of that nature! They have not the least common sense, beside thinking that it is perfectly easy to hire a chaise for midnight without making anyone suspicious! And it is *not!*' said Mr Hatherleigh, a strong sense of grievance overcoming him. 'Let alone the expense of it – and that, let me tell you, has pretty well made my pockets to let! I have had to go twenty miles to do it, because a rare flutter I should have set up if I'd bespoke a chaise to go to Scotland at the George, or the Sun! Why, my father would have had wind of it within the hour!

'And then I had to rack my brains to think how best to meet it, because it would never do to have it driving up to my home to pick me up, you know. Luckily old Thetford here is very much attached to our interests, so I told the post-boys in the end to come to this inn at half-past ten tonight. Annabella thinks everyone will be asleep by half-past eleven, or twelve at latest, and she is to meet me in the shrubbery. Shrubbery at midnight!' he repeated scornfully. 'I can tell you, it makes me feel like a great cake! Such flummery!'

He picked up the bottle again as he spoke, and poured some more brandy into his glass. Some of the liquor spilled on to the table. Mr Hatherleigh glared at it, and set the bottle down with precision.

'Do you know,' said Lord Stavely conversationally, 'if I were going to elope at midnight I believe I would not drink too much brandy at ten o'clock?'

Mr Hatherleigh eyed him austerely. 'If you think I'm foxed,' he enunciated, 'you're wrong! I have a very hard head.'

'I'm sure you have,' said his lordship. 'But if Miss Annabella were to detect the fumes on your breath she might not be quite pleased.'

'Well, she shouldn't have insisted on eloping with me!' retorted Mr Hatherleigh.

'She must be very much attached to you?'

'Of course she is. Why, she's known me all her life! All the same, she never would have taken this silly notion into her head if that peppery old fool hadn't asked this fellow to stay, and told her she was to marry him. I must say, I was shocked when Annabella told me of it. I dare say he must be fifty at least, and a dead bore! Besides, she has never clapped eyes on him! I quite saw that as a gentleman I must rescue her, though I never thought *then* that my uncle would invite me to stay with him in Yorkshire!'

'But surely even the most peppery of parents cannot in these days marry his daughter out of hand? Must you really elope?' said Lord Stavely.

'Annabella says so, and of course I am bound in honour to oblige her,' replied Mr Hatherleigh grandly. 'I dare say I shan't dislike being married so very much, once I get used to it.'

'I feel very strongly that you are making a mistake,' said his lordship, gently moving the bottle out of reach. 'Perhaps the dead bore will not wish to marry Annabella!'

'Then why is he coming to stay with the Abingdons?' demanded Mr Hatherleigh. 'I expect Sir Walter has it all arranged, in his famous style! My father says he is the most meddlesome, managing old fool in the county.' He drained his glass defiantly. ''T all events,' he pronounced, 'it'll be something to overset his precious plans!'

❦

Half an hour later, the landlord, coming in to inform Mr Tom that his chaise was at the door, found that young gentleman stertorously asleep, with his head on the table.

'I don't think,' said Lord Stavely, 'that Mr Tom is in a fit case for travel.'

'There, now, I knew how it would be!' exclaimed Thetford, looking down at Tom in some concern. 'Whatever can be the matter with him? When I see him this evening, I thought to myself: You're up to mischief, Mr Tom, or I don't know the signs! And here's a chaise and four come all the way from Whitworth to take him up! What's to be done?'

'You had better inform the postilions that Mr Tom is indisposed, and send them back to Whitworth,' said his lordship. 'And while you are about it, will you be so good as to inform my own postilions that I have changed my mind, and mean to go to Melbury Place tonight after all? Desire them to put the horses to at once, if you please.'

'Your lordship won't be staying here?' the landlord said, his face falling. 'And the bed made up, and a hot brick in it to air the sheets!'

'Carry Mr Tom up to it!' recommended Lord Stavely, with a smile. 'When he wakes –' He glanced down at Mr Tom's unconscious form. 'No, perhaps I had better leave a note for him.' He drew out his pocket-book, and after a moment's hesitation scribbled several lines in it in pencil, tore out the leaf, twisted it into a screw, and gave it to the landlord. 'When he wakes, give him that,' he said.

A quarter of an hour later, Thetford having furnished the post-boys with precise instructions, Lord Stavely was bowling along narrow country lanes to Melbury Place. When the gates came into sight, the post-boys would have turned in, but his lordship checked them, and said that he would get down.

They had long since decided that he was an eccentric, but this quite staggered them. 'It's Melbury Place right enough, my lord!' one assured him.

'I am aware. I have a fancy to stroll through the gardens in this exquisite moonlight. Wait here!'

He left them goggling after him. 'He must be as drunk as a wheelbarrow!' said one.

'Not him!' returned his fellow. 'Queer in his attic! I suspicioned it at the start.'

His lordship, meanwhile, was walking up the drive. He very soon left the gravel for the grass bordering it, so that no sound should betray his presence to anyone in the house. The air was heavy with the scent of roses, and the full moon, riding high overhead, cast ink-black shadows on the ground. It showed the house, outlined against a sky of deepest sapphire, and made it an easy matter for his lordship, traversing the flower gardens, to find the shrubbery. Here, neat walks meandered between high hedges, and several rustic seats were set at convenient spots. No one was present, and no light shone from the long, low house in the background. His lordship sat down to await events.

He had not long to wait. After perhaps twenty minutes, he heard the hush of skirts, and rose just as a cloaked figure came swiftly round a bend in the walk, carrying two bandboxes. He stepped forward, but before he could speak the newcomer exclaimed in a muted voice: 'I thought my aunt would never blow out her candle! But she is snoring now! Did you procure a chaise, Tom?'

Lord Stavely took off his hat, and the moonlight showed the lady the face of a complete stranger. She recoiled with a smothered shriek.

'Don't be afraid!' said his lordship reassuringly. 'I am Mr Hatherleigh's deputy. Let me take those boxes!'

'His *deputy*?' echoed Miss Abingdon, nervelessly relinquishing her baggage into his hands.

'Yes,' said Lord Stavely, setting the bandboxes down beside the seat. 'Shall we sit here while I explain it to you?'

'But who are you, and where is Tom?' demanded Miss Abingdon.

'Tom,' said his lordship diplomatically, 'is indisposed. He was good enough to confide his plans to me, and to – er – charge me with his deepest regrets.'

The lady's fright succumbed to a strong feeling of ill-usage. 'Well!' she said, her bosom swelling. 'If that is not the poorest spirited thing I ever heard! I suppose he was afraid?'

'Not at all!' said his lordship, gently propelling her towards the seat. 'He was overcome by a sudden illness.'

Miss Abingdon sat down, perforce, but peered suspiciously at him. 'It sounds to me like a fudge!' she said, not mincing matters. 'He was perfectly well yesterday!'

'His disorder attacked him unawares,' said Lord Stavely.

Miss Abingdon, who seemed to labour under few illusions, demanded forthrightly: 'Was he *foxed*?'

Lord Stavely did not answer for a moment. He looked at the lady, trying to see her face clearly in the moonlight. The hood had slipped back from her head. The uncertain light made it hard for him to decide whether her hair was dark or fair, but he was sure that it curled riotously, and that her eyes were both large and sparkling. He said: 'Foxed? Certainly not!'

'I don't believe you!' said Miss Abingdon. 'How could he be such a simpleton, on this of all nights?'

Lord Stavely returned no answer to this, and after pondering in silence for a few minutes, Miss Abingdon said: 'I did wonder if he quite liked the scheme. But why could he not have told me that he wanted to draw back from it?'

'That,' said Lord Stavely, 'is the last thing he meant to do. He informed me that you had plighted your troth many years ago.'

'Yes,' agreed Miss Abingdon. 'He cut my wrist with his knife, and we mixed our blood. He said I was chicken-hearted because I squeaked.'

'How very unfeeling of him!' said his lordship gravely. 'May I venture to ask if you love him very dearly?'

Miss Abingdon considered the matter. 'Well, I have always been prodigiously fond of him,' she answered at last. 'I dare say I might not have married him, in spite of the oath, had things not been so desperate, but what else could I do when my papa is behaving so abominably, and I am in such despair? I did hope that Papa would hire a house in London for the Season, for I am nearly twenty years old, and I have never been out of Shropshire, except to go to Bath, which I detest. And instead of that he means to marry me to a horrid old man I have never seen!'

'Yes, so Tom told me,' said his lordship. 'But – forgive me – it seems scarcely possible that he could do such a thing!'

'You don't know my papa!' said Miss Abingdon bitterly. 'He makes the most fantastic schemes, and forces everyone to fall in with them! And he says I must be civil to his odious friend, and if I am not he will pack me off to Bath to stay with my Aunt Charlotte! Sir, what could I do? Aunt Maria – who is Papa's other sister, and has lived with us since my mama died – will do nothing but say that I know what Papa is – and I *do*, and I dare say he would have not the least compunction in sending me to a stuffy house in Queen Square, with Aunt's pug wheezing at me, and Aunt scarcely stirring out of the house, but wishing me to play backgammon with her! *Backgammon!*' she reiterated, with loathing.

'That, certainly, is not to be thought of,' agreed his lordship. 'Yet I cannot help wondering if you are quite wise to elope to Gretna Green.'

'You don't think so?' Miss Abingdon said doubtfully.

'These Border marriages are not quite the thing, you know,' explained his lordship apologetically. 'Then, too, unless you are very much in love with Tom, you might not be perfectly happy with him.'

'No,' agreed Miss Abingdon, 'but how shocking it would be if I were to be an old maid!'

'If you will not think me very saucy for saying so,' said his lordship, a laugh in his voice, 'I cannot think that a very likely fate for you!'

'Yes, but it is!' she said earnestly. 'I have been kept cooped up here all my life, and Papa has not the least notion of taking me to London! He has made up his mind to it that his odious friend will be a very eligible match for me. He and this Lady Tenbury laid their heads together, I dare say –'

'So that was it!' interrupted his lordship. 'I should have guessed it, of course.'

Miss Abingdon was surprised. 'Are you acquainted with Lady Tenbury, sir?' she asked.

'My elder sister,' explained his lordship.

'Your – *w-what*?' gasped Miss Abingdon, recoiling.

'Don't be alarmed!' he begged. 'Though I shrink from owning to it, I think I must be your papa's odious friend. But

I assure you, Miss Abingdon, his and my meddling sister's schemes come as a complete surprise to me!'

Miss Abingdon swallowed convulsively. 'D-do you m-mean to tell me, sir, that you are Lord Stavely?'

'Yes,' confessed his lordship. He added: 'But though I may be a dead bore, I am not really so very old!'

'You should have told me!' said Miss Abingdon, deeply mortified.

'I know I should, but I could not help nourishing the hope that I might not, after all, be the odious old man you and Tom have described in such daunting terms.'

She turned her face away, saying in a stifled tone: 'I would never... Oh, how could you let me run on so?'

'Don't mind it!' he said, taking one of her hands in a comforting clasp. 'Only pray don't elope to Gretna just to escape from my attentions!'

'No, no, but –' She lifted her head and looked at him under brows which he guessed rather than saw to be knit. 'But how *can* you be a friend of my papa?' she asked.

'To tell you the truth, I didn't know that I had the right to call myself so,' he replied. 'He and my family have been upon terms any time these twenty years, I suppose, and I know that he is a close friend of my sister and her husband.'

Miss Abingdon still appeared to be dissatisfied. 'Then how did you come to visit me?'

'If I must answer truthfully,' said his lordship, 'I found it impossible to refuse your parent's repeated invitations with the least degree of civility!'

She seemed to find this understandable. She nodded, and said: 'And you haven't come to – I mean, you didn't know –'

'Until this evening, ma'am,' said his lordship, 'I did not know that you existed! My sister, you see, though quite as meddlesome as your father, has by far more tact.'

'It is the most infamous thing!' declared Miss Abingdon. 'He made me think it had all been arranged, and I had nothing to do but encourage your advances! So naturally I made up my mind to marry Tom rather!' She gave a little spurt of involuntary laughter. 'Was ever anything so nonsensical? I thought you had been fifty at least, and very likely fat!'

'I am thirty-five, and I do not *think* I am fat,' said his lordship meekly.

She was still more amused. 'No, I can see you are not! I am afraid I must seem the veriest goose to you! But Papa once thought for a whole month that he would like me to marry Sir Jasper Selkirk, and he is a widower, and has the gout besides! So there is never any telling what absurdity he may have taken into his head, you see.' A thought occurred to her; she turned more fully towards his lordship, and said: 'But how comes it that you are acquainted with Tom, and why are you so late? We were expecting you would arrive to dine, and Papa was in such a fume! And Aunt made them keep dinner back until the chickens were quite spoilt!'

'I cannot sufficiently apologize,' said Lord Stavely. 'A series of unfortunate accidents delayed me shockingly, and when I did at last reach Shropshire I found that your Papa's directions were not quite as helpful as I had supposed they would be. In fact, I lost my way.'

'It is a difficult country,' agreed Miss Abingdon. 'And of course Papa can never direct anyone properly. But how came you to meet Tom?'

'He was awaiting a chaise at the Green Dragon, where, being then so late, I stopped to dine. We fell into conversation, as one does, you know, and he was good enough to confide his intentions to me.'

'He *must* have been drunk!' interpolated Miss Abingdon.

'Let us say, rather, that he was a trifle worried over the propriety of eloping with you. I did what I could to persuade him against taking so ill-advised a step; he – er – succumbed to the disorder from which he was suffering, and I came here in his stead.'

'It was excessively kind of you, but I don't at all know why you should have taken so much trouble for me!'

He smiled. 'But I could not let you kick your heels in this shrubbery, could I? Besides, I had the liveliest curiosity to meet you, Miss Abingdon!'

She tried to see his face. 'Are you quizzing me?' she demanded.

'Not at all. You will allow that one's curiosity must be aroused when one learns that a lady is prepared to elope to escape from advances one had not the least intention of making!'

'It is quite dreadful!' she said, blushing. 'I wonder it did not give you the most shocking disgust of me! But indeed I did not think it would be improper to elope with Tom, because he is almost like a brother, you know – and it would have been such an adventure!'

She ended on a distinctly wistful note. Lord Stavely responded promptly: 'If your heart is set on the adventure, my chaise is waiting in the lane: you have only to command me!'

Another of her gurgling laughs escaped her. 'How can you be so absurd? As though I would elope with a stranger!'

'Well, I do feel it might be better if you gave up the notion,' he said. 'I fear I can hardly draw back now from Sir Walter's invitation, but if I give you my word not to press an unwanted suit upon you perhaps you may not find my visit insupportably distasteful.'

'No, no!' she assured him. 'But I very much fear that Papa may – may cause you a great deal of embarrassment, sir!'

'Quite impossible!' he said, smiling. 'Have no fear on that head!'

'You are the most truly amiable man I ever met!' she exclaimed warmly. 'Indeed, I am very much obliged to you, and quite ashamed to think I should have misjudged you so! You – you won't tell Papa?'

'Miss Abingdon, *that* is the unkindest thing you have yet said to me!'

'No. I know you would not!' she said quickly. She rose and held out her hand. 'I must go back to the house. But you?'

'In about twenty minutes' time,' said Lord Stavely, 'I shall drive up to the front door, with profuse apologies and excuses!'

'Oh, shall you indeed do that?' giggled Miss Abingdon. 'It must be close on midnight! Papa will be so cross!'

'Well, I must brave his wrath,' he said, raising her hand to his lips.

❧

Her hand clung to his; Miss Abingdon jerked up her head and stood listening. In another instant Lord Stavely had also heard what had startled her: footsteps which tried to be stealthy, and a voice whose owner seemed to imagine himself to be speaking under his breath: 'Do you go that way, Mullins, and I'll go this, and mind, no noise!'

'Papa!' breathed Miss Abingdon, in a panic. 'He must have heard me: I tripped on the gravel! Depend upon it, he thinks we are thieves: Sir Jasper was robbed last month! What am I to do?'

'Can you reach the house without being observed if I draw them off?' asked his lordship softly.

'Yes, yes, but you? Papa will very likely have his fowling piece!'

'Be sure I shall declare myself before he fires at me!' He picked up the bandboxes and gave them to her.

She clutched them and fled. Lord Stavely, having watched her disappear round a corner of the shrubbery, set his hat on his head and sauntered in the opposite direction, taking care to advertise his presence.

He emerged from the shrubbery into the rose garden, and was almost immediately challenged by an elderly gentleman who did indeed level a fowling-piece at him.

'Stand! I have you covered, rogue!' shouted Sir Walter. 'Mullins, you fool, here!'

Lord Stavely stood still, waiting for his host to approach him. This Sir Walter did not do until he had been reinforced by his butler, similarly armed, and sketchily attired in a nightshirt, a pair of breeches, and a greatcoat thrown over all. He then came forward, keeping his lordship covered, and said with gleeful satisfaction: 'Caught you, my lad!'

'How do you do, sir?' said Lord Stavely, holding out his hand. 'I must beg your pardon for presenting myself at this unconscionable hour, but I have been dogged by ill fortune all day. A broken lynch-pin and a lame horse must stand as my excuses.'

Sir Walter nearly dropped his piece. '*Stavely?*' he ejaculated, peering at his lordship in amazement.

Lord Stavely bowed.

'But what the devil are you doing in my garden?' Sir Walter demanded.

Lord Stavely waved an airy hand. 'Communing with Nature, sir, communing with Nature!'

'*Communing with Nature?*' echoed Sir Walter, his eyes fairly starting from his head.

'Roses bathed in moonlight!' said his lordship lyrically. 'Ah – must Mullins continue to point his piece at me?'

'Put it down, you fool!' commanded Sir Walter testily. 'Stavely, my dear fellow, are you feeling quite the thing?'

'Never better!' replied his lordship. 'Oh, you are thinking that I should have driven straight up to the house? Very true, sir, but I was lured out of my chaise by this exquisite scene. I am passionately fond of moonlight, and really, you know, your gardens present so charming a picture that I could not but yield to temptation, and explore them. I am sorry to have disturbed you!'

Sir Walter was staring at him with his jaw dropping almost as prodigiously as the butler's. 'Explore my gardens at midnight!' he uttered, in stupefied accents.

'Is it so late?' said his lordship. 'Yet I dare say one might see to read a book in this clear light!'

Sir Walter swallowed twice before venturing on a response. 'But where's your carriage?' he demanded.

'I told the post-boys to wait in the lane,' replied his lordship vaguely. 'I believe – yes, I believe I can detect the scent of jasmine!'

'Stavely,' said Sir Walter, laying an almost timid hand on his arm, 'do but come up to the house, and to bed! Everything is prepared, and this night air is most unwholesome!'

'On the contrary, I find that it awakens poetry in my soul,' said Lord Stavely. 'I am inspired to write a sonnet on roses drenched with moonshine.'

'Mullins, go and find his lordship's chaise, and direct the postilions to drive up to the house!' ordered Sir Walter, in an urgent under-voice. 'Sonnets, eh, Stavely? Yes, yes, I have been a rhymester in my time, too, but just come with me, my dear fellow, and you will soon feel better, I dare say! You have had a long and a tedious journey, that's what it is!'

He took his guest by the arm and firmly drew him towards the house. His lordship went with him unresisting, but maintained a slow pace, and frequently paused to admire some effect of trees against the night sky, or the sheen of moonlight on the lily-pond. Sir Walter, curbing his impatience, replied soothingly to these flights, and succeeded at last in coaxing him into the house, and upstairs to the chamber prepared for him. A suspicion that his noble guest had been imbibing too freely gave place to a far worse fear. Not until he was assured by the sound of my lord's deep breathing that he was sleeping soundly did Sir Walter retire from his post outside his guest's door and seek his own couch.

Lord Stavely and Miss Abingdon met officially at a late breakfast table. Sir Walter performed the introduction, eyeing his guest narrowly as he did so.

Lord Stavely, bowing first to Miss Maria Abingdon, apologized gracefully for having knocked the household up at such a late hour, and then turned to confront the heiress. For her part, she had been covertly studying him while he exchanged civilities with her aunt. She was very favourably impressed by what she saw. Lord Stavely was generally held to be a personable man. Miss Abingdon found no reason to quarrel with popular opinion. He had a pair of smiling grey eyes, a humorous mouth and an excellent figure. Both air and address were polished, and his raiment, without being dandified, was extremely elegant. He wore pantaloons and Hessians, which set off his legs to advantage; and Miss Abingdon noticed that his snow-white cravat was arranged in precise and intricate folds.

Miss Abingdon had surprised her aunt by choosing to wear quite her most becoming sprigged muslin gown. Miss Maria, who had despaired of detecting any such signs of docility in her niece, was further startled to observe that nothing could have been more demure than Annabella's behaviour. She seemed quite to have recovered from her sulks, curtsied shyly to the guest, and gave him her hand with the most enchanting and mischievous of smiles. Really, thought Miss Maria, watching her fondly, the child looked quite lovely!

Lord Stavely talked easily at the breakfast-table, ably assisted by both ladies. Sir Walter seemed a trifle preoccupied, and when they rose from the table, and his lordship begged leave to wander out into the sunlit garden, he acquiesced readily, and scarcely waited for his guest to step out through the long window before hurrying out of the room in his daughter's wake. He overtook her at the foot of the stairs, and peremptorily summoned her to his library. Shutting the door behind her, he said without preamble: 'Annabella, you need not be in a pet, for I have changed my plans for you! Yes, yes, I no longer think of Stavely for you, so let us have no more tantrums!'

Miss Abingdon's large blue eyes flew to his. 'Changed your plans for me, Papa?' she exclaimed.

He looked round cautiously, as though to be sure that his guest was not lurking in the room, and then said in an earnest tone: 'My dear, it is the most distressing circumstance! The poor fellow is deranged! You would never credit it, I dare say, but I found him wandering about the garden at midnight, talking of sonnets, and moonlight, and such stuff!'

Miss Abingdon lowered her gaze swiftly and faltered: 'Did you, Papa? How – how very strange, to be sure!'

'I was never more shocked in my life!' declared Sir Walter. 'I had not the least notion of such a thing, and I must say that I think Louisa Tenbury has not behaved as she should in concealing it from me!'

'It is very dreadful!' agreed Miss Abingdon. 'Yet he *seems* quite sane, Papa!'

'He seems sane *now*,' said her parent darkly, 'but we don't know what he may do when the moon is up! I believe some lunatics are only deranged at the full of the moon. And now I come to think of it, they used to say that his grandfather had some queer turns! Not that I believed it, but I see now that it may well have been so. I wish I had not pressed him to visit us! You had better take care, my child, not to be in his company unless I am at hand to protect you!'

Miss Abingdon, who, out of the tail of her eye, had seen Lord Stavely strolling in the direction of the rose garden, returned a dutiful answer, and proceeded without loss of time to follow his lordship.

She found him looking down at the sundial in the middle of a rose plot. He glanced up at her approach and smiled, moving to meet her. Her face was glowing with mischief, her eyes dancing. She said: 'Oh, my lord, Papa says you are mad, and he does not in the least wish me to marry you!'

He took her hands and held them. 'I know it. Now, what am I to do to convince him that I am in the fullest possession of my senses?'

'Why, what should it signify?' she asked. 'I am sure you do not care what he may think! I don't know how I kept my countenance! He says I must take care not to be in your company, unless he is at hand to protect me!'

'I see nothing to laugh at in that!' he protested.

She looked up innocently. 'I am so very sorry! But indeed I did not think that you would care!'

'On the contrary, it is of the first importance that your papa should think well of me.'

'Good gracious, why?'

'My dear Miss Abingdon, how can I persuade him to permit me to pay my addresses to you if he believes me to be mad?'

For a moment she stared at him; then her cheeks became suffused, and she pulled her hands away, saying faintly: '*Oh!* But you said you would not – you know you did!'

'I know nothing of the sort. I said I would not press an unwanted suit upon you. Do not take from me all hope of being able to make myself agreeable to you!'

Miss Abingdon, no longer meeting his eyes, murmured something not very intelligible, and began to nip off the faded blooms from a fine rose tree.

'I must study to please Sir Walter,' said his lordship. 'How is it to be done? I rely upon your superior knowledge of him!'

Miss Abingdon, bending down to pluck a half-blown rose, said haltingly: 'Well, if – if you don't wish him to believe you mad, perhaps – perhaps you had better remain with us for a little while, so that he may be brought to realize that you are quite sane!'

'An excellent plan!' approved his lordship. 'I shall be guided entirely by your advice, Miss Abingdon. May I have that rose?'

Sir Walter, informed by the gardener of the whereabouts of his guest and his daughter, came into the rose garden in time to see Miss Abingdon fix a pink rose-bud in the lapel of Lord Stavely's coat. His reflections on the perversity and undutifulness of females he was obliged to keep to himself, but he told Miss Abingdon, with some asperity, that her aunt was searching for her, and taking Lord Stavely by the arm, marched him off to inspect the stables.

Miss Abingdon found her aunt in a state of nervous flutter, having been informed by her brother of their guest's derangement. 'And I thought him such a sensible man! So handsome, too, and so truly amiable!'

'Oh, my dear aunt, is he not the most delightful creature?' confided Miss Abingdon, eyes and cheeks aglow. 'Only fancy his wishing to marry me!'

Miss Maria started. 'No, no, that is quite at an end! Your papa would never hear of it! And when I think that only yesterday you were vowing you would marry Tom Hatherleigh in spite of anything your papa could say, I declare I don't know what can have come over you!'

'Moon madness!' laughed Miss Abingdon. 'Just like Lord Stavely! *Poor* Papa!'

Sylvester

or The Wicked Uncle

SYLVESTER STOOD IN THE WINDOW OF HIS BREAKFAST parlour, leaning his hands on the ledge, and gazing out upon a fair prospect. No view of the ornamental water could be obtained from this, the east front of Chance, but the undulations of a lawn shaved all summer by scythemen were broken by a cedar, and beyond the lawn the stems of beech-trees, outliers of the Home Wood, shimmered in wintry sunlight. They still held their lure for Sylvester, though they beckoned him now to his coverts rather than to a land where every thicket concealed a dragon, and false knights came pricking down the rides. He and Harry, his twin, had slain the dragons, and ridden great wallops at the knights. There were none left now, and Harry had been dead for almost four years; but there were pheasants to tempt Sylvester forth, and they did tempt him, for a succession of black frosts had made the ground iron-hard, robbing him of two hunting days; and a blusterous north wind would not have invited the most ardent of sportsmen to take a gun out. It was still very cold, but the wind had dropped, and the sun shone, and what a bore it was that he should have decided that this day, out of all the inclement ones that had preceded it, should be devoted to business. He could change his mind, of course, telling his butler to inform the various persons now awaiting his pleasure that he would see them on the following day. His agent-in-chief and his man of business had come all the way from London to attend upon him, but it did not occur to Sylvester that they could find any cause for complaint in being kept kicking their heels. They were in his employ, and had no other concern than to serve his interests; they would accept his change of mind as the caprice to be expected from a noble and wealthy master.

But Sylvester was not capricious, and he had no intention of succumbing to temptation. Caprice bred bad servants, and where the management of vast estates was concerned good service was essential. Sylvester had only just entered his twenty-eighth year, but he had succeeded to his huge inheritance when he was nineteen, and whatever follies and extravagances he had committed they had never led him to treat that inheritance as his plaything, or to evade the least one of its responsibilities. He had been born to a great position, reared to fill it in a manner worthy of a long line of distinguished forebears, and as little as he questioned his right to command the obedience of all the persons whose names were inscribed on his staggering payroll did he question the inescapability of the duties which had been laid on his shoulders. Had he been asked if he enjoyed his consequence he would have replied truthfully that he never thought of it; but he would certainly have disliked very much to have had it suddenly removed.

No one was in the least likely to ask him such a question, of course. He was generally considered to be a singularly fortunate young man, endowed with rank, wealth, and elegance. No bad fairy had attended his christening to leaven his luck with the gift of a hunchback or a harelip; though not above medium height he was well proportioned, with good shoulders, a pair of shapely legs, and a countenance sufficiently pleasing to make the epithet *handsome*, frequently bestowed on it, not altogether ridiculous.

In a lesser man the oddity of eyes set with the suspicion of a slant under flying black brows might have been accounted a blemish; in the Duke of Salford they were naturally held to lend distinction; and those who had admired his mother in her heyday remembered that she too had that thin, soaring line of eyebrow. It was just as though the brows had been added with a paintbrush, drawn in a sleek line upwards towards the temples. In the Duchess this peculiarity was charming; in Sylvester it was less attractive. It gave him, when he was vexed, and the upward trend was exaggerated by a frown, a slight look of a satyr.

He was about to turn away from the window when his attention was caught by a small, scampering figure. Emerging from the shelter of a yew hedge, a little boy with a cluster of golden curls set off across the lawn in the direction of the Home Wood, his nankeen-covered legs twinkling over the grass, and the freshly laundered frill of his shirt rucked up under one ear by a duffle coat, dragged over his little blue jacket by hurried and inexpert hands.

Sylvester laughed, throwing up the window. His impulse was to wish Edmund success in his adventure, but even as he leaned out he checked it. Though Edmund would not stop for his nurse or his tutor he would do so if his uncle called to him, and since he seemed to have made good his escape from these persons it would be unsportsmanlike to check him when his goal was within sight. To keep him dallying under the window would put him in grave danger of being captured, and that, reflected Sylvester, would lead to one of those scenes which bored him to death. Edmund would beg his leave to go off to the woods, and whether he gave it or withheld it he would be obliged to endure the reproaches of his widowed sister-in-law. He would be accused of treating poor little Edmund either with brutal severity, or with a heartless unconcern for his welfare; for Lady Henry Rayne could never bring herself to forgive him for having persuaded his brother (as she obstinately affirmed) to leave Edmund to his sole guardianship. It was of no use for anyone to tell Lady Henry that Harry's will had been drawn up on the occasion of his marriage, merely to ensure, in the event of accident, which no one had thought more unlikely than Harry himself, that any offspring of the match would be safe under the protection of the head of his house. However stupid Sylvester might think her she hoped she was not so green as to imagine that his attorney would have dared to insert so infamous a clause except at his express command. Sylvester, with the wound of Harry's death still raw, had allowed himself to be goaded into bitter retort: 'If you imagine that I wished to have the brat thrust on to me you are even greener than I had supposed!'

He was to regret those hasty words, for although he had immediately retracted them he had never been allowed to forget them; and they formed today, when the custody of Edmund had become a matter of acute importance, the foundation-stone of Lady Henry's arguments. 'You never wanted him,' she reminded him. 'You said so yourself.'

It had been partly true, of course: except as Harry's son he had had very little interest in a two-year-old infant, and had paid no more heed to him than might have been expected of a young man. When Edmund began to grow out of babyhood, however, he saw rather more of him, for Edmund's first object, whenever his magnificent uncle was at Chance, was to attach himself as firmly as possible to him. He had qualities wholly lacking in Button, Edmund's nurse (and his father's and uncle's before him), or in Mama. He showed no disposition to fondle his nephew; he was indifferent to torn clothes; such conversation as he addressed to Edmund was brief and to the point; and while he might, in an unpropitious mood, send him somewhat peremptorily about his business, it was always possible that he would hoist him up on to his saddle before him, and canter off with him through the park. These attributes were accompanied by a less agreeable but equally godlike idiosyncrasy: he exacted instant obedience to his commands, and he had a short way of dealing with recalcitrants.

Sylvester thought that Ianthe and Button were doing their best to spoil Edmund, but while he did not hesitate to make plain to that astute young gentleman the unwisdom of employing with him the tactics that succeeded so well in the nursery it was rarely that he interfered with his upbringing. He saw no faults in Edmund that could not speedily be cured when he was rather older; and by the time he was six had grown to like him as much for his own sake as for his father's.

Edmund had disappeared from view. Sylvester pulled the window down again, thinking that he really ought to provide the brat with a livelier tutor than the Reverend Loftus Leyburn, the elderly and rather infirm cleric who was his – or, more accurately, his mother's – chaplain. He had thought it a poor arrangement when Ianthe had begged Mr Loftus to teach Edmund his first lessons, but not a matter of sufficient moment to make it necessary for him to provoke her by refusing to agree to the scheme. Now she was complaining that Edmund haunted the stables, and learned the most vulgar language there. What the devil did she expect? wondered Sylvester.

He turned from the window as the door opened, and his butler came in, followed by a young footman, who began to clear away the remains of a substantial breakfast.

'I'll see Mr Ossett and Pewsey at noon, Reeth,' Sylvester said. 'Chale and Brough may bring their books in to me at the same time. I am going up to sit with her grace now. You might send down a message to Trent, warning him that I may want –' He paused, glancing towards the window. 'No, never mind that! The light will be gone by four o'clock.'

'It seems a pity your grace should be cooped up in the office on such a fine day,' said Reeth suggestively.

'A great pity, but it can't be helped.' He found that he had dropped his handkerchief, and that the footman had hurried to pick it up for him. He said, 'Thank you', as he took it, and accompanied the words with a slight smile. He had a singularly charming smile, and it ensured for him, no matter how exacting might be his demands, the uncomplaining exertions of his servants. He was perfectly well aware of that, just as he was aware of the value of the word of praise dropped at exactly the right moment; and he would have thought himself extremely stupid to withhold what cost him so little and was productive of such desirable results.

Leaving the breakfast-parlour, he made his way to the main hall, and (it might have been thought) to another century, since this central portion of a pile that sprawled over several acres was all that remained of the original structure. Rugged beams, plastered walls, and a floor of uneven flagstones lingered on here in odd but not infelicitous contrast to the suave elegance of the more modern parts of the great house. The winged staircase of Tudor origin that led up from the hall to a surrounding gallery was guarded by two figures in full armour; the walls were embellished with clusters of antique weapons; the windows were of armorial glass; and under an enormous hood a pile of hot ashes supported several blazing logs. Before this fire a liver-and-white spaniel lay in an attitude of watchful expectancy. She raised her head when she heard Sylvester's step, and began to wag her tail; but when he came into the hall her tail sank, and although she bundled across the floor to meet him, and looked adoringly up at him when he stooped to pat her, she neither frisked about him nor uttered barks of joyful anticipation. His valet was hardly more familiar with his wardrobe than she, and she knew well that pantaloons and Hessian boots meant that the most she could hope for was to be permitted to lie at his feet in the library.

The Duchess's apartments comprised, besides her bedchamber, and the dressing-room occupied by her maid, an antechamber which led into a large, sunny apartment, known to the household as the Duchess's Drawing-room. She rarely went beyond it, for she had been for many years the victim of an arthritic complaint which none of the eminent physicians who had attended her, or any of the cures she had undergone, had been able to arrest. She could still manage, supported by her attendants, to drag herself from her bedchamber to her drawing-room, but once lowered into her chair she could not rise from it without assistance. What degree of pain she suffered no one knew, for she never complained, or asked for sympathy. 'Very well' was her invariable reply to solicitous enquiries; and if anyone deplored the monotony of her existence she laughed, and said that pity was wasted on her, and would be better bestowed on those who danced attendance on her. As for herself, with her son to bring her all the London on-dits, her grandson to amuse her with his pranks, her daughter-in-law to discuss the latest fashions with her, her patient cousin to bear with her crotchets, her devoted maid to cosset her, and her old friend, Mr Leyburn, to browse with her amongst her books she thought she was rather to be envied than pitied. Except to her intimates she did not mention her poems, but the fact was that the Duchess was an author. Mr Blackwell had published two volumes of her verses, and these had enjoyed quite a vogue amongst members of the ton; for although they were, of course, published anonymously the secret of their authorship soon leaked out, and was thought to lend considerable interest to them.

She was engaged in writing when Sylvester entered the room, on the table so cleverly made by the estate carpenter to fit across the arms of her wing-chair; but as soon as she saw who had come in she laid down her pen, and welcomed Sylvester with a smile more charming than his own because so much warmer, and exclaimed: 'Ah, how delightful! But so vexatious for you, love, to be obliged to stay at home on the first good shooting-day we have had in a se'enight!'

'A dead bore, isn't it?' he responded, bending over her to kiss her cheek. She put up her hand to lay it on his shoulder, and he stayed for a moment, scanning her face. Apparently he was satisfied with what he saw there, for he let his eyes travel to the delicate lace confection set on her silvered black hair, and said: 'A new touch, Mama? That's a very fetching cap!'

The ready laughter sprang to her eyes. 'Confess that Anna warned you to take notice of my finery!'

'Certainly not! Do you think I must be told by your maid when you are looking in great beauty?'

'Sylvester, you make love so charmingly that I fear you must be the most outrageous flirt!'

Venetia

'A FOX GOT IN AMONGST THE HENS LAST NIGHT, AND ravished our best layer,' remarked Miss Lanyon. 'A great-grandmother, too! You'd think he would be ashamed!' Receiving no answer, she continued, in an altered voice: 'Indeed, you would! It is a great deal too bad. What is to be done?'

His attention caught, her companion raised his eyes from the book which lay open beside him on the table and directed them upon her in a look of aloof enquiry. 'What's that? Did you say something to me, Venetia?'

'Yes, love,' responded his sister cheerfully, 'but it wasn't of the least consequence, and in any event I answered for you. You would be astonished, I daresay, if you knew what interesting conversations I enjoy with myself.'

'I was reading.'

'So you were – and have let your coffee grow cold, besides abandoning that slice of bread-and-butter. Do eat it up! I'm persuaded I ought not to permit you to read at table.'

'Oh, the *breakfast*-table!' he said disparagingly. 'Try if you can stop me!'

'I can't, of course. What is it?' she returned, glancing at the volume. 'Ah, Greek! Some improving tale, I don't doubt.'

'The *Medea*,' he said repressively. 'Porson's edition, which Mr Appersett lent to me.'

'*I* know! She was the delightful creature who cut up her brother, and cast the pieces in her papa's way, wasn't she? I daresay perfectly amiable when one came to know her.'

He hunched an impatient shoulder, and replied contemptuously: 'You don't understand, and it's a waste of time to try to make you.'

Her eyes twinkled at him. 'But I promise you I do! Yes, and sympathise with her, besides wishing I had her resolution! Though I think I should rather have buried *your* remains tidily in the garden, my dear!'

This sally drew a grin from him, but he merely said, before turning back to his book, that to order her to do so would certainly have been all the heed their parent would have paid.

Inured to his habits, his sister made no further attempt to engage his attention. The slice of bread-and-butter, which was all the food he would accept that morning, lay half-eaten on his plate, but to expostulate would be a waste of time, and to venture on an enquiry about the state of his health would serve only to set up his hackles.

He was a thin boy, rather undersized, by no means ill-looking, but with a countenance sharpened and lined beyond his years. A stranger would have found these hard to compute, his body's immaturity being oddly belied by his face and his manners. In point of fact he had not long entered on his seventeenth year, but physical suffering had dug the lines in his face, and association with none but his seniors, coupled with an intellect at once scholarly and powerful, had made him precocious. A disease of the hip-joint had kept him away from Eton, where his brother Conway, his senior by six years, had been educated, and this (or, as his sister sometimes thought, the various treatments to which he had been subjected) had resulted in a shortening of one leg.

When he walked it was with a pronounced and ugly limp; and although the disease was said to have been arrested the joint still pained him in inclement weather, or when he had over-exerted himself. Such sports as his brother delighted in were denied him, but he was a gallant rider, and a fair shot, and only he knew, and Venetia guessed, how bitterly he loathed his infirmity.

A boyhood of enforced physical inertia had strengthened a natural turn for scholarship. By the time he was fourteen if he had not outstripped his tutor in learning he had done so in understanding; and it was recognised by that worthy man that more advanced coaching than he felt himself able to supply was needed. Fortunately, the means of obtaining it were at hand. The incumbent of the parish was a notable scholar, and had for long observed with a sort of wistful delight Aubrey Lanyon's progress. He offered to prepare the boy for Cambridge; Sir Francis Lanyon, relieved to be spared the necessity of admitting a new tutor into his household, acquiesced in the arrangement; and Aubrey, by that time able to bestride a horse, thereafter spent the better part of his days at the Parsonage, poring over texts in the Reverend Julius Appersett's dim bookroom, eagerly absorbing his gentle preceptor's wide lore, and filling him with an ever-increasing belief in his ability to excel. He was entered already at Trinity College, where he would be admitted at Michaelmas in the following year; and Mr Appersett had little doubt that young though he would still be he would very soon be elected a scholar.

Neither his sister nor his elder brother cherished doubts on this head. Venetia knew his intellect to be superior; and Conway, himself a splendidly robust young sportsman to whom the writing of a letter was an intolerable labour, regarded him with as much awe as compassion. To win a Fellowship seemed to Conway a strange ambition, but he sincerely hoped Aubrey would achieve it, for what else (he once said to Venetia) could the poor little lad do but stick to his books?

For her part, Venetia thought he stuck too closely to them, and was showing at an alarmingly early age every sign of becoming just such an obstinate recluse as their father had been. He was supposed, at the moment, to be enjoying a holiday, for Mr Appersett was in Bath, recuperating from a severe illness, a cousin, with whom he had fortunately been able to exchange, performing his duties for him. Any other boy would have thrust his books on to a shelf and equipped himself instead with his rod. Aubrey brought books even to the breakfast-table, and let his coffee grow cold while he sat propping his broad, delicate brow on his hand, his eyes bent on the printed page, his brain so much concentrated on what he read that one might speak his name a dozen times and still win no response. It did not occur to him that such absorption made him a poor companion. It occurred forcibly to Venetia, but since she had long since recognised that he was quite as selfish as his father or his brother she was able to accept his odd ways with perfect equanimity, and to go on holding him in affection without suffering any of the pangs of disillusionment.

She was nine years his senior, the eldest of the three surviving children of a Yorkshire landowner of long lineage, comfortable fortune, and eccentric habits. The loss of his wife before Aubrey was out of short coats had caused Sir Francis to immure himself in the fastness of his manor, some fifteen miles from York, and to remain there, sublimely indifferent to the welfare of his offspring, abjuring the society of his fellows. Venetia could only suppose that the trend of his nature must always have been towards solitude, for she was quite unable to believe that such extravagant conduct had arisen from a broken heart. Sir Francis had been a man of rigid pride, but never one of sensibility, and that his marriage had been one of unmixed bliss was an amiable fiction his clear-sighted daughter was quite unable to believe. Her memories of her mother were vague, but they included the echoes of bitter quarrels, slammed doors, and painful fits of hysteria. She could remember being admitted to her mother's scented bedchamber to see her dressed for a ball at Castle Howard; she could remember a beautiful discontented face; a welter of expensive dresses; a French maid; but not one recollection could she summon up of maternal concern or affection. It was certain that Lady Lanyon had not shared her husband's love of country life. Every spring had seen the ill-assorted pair in London; early summer took them to Brighton; when they returned to Undershaw it was not long before her ladyship became moped; and when winter closed down on Yorkshire she was unable to support the rigours of the climate, and was off with her reluctant spouse to visit friends. No one could think that such a butterfly's existence suited Sir Francis, yet when a sudden illness had carried her off he had come home a stricken man, unable to bear the sight of her portrait on the wall, or to hear her name mentioned.

His children grew up in the desert of his creating, only Conway, sent to Eton, and passing thence into the -th Foot, escaping into a larger world. Neither Venetia nor Aubrey had been farther from Undershaw than Scarborough, and their acquaintance was limited to the few families living within reach of the Manor. Neither repined, Aubrey because he shrank from going amongst strangers, Venetia because it was not in her nature to do so. She had only once been disconsolate: that was when she was seventeen, and Sir Francis had refused to let her go to his sister, in London, to be presented, and brought out into Society. It had seemed hard, and some tears had been shed. However, a very little reflection had sufficed to convince her that the scheme was really quite impractical. She could not leave Aubrey, a sickly eight-year-old, to Nurse's sole care: that excellent creature's devotion would have driven him into a madhouse. So she had dried her eyes, and made the best of things. Papa, after all, was not unreasonable: though he would not consent to a London Season he raised no objection to her attending the Assemblies in York, or even in Harrogate, whenever Lady Denny, or Mrs Yardley, invited her to go with them, which they quite frequently did, the one from kindness, the other under compulsion from her determined son. Nor was Papa at all mean: he never questioned her household expenditure, bestowed a handsome allowance on her, and, somewhat to her surprise, left her, at his death, a very respectable competence.

This event had occurred three years previously, within a month of the glorious victory at Waterloo, and quite unexpectedly, of a fatal stroke. It had been a shock to his children, but not a grief. 'In fact,' said Venetia, scandalising kind Lady Denny, 'we go on very much better without him.'

'My dear!' gasped her ladyship, who had come to the Manor prepared to clasp the orphans to her sentimental bosom. 'You are overwrought!'

'Indeed I'm not!' Venetia replied, laughing. 'Why, ma'am, how many times have you declared him to have been the most unnatural parent?'

'But he's *dead*, Venetia!'

'Yes, but I don't suppose he has any more fondness for us now than he had when he was alive, ma'am. He never made the least push to engage our affections, you know, so he really *cannot* expect us to grieve for him.'

Finding this unanswerable Lady Denny merely begged her not to say such things, and made haste to ask what she now meant to do. Venetia had said that it all depended on Conway. Until he came home to take up his inheritance there was nothing she could do but continue in the old way. 'Except, of course, that I shall now be able to entertain our friends at the Manor, which will be very much more comfortable than it was when

Papa would allow none but Edward Yardley and Dr Benworth to cross the threshold.'

Three years later Venetia was still awaiting Conway's return, and Lady Denny had almost ceased to inveigh against his self-ishness in leaving the burden of his affairs on her shoulders. No one had been surprised that he had at first found it impossible to return to England, for no doubt everything must have been at sixes and sevens in Belgium and France, and all our regi-ments sadly depleted after so sanguinary a battle as Waterloo. But as the months slid by, and all the news that was to be had of Conway came in a brief scrawl to his sister assuring her that he had every confidence in her ability to do just as she ought at Undershaw, and would write to her again when he had more time to devote to the task, it began to be gener-ally felt that his continued absence arose less from a sense of duty than from reluctance to abandon a life that seemed (from accounts gleaned from visitors to the Army of Occupation) to consist largely of cricket-matches and balls. When last heard of, Conway had had the good fortune to be appointed to Lord Hill's staff, and was stationed at Cambray. He had been unable to write at much length to Venetia because the Great Man was expected, and there was to be a Review, followed by a dinner-party, which meant that the staff was kept busy. He knew she would understand exactly how it was, and he remained her affectionate brother Conway. *P.S. I don't know which field you mean — you had best do what Powick thinks right.*

'And for anything he cares she may live all her days at Undershaw, and die an old maid!' tearfully declared Lady Denny.

'She is more likely to marry Edward Yardley,' responded her lord prosaically.

'I have nothing to say against Edward Yardley — indeed, I believe him to be a truly estimable person! — but I have always said, and I always *shall* say, that it would be throwing herself away! If only our own dear Oswald were ten years older, Sir John!'

But here the conversation took an abrupt turn, Sir John's evil genius prompting him to exclaim that he hoped such a fine-looking girl had more sense than to look twice at the silliest puppy in the county. As he added a rider to the effect that it was high time his wife stopped encouraging Oswald to make a cake of himself with his play-acting ways, Venetia was forgotten in a pretty spirited interchange of conflicting opinions.

None would have denied that Venetia was a fine-looking girl; most would not have hesitated to call her beautiful. Amongst the pick of the débutantes at Almack's she must have attracted attention; in the more restricted society in which she dwelt she was a nonpareil. It was not only the size and brilliance of her eyes which excited admiration, or the glory of her shining guinea-gold hair, or even the enchanting arch of her pretty mouth: there was something very taking in her face which owed nothing to the excellence of her features: an expression of sweetness, a sparkle of irrepressible fun, an unusually open look, quite devoid of self-consciousness.

About the Author

Author of over fifty books, Georgette Heyer is one of the best-known and best-loved of all historical novelists, making the Regency period her own. Her first novel, *The Black Moth*, published in 1921, was written at the age of seventeen to amuse her convalescent brother; her last was *My Lord John*. Although most famous for her historical novels, she also wrote twelve detective stories. Georgette Heyer died in 1974 at the age of seventy-one.

The Private World of Georgette Heyer

by Jane Aiken Hodge

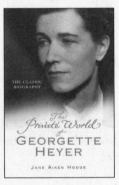

An internationally bestselling phenomenon and queen of the Regency romance, Georgette Heyer is one of the most beloved historical novelists of our time. She wrote more than fifty novels, yet her private life was inaccessible to any but her nearest friends and relatives.

Lavishly illustrated and with access to private papers, correspondence and family archives, this classic biography opens a window into Georgette Heyer's world and that of her most memorable characters, revealing a formidable, energetic woman with an impeccable sense of style and, beyond everything, a love for all things Regency.

Praise for **The Private World of Georgette Heyer:**

"The Georgette Heyer bible...
This is a must-have book for any Georgette
Heyer lover." —*Historically Obsessed*

For more Jane Aiken Hodge books, visit:

www.sourcebooks.com